KATE LL

REINVENTING

Ruthie

KATE LLOYD

UNION BAY
PUBLISHING

Reinventing Ruthie

© 2023 by Kate Lloyd

KATELLOYD.COM

ISBN 978-1-7352411-6-6
ISBN 978-1-7352411-7-3 (ebook)

This is a work of fiction. Names, characters, places, and events are products of the author's imagination, and any resemblances to actual events or places or persons, living or dead, is entirely coincidental.

Cover Design: Kimberly Denando
Interior design: Colleen Sheehan, Bookery / Kimberly Denando

Printed in the United States of America

Dedicated to Mary Jackson

1

B ITTERNESS CLAWED THROUGH my chest as it had a thousand times since Drew left me. I pictured his empty side of our bed, his vacant half of the closet, and only one car out front of the brick Tudor that was to be our haven in retirement.

"I want out of the marriage." He'd checked his iPhone as casually as if he were heading off to work. At first I thought he was joking.

"I'm serious." He sent me a patronizing glare.

I'd ransacked my mind for things he didn't like about me. When I was nervous I talked too much, like I'm doing now. Once a month I allowed PMS to rule my mood. I'd get weepy eyed over the smallest things, like seeing a dead squirrel by the side of the road or hearing an Irish tenor singing *Oh Danny Boy*. And I admit I sometimes thwarted Drew's amorous advances for no reason other than he hadn't taken out the garbage or he'd left the toilet seat up. But none of that seemed substantial enough to make him call it quits. I finally decided he was flailing through a midlife crisis that would pass in a few days.

"Let's try counseling." I'd taken his forearm, but he shook it free.

"It's too late for that now." He gave me a one-shouldered shrug. "I've met someone."

And my world faded to black-and-white.

"CAN YOU HEAR me?"

I recognized my elder daughter's voice, but her words sank beneath the sound of lapping water and seagulls' bleating calls.

"Mom, wake up."

I tried to answer Nichole, but my lips were glued together, my tongue a lifeless appendage.

"Is she going to be all right?" She sounded frightened.

"As far as we can tell your mother has no internal injuries," a man with a nasally voice said. "Her head's suffered trauma, but the CT scan was normal. We'll know more when she regains consciousness."

"But her face—"

"That's superficial, nothing to worry about."

I felt something resting under my nostrils and pressure on the tip of my index finger. Red-hot sunlight filtered through my eyelids, but goose bumps prickled my skin. What kind of a creepy dream was this? Trying to rouse myself, all I could manage was to swallow.

"When will she come around?" Nichole asked, but he didn't answer.

I felt one eyelid being pried open and a moment later saw bushy eyebrows behind a flashlight beam.

"Mrs. Templeton?" the man said. "Ruth Ann?"

As soon as he let go of my lid, it flopped shut again, and I was left floating in darkness. My thoughts rambled like the incoming tide. Were my groceries still in the car? I was planning to cook lasagna, Drew's favorite. I knew the dinner was a waste of time. He'd resisted every overture—even the lacy negligee and the perfume I'd spent hours picking out with dreams of enticing him back into my arms. My soon-to-be ex-husband was only coming by to sign divorce-related documents, to tie up loose ends, as he put it. I would get the house and he the business. I had an office job and I hoped enough income to get by. I wouldn't need to rely on Drew, now or ever again.

The seagulls' shrieks turned into an incessant bleeping. I tried to clap my hands over my ears to quiet them, but a band was restraining one arm.

"Doctor," Nichole said. "She moved."

I felt a draft, then heard my younger daughter speak. "She looks gross." Harriet's voice was acrid, as always.

Nichole shushed her. "Be quiet, she might be able to hear you."

"So, what's she going to do? Send me to my room for a time out?"

"For once, can't you show compassion?"

"Like you show it to me?"

A cuff encircling my upper arm tightened, making me feel like a snared rabbit. As I attempted to break free, my eyes shot open and I saw a nurse taking my blood pressure.

Next to her stood long-legged Nichole, her ash-blond hair loose around her shoulders. "Mom, you're awake."

My jaw fell open and I gasped a mouthful of air. Inflating my lungs, my chest and ribs ached like I'd been lifting one-hundred-pound weights, when in fact I hadn't set foot in the gym for months. I noticed tubes running out of my body like serpents, a drip-bag hanging from a metal rack, and a box with digital numbers. A heart monitor? Scanning the stark cubicle, I realized what I thought was the sun was a fluorescent light hanging overhead. Harriet, a swatch of belly parading out between her cropped sweater and low-riding jeans, hovered at a distance.

I struggled for equilibrium. "Where am I?" I sounded puny, like a child speaking from another room.

"Northwest Hospital," said the balding man dressed in light blue standing at the foot of the bed. "I'm Doctor Kirshbaum." The corners of his mouth lifted, but his face remained a tinted window, which I could see partially through—enough to detect concern.

"Why— am I here?" My rubbery tongue slurred my words.

"You were in a car accident. You arrived by ambulance."

"Impossible."

Nichole leaned against the bed's railing. "That's what the state patrolman said when he called." Her sentence came out deliberately, as if she were conversing with a foreigner.

I tried to lift my head, but a splinter of pain shot from my shoulder up my neck. "Where was I?"

"On the freeway."

Nothing made sense. I prided myself on being a careful driver. Sure, I'd slid through many an amber-turning-to-red light, but I'd never received a speeding ticket or even been in a fender bender. Had an SUV or a truck inadvertently forced my car off the road?

"Was another vehicle involved?" I asked.

"No." Nichole remained close by. "The patrolman reported you lost control of the wheel."

"How does he know?"

"The people driving behind you saw the whole thing."

"They must have been mistaken." My muddled brain tried to recreate a non-existent auto-wreck without success. "Is it possible the witnesses were under the influence of drugs or alcohol?"

Harriet, her hair recently dyed fiery red, edged nearer like a raven preparing to peck at a wounded bird. "Why must you always assume someone else is to blame?"

Ignoring her barbed words, I shifted my gaze to see Dr. Kirshbaum jotting something down on an iPad.

"Am I going to be okay?" I asked him.

"Yes, thanks to your seatbelt."

"Our mother always wears one." Harriet's jagged bangs fell across one of her eyes like a curtain shutting me out. "She's constantly on my case to use mine."

"And this proves she's right," Nichole said.

"Thank you, Miss Perfect. All I need is another parent."

Their words ricocheted off the walls like those little bouncy-balls Harriet used to toss around the house.

"Girls, please try to get along." I focused my attention on Dr. Kirshbaum and noted a hooked nose and horn-rimmed spectacles. "How long have I been here?" I asked him.

"Several hours." He checked his iPad. "You were admitted at 4:30 p.m."

I squeezed my eyes shut as my thoughts spun back in time. Retracing my steps in circle-eights, I tried to reconstruct my

day, but my mind was like an endless tunnel. I knew one plus
one equaled two, and A was followed by B. But logic didn't
seem to matter anymore.

WHEN I AWOKE, I saw a black nurse gazing down at me
with kind eyes.

"Good morning, I'm Jackie." She spoke in a husky contralto
voice.

Morning? Had a night elapsed? I glanced around to find
myself in a different room. I vaguely remembered my bed rattling against an elevator door and a bumpy ride down the hall.
Out the window I saw a bright, hard sky—a rarity in Seattle.

"How are you doing?" She patted my good arm.

Never complain, never explain, my father often said, but it felt
like my frontal lobe had swollen larger than my skull and was
about to pound out my ears.

"My head feels clamped in a vice." My speech came out slug-
gishly, like I had a mouthful of peanut butter. I stretched and
the throbbing increased.

"I'll get you something for the pain," she said. "Your daughter's resting out in the waiting room. Shall I wake her?"

I didn't have to ask which daughter. I envisioned willowy
Nichole sacked out on a couch. "No, that's okay. Let her sleep."

"And your husband called several times."

"Are you sure?" Most likely it was my father, whom I'd
dubbed Pop.

"He said his name was Drew Templeton, and he asked us
to contact him the moment you woke up." Her hand glided
toward the telephone by the bed.

"No, please don't." The truth was I still loved him, which was idiotic. I mean, if a man treated one of my daughters the way Drew treated me, I would have been outraged.

"All right, the doctor will be in soon." She adjusted my pillow and checked my vitals. "Are you sure you don't want me to call your husband?"

"Yes, I'm positive."

I recognized Dr. Kirshbaum entering the room several minutes later. The ceiling lights reflected off his domed forehead and his neck sloped forward, like a tortoise.

"How do you feel?" he asked.

"I've been better." As I rolled onto my side, a slice of pain raged from my hand up my arm. I let out a small gasp.

He moved closer. "There's swelling around your wrist. We'll get that x-rayed."

"Then can I go home?" Where was my purse? And what about my clothes? I couldn't wait to get out of this hospital gown.

"No, we'll need to keep you through tomorrow." He slipped a small flashlight from his pocket, flicked it on to inspect my eye.

Staring blindly into the shaft of light, my mind ground with worry. Would Nichole remember to bolt the front door and put on the porch light? Could she keep fifteen-year-old Harriet out of trouble? Would she feed Bonnie, our Welsh corgi?

"I have two teenagers who need me," I explained.

He examined the other eye. "What about your husband? Can't he handle things for a few days?"

"My husband doesn't live with us."

"I see." I noticed his well-worn wedding band and doubted he understood. He looked like a nice, sweet guy who probably adored his wife.

Nichole trudged in, her sandy hair matted on one side and her eyes rimmed with purplish fatigue.

"Sweetheart." I wanted to jump to my feet. "You should have gone home, you look exhausted."

"I thought you might need me."

"But Harriet—"

"She's fine." She paused, as if searching for the proper words. "There's nothing for you to worry about except getting better." She glanced at the clock on the wall. "It's almost 7:00, I'd better go."

"Yes, get to school, sweetheart, and please make sure your little sister does, too." I'd saddled her with a formidable task. "And take something out of the freezer for supper. There's a container of beef stew that would be perfect for two people. The noodles are in a plastic bin in the pantry."

"Mom." She bent and left a kissed near my cheek. "I know where everything is, we'll be fine."

"Of course, you're a capable young woman. It's your sister I should be concerned about."

Appearing in a hurry, Dr. Kirshbaum started to leave. Nichole followed him. "May I speak to you for a moment?"

"Yes, sure,"

They stepped into the hall. Through the doorway, I could see her slender back and the top of Dr. Kirshbaum's head, which moved as he spoke. I tried to catch their words but couldn't. Then they turned away from each other to walk down the hall in opposite directions.

I sighed as I realized how helpless I was—like a baby waiting for its bottle.

The telephone sitting on the side table rang. I managed to answer it with my good hand. "Hello."

"Ruth Ann, dear," my mother said. "I just found out. I heard the phone ringing last night, but I was busy with your father and couldn't answer it. Then, I forgot to listen to the message until just now. I'm terribly sorry."

"Mom, I'm okay."

In the background, I heard my father bellowing, "Mildred? Mildred?" which struck me as odd. I'd never heard him raise his voice at my mother before.

"Just a minute," she said. "I'm talking to Ruth Ann."

"Who?"

"Your daughter. Remember, I told you she was in the hospital."

"Another baby?"

Knowing my father loved to tease, I chortled. "Tell Pop there's no chance of that."

She ignored my comment. "Ruth Ann, I'll try coming by this afternoon, but I will have to bring your father with me. I don't think I should leave him alone."

Even though we only lived across town from each other, I hadn't spoken to him one-on-one in months and I missed our chats.

"Why not?" I pressed the receiver to my ear. "What do you mean?" I could hear Pop jabbering in the background.

"I'll fill you in later, dear. I need to run."

Before I could say good-bye, the dial tone blared in my ear. "That was weird." Mom had sounded frazzled, not her usual patient self.

Jackie sauntered back into the room. "Let's see if this helps." She came over to the bed and took the receiver from my hand, replaced it on the phone. Then she jiggled the tube in the back of my hand. Moments later, I felt coolness, then less pain.

"Better?" She nodded her head even though I hadn't replied. "Your daughters will be fine." Her voice sounded like amber—smooth and warm. She straightened the covers and for a moment stood by the bed. Then she smiled in a caring way that made me want to weep.

I WAS RESTING on water as flat as the sky. Under its tranquil surface, fish swarmed, darting back and forth—the larger species devouring the small ones, hiding or seeking.

I thought about Drew's love shack luxuriating on the banks of Lake Washington. His paramour, Kristi, probably lived with him, but I'd refused to ask. Her age was still a mystery, too. The girls had both met her, but their descriptions remained vague. They'd used words like *about your age* and *average looking*. I figured Nichole, anyway, was trying to save my feelings. Yet I hoped Drew hadn't ditched me for someone mediocre. Unless I was second-rate. No, I wouldn't let myself think that way. There was nothing wrong with me, except my naïveté.

I remembered times in our marriage when it seemed as though we had nothing. Now I realized we had everything. Scrimping and wanting things that were beyond our grasp, we'd enjoyed small triumphs: quiet moments in front of the TV when we couldn't afford a movie—eating popcorn, snuggling together. Those were our finest hours. Then, money started flowing in as Drew's new software company took off. More money, more work, a faster life, and bigger needs. He became a sponge, never sated and still expanding.

"Ruthie, it's me," Drew said.

I inhaled a whiff of his citrus-scented aftershave, then opened my eyes to see his face several feet away, closer than it had been for six months.

Even though I longed for his touch, I felt hard inside. Dried out. "What are you doing here?"

"Nichole called me right away. I stayed with Harriet last night."

"In my house?" flared out with a sting, but I decided there was no reason to contain my anger any longer. He didn't care about me and never would again. "You have no right to stroll in there whenever you feel like it. You promised to ask my permission before you came over."

"I figured this was a special circumstance. You could have died."

He probably wished I had, then all his problems would be solved. We were still legally married. Since I didn't have a will, he'd inherit everything I owned, and be able to move back home like I never existed.

"My health is none of your concern," I said.

"Are you kidding?" He took my hand and massaged it with his thumb. "You're the mother of my children."

I examined his face to see pinched blue eyes against a chalky complexion. Was this fear? Maybe he thought God was going to come down and smack him one.

"Where's Kristi?" Her name tasted like unsweetened grape-fruit, making my mouth pucker. "Out in the waiting room mending your socks?"

"No, she's at work." He squeezed my fingers too hard.

"Ouch." I yanked my hand away. "Are you here to inflict more pain on me?"

"No, just the opposite. I wanted to say I'm sorry."

My optimistic mother had claimed Drew would eventually beg for forgiveness, but I assumed he never would. I held my breath and waited for him to go on, to declare he still loved me and wanted me back more than anything. But he pressed his lips together like a clothespin, then started cleaning under his thumbnail, a habit I'd always found annoying.

I hated myself for caring what was on his mind, I really did. But I couldn't resist saying, "Drew, what are you trying to tell me?"

"That I regret hurting you." He stared at a spot on my shoulder. Couldn't he even muster up eye contact?

"Aren't you the thoughtful one." I narrowed my eyes, and finally his gaze met mine.

"Ruthie, I'm trying to apologize."

"Let me get this straight—you're apologizing for hurting me." Not to mention breaking my heart. "But you're not sorry for wrenching our family apart?"

He sucked air in through his mouth and started working his thumbnail again.

"It sounds like you're hoping to ease your guilt." I felt heat building under my armpits. "Trying to make yourself feel better at my expense." While I was too compromised to defend myself.

"Maybe I shouldn't have come." He tugged his earlobe. "But I thought you might want something."

"The only thing I want from you is to leave me alone." I wasn't sure I meant it, but the words gave me a sense of power, like I was calling the shots.

When he said nothing, I turned my eyes to the window and noticed a film of haze graying the sky. I thought about all the chores I needed to complete before the holidays. Thanksgiving always tumbled into December, then a mad frenzy followed until Christmas.

"I guess I should go." He stood. "Do you want me to turn on the TV?"

"No, although I could use a weather report."

"It's supposed to rain tonight and the rest of the week."

I remembered the mountain of leaves accumulating under the maple tree in the front yard. "I need to hire someone to look after the yard. The rain will turn the leaves into mush and flatten the grass."

He lowered himself back into the chair. "What do you mean?"

"Don't worry, I'm not asking you to rake." A rush of adrenaline caused a pulsing in my right temple. "The girls and I can handle everything. This Thanksgiving we'll fix a twenty-pound turkey without your famous oyster dressing I never really liked. Then we'll toss away that phony Christmas tree you insist saves you from asthmatic attacks and buy a noble fir. We'll have the best time ever."

Drew blinked in slow motion. "But, Ruthie, it's only April." He turned back his shirtsleeve to expose the wristwatch I'd given him on his birthday several years ago. "It's April twentieth. You were admitted yesterday."

I felt like I was toppling off a cliff, but kept my features from revealing my confusion. "Of course," I finally said as the whole ugly holiday season replayed itself in my mind. Drew had shown up Christmas morning with an armload of extravagant gifts for the girls, then whisked them off for the rest of the day. I'd sat alone watching movies with over-the-top happy endings on TV so I'd have an excuse to cry.

"Daddy, can we go now?"

Harriet's voice made me start. I looked up to see my younger daughter's angular shape as she lumbered into the room.

"Hi, I didn't realize you were here." I faked a smile.

She clutched a glazed doughnut, held it up like a trophy for me to view. "I was getting something to eat."

I checked the clock to see it was 9:30. "Sweetie, why aren't you in school?"

"Don't have a cow." She tore off a chunk of dough, popped it into her mouth past pink frosted lips, then spoke through the crumbs. "We have a late start today."

"Late start? I've never heard of that."

She stared at the floor for a moment. "Some sort of teachers' meeting."

"I didn't see it on the calendar." Or did I? At that moment I couldn't remember if we even had a school calendar.

"They sent a notice home last week, but I guess I forgot to give it to you."

"Hmm." It still sounded fishy, and it wouldn't be the first time she'd tried to fool me.

Drew's cell phone chirped. He stood to answer it, then slunk into the hall. No doubt Kristi was setting her baited hook and reeling in her line.

"How are things going on the home front?" I asked Harriet.

"Fine."

I was used to drudging for scraps of information from this secretive girl. "Anything more you can tell me?"

She chewed off another morsel. "Daddy's staying with us."

"So I hear."

"He cooked baked blueberry French toast and sausage this morning."

"Sounds delicious." This man who'd abandoned his family was playing the role of Danny Tanner. Knowing Drew, he'd left the kitchen a disaster area. I imagined our Welsh corgi, Bonnie, snuffling up debris from the floor, and her water dish sitting empty.

"Did anyone feed Bonnie?" I asked. "She needs a daily walk and her eye drops." Or was it diabetes medication?

"Nichole's taking care of her."

"That's good." What would I do without dependable Nichole? "Say, what day is it, anyway?"

"Like, Wednesday." She omitted *You loser*, but I could read the sentiment on her face.

"Don't forget tomorrow's garbage and recycle day," I said.

Harriet's shoulder tattoo—a spider encircled by a coil of barbed wire that I found abhorrent—peeked out from behind her sleeveless tank top. "Yes, Mommy, dearest."

I pursed my lips as I watched her pick between her teeth with a lacquered-black fingernail. This girl was of my flesh, I reminded myself. I remembered her thrashing in my abdomen, kicking all night the last few months of my pregnancy. Her face a scarlet red, she'd finally emerged two weeks late and was christened with the name Natalie. As an infant, she'd fussed whenever I left the room, shrieked when I spoke on the phone, and refused to take naps. Then, at age four, the girl turned independent. "You can't make me!" was her answer to most every request, and she insisted her name was Harriet. And lenient Drew went along with it.

"Did your father happen to mention if he's coming back tonight?" There was no way around it; I needed his assistance keeping the household on track.

"Yeah, he's taking us out for Thai food."

I supposed Drew would request our favorite booth at our usual haunt. As I considered which girl would sit next to her father, a ghastly thought entered my mind. "Anyone else coming along?"

"You mean Kristi?" she shot back, as if speaking the woman's name were the most natural thing. "I don't think so, but you never know. Things sure would be easier if you'd held your marriage together and Dad still lived with us."

My legs stiffened like two wooden planks. "Excuse me if I didn't make things clear. Your father walked out on me. I practically groveled at his feet begging him to stay." Sad to say, I wasn't exaggerating.

"That was the wrong tactic. You should have gone on a diet or found some hunk to make him jealous over instead of acting like a wimp."

As if this teenager would know anything about men. She'd never even had a boyfriend.

"I did my best," I said. "I'm not the one who broke his wedding vows."

Harriet finished off the donut and wiped her fingers on the corner of my blanket. "Mother, you can be so dense. Men need more than promises to keep them around."

A man's as good as his word, Pop said many a time. I wanted to refute Harriet's statement, to say my father would never break a promise, but at this moment I wasn't sure of anything.

2

AN EAGLE BARELY moves its wings when gliding on the crest of the wind. Floating, his eyes remain alert as he scans the water's surface. Below, a blue heron stands like a bronze statue in water as shiny as a mirror. I had probably ambled right by the giant bird many times, just as I'd walked past Drew's cheating—my gaze aimed downward, looking for agates, not noticing the obvious.

I'd been a colossal chump—for the last time.

I heard people speaking in the hallway, their words rippling in my ears like a radio with poor reception. I recalled the sound of rocks churning beneath my feet as I trekked along the shore at the island. Millions of rocks, and every single one was unique. "That's a sugar stone," I told four-year-old Nichole many years ago. "When it's wet, it may look like an agate, but when it dries, the surface turns dull." Nichole had rubbed the pebble between her small pink fingers. "No matter how long it's polished," I said, "it will never be smooth and shiny like a real agate."

Strolling up and down the beach, the seasons and years melded together. Drew and I had bought the cabin right after Nichole's birth. My heart had swelled with gladness our first evening there. I nestled on the couch with my head on Drew's shoulder, and watched the setting sun cast an orangy-peach veil over the distant hills across the bay. A wide horizon of happiness expanded across my future. The sun rose and set, the tide meandered in and out on a fixed schedule, and I'd believed in my future with Drew as surely as those facts.

Clomping footsteps snagged my attention, lassoing me back to the present. I opened my eyes to see a lanky brunette enter the room. As if invited, she maneuvered a chair to my bedside.

"Good morning." She sat and scooted the chair closer. "I'm Isolda Browning, intern chaplain. How are you?"

A minister in training? I had no use for religion of any brand. Save my mother, the last person who'd prayed over me was the minister at Drew's and my wedding. "To whom God hath joined, let no man put asunder," he'd stated with authority. Obviously, his pronouncement hadn't worked. Till death do us part? What a laugh.

"I think you're in the wrong room." I wanted her to vamoose.

"Are you Ruth Ann Templeton?"

"Yes."

She adjusted her horn-rimmed glasses. "It says on your chart that you're Presbyterian."

"One of my daughters must have written that. I go twice a year—Easter and Christmas—only to make my mother happy."

She smiled, exposing bucky front teeth. "That's a good start."

I considered myself a broad-minded person but knew better than to engage a religious zealot in conversation. I'd been stuck in that verbal loop too many times with my well-meaning mother. I took in Isolda's narrow face, and estimated she was barely old enough to be out of college. She'd probably never been imprisoned by love or experienced heartache, let alone landed in the hospital.

"It looks like the world hasn't been treating you very well," she said.

"I must resemble a grizzly bear that just crawled out of a cave." I fluffed my hair. "I haven't washed my face since yesterday." I dabbed my tongue around the inside of my mouth and realized I needed to brush my teeth. "You could do me a favor." I wanted to add *Before you leave*. "Check and see if there's a mirror in that bed table."

"I don't think I should." She rose, her hands wringing each other. "I'll get the nurse."

I pressed a button to elevate my head. "She's busy, I don't want to bother her."

"But I don't think I'm allowed."

I sent her a woeful look. "Please, don't make me get out of bed to find a mirror, myself."

She was stalling. "You realize you've been in an accident?"

"I'm not here for a tummy tuck." I grinned at my humor, although she didn't respond to my levity.

"All right." She stood and pushed the overbed table to me. Her features tightened as she raised the lid to reveal a mirror affixed to its bottom.

My eyes strained to see my reflection. I must have injured them in the accident—that Halloween mask couldn't be me. I adjusted my position so the light slanting in from the window illuminated my face. Then I stared into the mirror again.

"No, no!" gushed out of my mouth. I looked like I'd been mugged, then thrown into an incinerator. The flesh around my eyes was swollen and black, my cheeks the color of dried blood and my lips like chapped leather. Only my green irises remained recognizable.

"Mrs. Templeton, it's going to be all right."

I imagined myself through Drew's eyes. He must have been repulsed, as anyone would be. "I'm hideous."

"No, you're not. People come in here looking much worse than this. Black and blue turns to green, then yellow, and pretty soon, your face will be as beautiful as ever."

My chest felt like it was caving in. I couldn't face people like this. I'd have to hide out until the bruises healed, if they did.

"I'll be right back." She fled into the hall and a minute later followed Jackie back into the room.

"I hear you got a look at yourself," Jackie said.

I nodded, tears seeping out.

"I'm so sorry, please forgive me." Isolda massaged her palm. "I'll never do that again, I promise."

Jackie's chestnut brown eyes were larger than any I had ever seen, full of compassion without pity.

"Not to worry." She retrieved my pillow, which had fallen off to the side. "That first look is never any fun."

Sadness tunneled through me. Hadn't I already sunk to the bottom of the pit over the last few months? I'd thought I couldn't submerge any lower, that I couldn't continue living if I felt worse. Yet here I was.

"What happened to me?"

"I'm guessing your airbag slapped you hard. It probably yanked that wrist of yours, too."

I dove into the recesses of my brain trying to recall the moment of impact—the swooshing sound of the airbag inflating, the jolt as it mashed me against the seat—but I came up empty.

"How long will I look like this? Is there anything I can do?"

"We've notified your primary physician," Jackie said. "He should come by today and answer all your questions."

"Dr. Garcia's a woman." I recalled my last visit to her office. Right after Drew took off, I began suffering from crushing insomnia, causing my days and nights to merge into an ocean of exhaustion. Instead of the sleeping pills I requested, my doctor recommended I try an antidepressant. But I'd refused, telling her, "I'm not depressed, just furious. And I have every right to be."

"Mrs. Templeton has two lovely daughters," Jackie said. "And her eldest mentioned they attend the same high school as my son."

"How wonderful." Isolda plopped into the chair like we were old friends. "You must be very proud."

"Yes, I am." Of one of them, anyway. I embraced the girls in my thoughts. "I'm thankful I'm in here and not one of them."

"Funny how there's always some good in everything." Isolda crossed her legs at the knee. "I mean, look how well you are. You're awake and alive. And life is good."

"I'm not sure how good it is."

She soaked in my words, then nodded. "Sometimes our troubles seem to overshadow our blessings. But the sun's still shining up there somewhere."

I glanced to the window to see raindrops slithering down the glass. "I'll try to keep that in mind."

"Buzz me if you need anything." Jackie took a step toward the door.

"Before you go, I have a question." I rehashed my conversation with Drew. "Something weird happened earlier." My mind floundered as it tried to leave this room, which now seemed like my entire world. "I feel a little mixed up," I added, not knowing how to describe my blurred thinking without sounding batty. "Like a ninety-nine-year-old woman who can't remember her last name."

"Memory loss?" Jackie moved to my bedside. "When Dr. Kirshbaum returns, we'll ask him what that means. If you have a concussion, it may take a while to get your bearings back. Say, I hear your husband was here."

"Yeah, and now I understand why he stared at me. I don't know why I care what he thinks. He threw me away like yesterday's newspaper."

"Any chance you'll get back together?" Isolda straightened her glasses.

"Nah, he's got a new honey." I did my best to sound as if I found his antics amusing. "And get this, he thinks she and I will like each other. Isn't that peachy? We'll be one big happy family. He's an amazing man."

"He must be, to have someone like you love him."

Isolda's kind words fastened onto my heart. I was surprised to feel my bottom lip trembling.

"Now, now." Jackie lay a hand on my arm. "Let's not worry about him right now. Treat your time here like a vacation. All you have to do is rest and let others take care of you."

"Okay, that sounds good." But I didn't think so. I'd never liked people waiting on me. Pride or guilt always filed in, making me want to spring to my feet to serve them.

"I ordered you some gourmet cuisine." Jackie sent me a wry smile. "Feel like you could eat lunch?"

I heard a cart rattling out in the hall. The thick aroma of package-made gravy wafted in and I grimaced as the smell took me back to my high school cafeteria where I often sat alone, pretending I was there by choice.

"We'll see how you feel when it gets here," Jackie said.

A man carrying a food tray padded in and set it on the overbed table, then removed the metal lid to expose a slab of meatloaf, a lump of mashed potatoes, and a blob of limp broccoli.

A wave of nausea gurgled through my stomach. "I guess I'm not hungry."

Jackie lifted the tray. "All right, I'll take this away."

Isolda's expression turned playful as she whisked a plate housing a chocolate-chip cookie, a small carton of milk, and a glass of water off the tray. "Let's keep these, just in case."

Jackie chuckled as she breezed into the hall.

Isolda placed the cookie, milk, and water on my bedside table. "I'll stop by later. If you get hungry, I'll run down to the cafeteria and buy you a sandwich."

"You're kind, but you don't need to do that."

"I want to." She proceeded into the corridor, where I heard her speaking to someone. A moment later a silver-haired woman about my mother's age stepped through the doorway.

"May we come in?" She looked me full on for a moment, then averted her gaze ever so slightly. Not that I blamed her, mind you. I'd done the same thing when meeting someone with a disfigured face or even confined to a wheelchair. I was filled with a new empathy followed by shame for my coward-ice. I swore to myself I'd never turn away like that again.

"We're the Morrisons, Frank and Martha," she said. "The people who called 911."

A gentleman with tufts of hair scraggling from either side of his balding skull followed Martha into the room. He, too, seemed shaken by my appearance.

"We've been wondering how you're doing," he said.

I inhaled the aroma of Martha's lilac-scented perfume. "Except for my face, pretty well. Just a sprained wrist. I'm glad you're here, so I can thank you."

"We were happy to be of assistance," Martha said.

I appraised the couple and decided they looked like reliable witnesses. Frank wore a tweed jacket, slacks, and a neatly pressed shirt, and Martha a flowered dress—the kind Mom would like.

"Can you fill me in on what happened?" I tried to sound nonchalant.

"Sure," Martha said, then glanced to Frank.

"We were up north in Arlington at that little restaurant at the airport watching the planes take off and land, having a late lunch."

"Or was that an early supper?" She smiled. "I know what you're thinking, it's a long drive from Seattle. But when you're our age, you can indulge yourself and eat whenever you want."

"We've got nothing else to do," Frank said.

"What time was it?" My words flew out of my mouth with urgency.

"About 3:30?" He turned to Martha and she nodded. "We saw you cruise onto the freeway up ahead of us," he said, his voice gathering tension.

"Where was I?"

Frank's face creased with concern. "Why, Edmonds."

I sat for a moment in stunned disbelief. I couldn't imagine what I was doing ten miles north of town. The last thing I remembered was driving out of the QFC grocery store parking lot with a trunk full of food.

"Which direction was I traveling?" I asked.

"South, same way as us." Frank's weight swayed back and forth as he spoke. "You seemed to be in quite a hurry."

I wondered if they thought I'd been high on something. They had no way of knowing I'd all but given up alcohol in college, after a gut-wrenching hangover. Pop taught me: *Moderation in all things.*

Martha wove her fingers together. "You crossed two lanes right in front of us."

"We followed you for a minute." Frank hesitated. "Then your car started veering to the left." He fingered the change in his pocket. "A moment later, it flipped off the road into the median."

The room resounded with brittle silence. Finally, Martha said, "Your car turned over twice." She noticed me flinch. "We pulled onto the shoulder. Frank scrambled down the bank and turned off your ignition while I called the State Patrol."

I was panicky in the back of my throat, as if I couldn't get enough air. "I wonder if my steering wheel malfunctioned." I tried to use the left side of my brain, where common sense resided. "Or maybe my brakes went out."

"I don't think so," Frank said. "We didn't see any swerving, nor did we see your brake lights."

I felt like I was on trial and the prosecutor had just presented another piece of damaging evidence against me. I wouldn't have been surprised to hear the judge's gavel drop to pronounce me guilty of a crime that for the life of me I couldn't remember.

3

IT WAS DOWNRIGHT odd watching Drew use his house key to unlock the front door as if it were any old afternoon. I supposed I needed to take it away from him before he left. After all, I didn't own a key to his fancy schmancy apartment. I'd certainly thought about sneaking by his place to see if he was entertaining Kristi more times than I care to admit, but I'd had the good sense to stop myself. Anyway, he lived up on the third floor facing the lake, according to the girls. And why torture myself? If he wasn't with Kristi, then someone else.

He swung the door open, then stepped aside to give me space to cross the threshold. Rust-colored Bonnie came scampering from the kitchen and through the dining room; her stubby legs clamored across the hardwood floor.

I'd always loved dogs—their exuberance and unwavering loyalty. It occurred to me that humans could take a lesson from them.

"Good girl," I said, bending to stroke Bonnie's silky head. "Did you miss me?" I could always count on my dear corgi to remain loyal.

She yapped in return, her body wriggling with excitement.

When I straightened my spine, my head began spinning. I reached for the banister to steady myself.

"Easy, Ruthie." Drew moved in behind me, anchoring his hands at my waist to support part of my weight.

Here's something crazy: I cared what his hands felt. I was glad I'd kept off the five pounds I'd lost when I was too despondent to eat.

I didn't have the strength to make it to the second floor. I'd felt energetic when leaving the hospital thirty minutes earlier; I'd even joked with Jackie that I'd be back next time I needed a little R and R. But the ride home had been an ordeal, each bump stabbing up my arm and pounding into my temple.

He kept his hold on me. "Let's sit you down and get your feet up."

The couch, through the front hall and halfway across the living room, seemed miles away. As I shuffled toward it, Bonnie pranced ahead of me. I scanned the room, with its painted-brick fireplace and aged Persian carpet I'd found at a garage sale. Drew's briefcase sat on one of the two armchairs, strange magazines fanned across the oak coffee table, and a half-empty water glass without a coaster sat on the table's corner.

I settled myself on the couch while Drew returned to his car to retrieve my floral arrangements—one from the office, an architectural firm; and one from my best friend, Gloria. He placed them on the end of the coffee table, then parked himself on the vacant armchair.

"Thanks for the ride," I forced myself to say. I refused to thank him for spending the night with his own children. He'd barely seen them since he'd moved out.

"Not a problem."

"You can go now." I was sure he couldn't wait to hit the road, and this made me want him to leave.

"That's all right, I have the afternoon off. I told Harriet I'd be here when she got home from school. She's got a math test tomorrow, and I promised to explain the quadratic formula."

My arithmetic skills were minimal compared to what kids study these days, but I said, "I'll help Harriet with her homework."

"No, I'm sticking around." He unlaced his shoes, kicked them off, then began sorting through the magazines. "Anyway, I dropped by the grocery store earlier and bought dinner fixings. I can't see you cooking for a while."

"I'm sure we'll manage just fine. We have been."

He selected *Travel & Leisure* and started flipping through the pages. Since when did he read travel magazines? Was he planning the trip to Rome and Tuscany we'd talked about for years? Would he take Kristi there instead of me?

"Nichole can throw dinner together," I said. "And I can always call Mom."

Not that my mother had been enthusiastic about driving me home today. "If Drew's willing to give you a lift, please take him up on it, won't you?" she'd said. And Mom had only stopped by my hospital room once, then departed ten minutes later saying she'd taken a chance leaving my father home by himself.

"Sounds like your mother has her hands full." Drew leafed through the pages, stopping somewhere in the middle. "I talked to her yesterday. She said your father's worse. He doesn't have a clue who's president and couldn't care less. And the other day he put on a suit and tie, and thought he was late for work."

So what if Pop was getting a little forgetful? How dare Drew say anything negative about him? Why, my father was twice the man Drew would ever be.

"He's just bored." I craned my neck to see what he was looking at but couldn't. "Pop never has adjusted to retirement."

As Drew glanced up his mouth dragged to one side. "It's been almost ten years since we threw his retirement party. And, let's face it, he's in his eighties."

"That's not so old anymore. Last month on a PBS documentary on longevity they showed photos of people one-hundred-years-old and over. They're doing crossword puzzles and reading books." I'd enjoyed hearing their old-fashioned names, like Annabelle and Wilber, and learning about their favorite pastimes.

"I hope you're right." He clapped the magazine shut and tossed it on the table. "Hey, this is wonderful, you and I chatting. I'm glad we can be friends."

Some friend. I knew he was only here for the kids' benefit.

"I wouldn't call us best buddies." My head felt as heavy as a block of hardening cement. I let it slump against the back of the couch and closed my eyes for a moment. When I opened them, I found him scrutinizing my face.

"I'll be staying longer," he said. When I glowered, he added, "Until the divorce goes through, this is still half my house."

I remembered how for months after he'd left, I staggered like a zombie through long days and sleepless nights. Tears ripping down my cheeks, I'd almost suffocated beneath the grief-infested waters. If Drew thought he was going to swing by whenever he pleased and climb into my bed, he had another think coming.

"I'm using the bedroom," I said.

He grinned in a way that used to fill me with tenderness, but I refused to smile back.

"Calm down," he said. "I'm camped out in the guest room."

The back door rattled, then slammed shut. Bonnie, her tail-less rear end bobbing up and down, cantered into the kitchen. I could hear Harriet cooing over the dog. She had her sweet moments.

She jabbed her head around the corner. "I'm home."

"Hi," Drew and I said in unison.

Harriet sashayed across the room wearing a skirt that hung inches shorter than the last time I saw it. Apparently she was doing her own hemming.

She perched on the arm of Drew's chair, snuggled up against him, and then swung around to speak to me. "Where's the car?"

Feeling my cheeks warm, I looked to Drew for help. While in the hospital, I'd forgotten I even owned my ten-year-old Honda.

"It's in the body shop," he said. "The insurance company thinks it can be repaired, but it looks totaled to me."

He must have gone to inspect my automobile, which I had to acknowledge was a generous act. I was in no shape to venture out.

Or maybe he was just worried about our insurance rates hiking up.

He sat forward, elbows on knees. "What did happen, Ruthie? The car looks like it got it from all sides."

"I can't remember."

"How's that possible?" He shot me a look of disbelief.

I resented his grilling me in front of Harriet. "I was sane and sober."

"I wasn't inferring otherwise. Don't put words in my mouth."

His cell phone warbled, saving me from further questions. Before answering, he jumped up and roamed into the kitchen with Bonnie dancing at his heels. The dog had missed him fiercely when he left and must have assumed her master was home to stay.

Harriet slouched onto the chair like her bones were going soft. "How long before you go back to work?" she asked me.

"I don't know. Maybe a couple of weeks." It wasn't only my wrist that impeded my return, but also my sluggish thinking. And how would I get there?

"That stinks." Her voice picked up volume. "How are we going to have enough money?"

"We'll get by." Somehow.

"But you said we went overboard at Christmas and you still owe a bundle on your Visa card."

"We'll just have to spend less."

"We already do. You won't give me money for Starbucks and you haven't taken me shopping for clothes in months." She pulled herself upright and fired her words at me point blank. "And don't tell me to wear Nichole's old rags. I'll look like a weirdo."

Drew strode back into the room as he stashed his phone in his pocket. He must have heard her raised voice because he said, "Something wrong, Kitten?"

Harriet sprang to her feet and snaked her arm around his waist. "Daddy, I don't have anything to wear."

"You have a closet full of nice clothes," I interjected. Although most of her clothing lay dirty on her floor.

"I've worn those outfits a thousand times."

"I remember what it was like," I said, trying to demonstrate support while my annoyance grew. "I couldn't be caught in the same outfit more than once a week." The fact that cute clothes hadn't elevated me to the popular crowd was something I wouldn't admit.

She screwed up her mouth as disgust contorted her face. "That was back in the dark ages. It's ten times worse now. If you don't keep up with the trends, all the kids make fun of you."

I was all too aware how it felt to be excluded. "Good friends don't care what you wear." I knew she had several, for which I was thankful.

She gave her father the waifish look she saved only for him. "Daddy, could we go to the mall?"

"Sure, why not?"

I folded my arms; my chest remained tender where the airbag punched me. And the seatbelt had left a bruise. "She needs to do her homework first."

"Nah, it's still early." His arm curved across her shoulder. "We have time before dinner."

She smooched his cheek, leaving an eggplant-colored imprint of her lips. "I love you, Daddy, I love you." She'd never said those precious words to me. Even when I caved in to her demands and acted like her servant, she'd treated me like the enemy.

"With you in the car, I can drive."

Drew's face took on a terrified look—his eyes bulging and the corners of his mouth pulling back. But it was my turn to smile. Let him be carted around by a hyperactive girl with a month-old learner's permit.

As Drew jogged upstairs to grab a sweater, Harriet skulked closer to me. "You know, this is your chance to win Daddy back."

"What makes you think I want him?" That would be like hoping the Easter Bunny was real.

"You do and you know it."

Raising my chin, I tried to adopt an air of dignity. "As a matter of fact, I'm happy the way things are." If I said it enough times, I'd believe it.

"That's because you're selfish."

"Me?" I felt myself being sucked into her turbulent eddy. "I gave up earning my master's degree so your father could get his. That's why he can afford to buy you stuff and I can't. I stayed home to take care of you kids until you were old enough for school, then took a part-time job so I could be home in the afternoon."

"You're doing it again, Mother—talking about yourself. It's always about you."

My brain groped for the right words, but I knew nothing I said would be good enough to influence Harriet.

"This is a moot point," I said. "Your father made his choice."

AS I LISTENED to Drew's BMW rocket down the street, I glanced at my right arm. The brace holding my sprained wrist reminded me I'd be useless at work. I couldn't even answer the phone efficiently.

I gazed at the lilies and irises sent by the office. They'd hired a temp, the card said, but wanted me back the moment I was well. The other arrangement, composed of lavender freesia, asters, and larkspur, was from my best girlfriend. I dislodged the card and opened it to read, *Get well soon, Gloria.*

I'd called Gloria from my hospital bed. "How awful," she'd said, her voice mingling with her two-year-old's nattering. "Where are you?" When I told her, she said, "I wish I could come by, but Shelby's sick and can't go to day care. Which is ridiculous, because I'm sure that's where she caught the bug."

"That's okay, take care of that little cutie." In the past, I'd encouraged her to quit her job and stay home to raise her daughter. In the old days, I believed there was more than one way to spell success. But Gloria, a thirty-five-year-old attorney on the rise, made it clear she had no intention of pausing her career. And maybe she was right; if her husband took off, she could support herself far better than I.

The doorbell jangled and I dragged myself to my feet. Out the front window I saw Mom's beige-metallic Buick gathering moisture under the drizzling sky.

Bonnie barked as I opened the door to find my mother carrying a rectangular Tupperware container. Her hair, normally coiffed short and neatly combed, was flyaway and in need of a trim. And a stripe of inch-long gray roots stood out at the part line, which wasn't like her—she usually kept her brown hair a shade lighter than mine.

"I made a Danish." She brought in with her the aroma of confectioner's sugar glaze.

"Yummy, comfort food. Just what I needed."

She folded her raincoat over the banister. As I led her through the dining room, an area barely large enough to contain the table and four chairs, I noticed several unopened bills and pieces of junk mail littering the table's surface. My Visa bill balanced on top, as if trying to flag me down. Below it lay an envelope from the mortgage company.

Mom slowed her pace. I glanced back to see her eyeing the letters. I continued into the kitchen. There was no way I'd discuss my finances with her again; it only made her worry—which was contagious.

"You look better today." She lifted the Danish out of the plastic container, placed it on the counter. She found a serrated knife and began slicing the pastry into even rows. "God's been watching after you."

I was used to Mom's religious prattling but couldn't let it go by unchallenged.

"Oh, yeah?" Using my left hand, I flushed tap water into the kettle, then set it on the stove. "If he was, couldn't he have kept me on the road?"

"Now, don't be like that. My only daughter's alive and I'm grateful."

"Thanks, Mom, but I wonder if Harriet would have been just as happy if I'd never come home. It seems I've been replaced by Drew."

"I'm sure that's not true. She needs her mother. All girls do."

"Harriet's mission in life is to be the opposite of other girls." I listened to the kettle murmur. "Did you know Drew's staying here?"

Her eyebrows lifted, etching lines across her forehead.

"It doesn't mean a thing." I wished I hadn't brought up the subject. This was a good example of my rattling off at the mouth. "He still has his bimbo girlfriend. He's just trying to impress the kids."

"Maybe you two—"

I put up a hand to silence her. "Please, Mom, it's not going to happen."

The kettle started whistling; I transferred it to a cold burner.

"Have a seat and I'll make us tea."

"No thanks, I'd better get home. Sometimes your father fixes himself soup, then forgets to turn off the stove."

"Big deal. One burner couldn't use up that much electricity." Most likely my conscientious father had left it on once over the last twenty years. I'd bet Mom had done the same thing.

I nabbed a mouth-sized piece of Danish as I followed her to the front hall. Biting into the sweet dough, I savored the blend of butter, sugar, and sliced almonds sprinkled over the top. It reminded me of childhood, of coming home after school to find Mom had baked something special. If I haven't mentioned it before, I got lucky in the parent department. They weren't perfect, but who is?

"I'm serious." Mom located her purse. "With your father's memory on the decline, I don't trust him at home by himself."

I couldn't imagine what kind of trouble a grown man could get into in his own house. So what if he couldn't remember all the crossword puzzle answers anymore? "Could he go to a friend's house?" I envisioned two men playing cards and enjoying a cigar.

"I can't think of anyone. His pal Sam died last year, and Chet and his wife moved to Arizona to be closer to their grandchildren. That leaves Horace, who's out on the golf course every day."

"If it would give you more freedom, maybe you should pay someone to stay with him."

"You mean a babysitter? He's not sick enough for a nurse." She dug through her handbag and plucked out the beaded keychain Harriet fashioned for her in third grade. My younger daughter was talented at crafts, although it had been years since I'd seen her make anything.

"Did I mention your father's seeing a neurologist?" Mom said.

"What for?"

She jiggled her keys. "His general practitioner is young enough to be our grandson. He's no help." Her words became clipped. "He calls Ed's memory lapses all part of growing old, which seems to be his answer to everything. I decided it was time to get a second opinion."

My mother was a mama bird, I thought, remembering how she used to bundle up my brother, Jeff, and me while the other kids wore shorts and T-shirts. With her chickadees out of the nest, maybe she needed someone to fuss over.

"That sounds like a good idea," I said. Their insurance would pay for it. "I have an appointment with Dr. Kirshbaum in a few days, but I may cancel it. I'd rather see my own doctor."

"Why? Dr. Kirshbaum's the expert."

"Because he's always blinding me with his flashlight, then peering at me like I'm two steps from the grave."

"Ruth Ann, you'd save me a world of worry if you saw him one more time. He and your father's neurologist, Dr. Huff, are in the same office. I'll drive you and take your father in to get blood work done while you're there." She pushed her arms into her coat sleeves. "Maybe you could speak to Dr. Huff, too. It would help me to have another set of ears."

I could tell she wasn't going to let me win this one. And I was curious what Pop's doctor had to say about him.

"Okay, I'll do it." I clasped her in a quick embrace, then opened the door. "Bye, Mom. I love you."

As she strode outside, her toe caught on the door jam. She stumbled forward, staggering several feet across the porch. Inches before the first step, she righted herself.

Near calamity happened so quickly all I could do was watch. Then I rushed out and grabbed her elbow with my good arm. "Are you all right?" I held her elbow for a moment longer, until I was sure she was safe.

She brushed my hand away. "Sure. Silly me."

I scooped up her pocketbook, which had somehow landed right side up on the middle step, and handed it to her.

"I've been having a little trouble with depth perception. Nothing serious." She took hold of the purse's handle. "As Ed's doctor would say, it's all part of getting old."

I descended the stairs to pick up her keys that lay sprawled on the cement walkway. As she proceeded down the steps, I studied her face. Fifteen years younger than Pop, she had always been a head-turner, but today I noticed sunken cheeks and a bluish cast to her complexion. Had I been so immersed in self-pity I hadn't seen her decline?

"Are you sure you can drive?" I still grasped the keys. Not that I could run her home in my shape.

"Of course." In a swift motion, she swiped them from me. "Remember, I came here to look after you."

A moment later I watched her drive away, the top of her head barely visible above the headrest. I wondered how long it would be before I said those exact words to her.

4

I COULDN'T BELIEVE I'D slept in while the girls got themselves off to school. That was a first. *You've wasted the best hours of the day*, Pop would say.

I tottered down to the first floor and into the kitchen to find it empty, save for Bonnie sleeping in her basket with her legs twitching as she chased the neighbor's cat in her dreams. I noticed brown liquid in the coffee urn and poured some into a mug, then placed it in the microwave. As I listened to the oven drone, I looked around the room to see the dishwasher's door hanging open. Someone had removed the clean dinner dishes and replaced them with breakfast plates. Another first.

As I removed the cup and took a careful sip, I considered whether I felt good enough to drive to the grocery store. No, and even with layers of makeup, my face would bring horrified stares. And with my right arm out of commission, how would I navigate the cart, let alone the car? Everything seemed like too much work.

I wandered into the dining room, picked up my Visa bill and tore open the envelope to see $3,572 was due in a week. The sum assaulted me like a slap on the cheek. I'd attempted to pay the balance down, but when compounded with the interest charge and occasional late fee it continued to increase.

I set the bill aside to see a letter from my attorney, Sue McDonald, whom Gloria had recommended as easygoing, but no pushover. "Take your time, don't let Drew rush you," Sue had urged me in her office a couple months ago. "If he wants a divorce so much, let him bring major concessions to the table." But in the meantime, I had to pay for an attorney I never wanted.

The remaining envelope had Roosevelt High School printed across the upper left corner. I ripped it open and read: Dear Mr. and Mrs. Templeton, Your daughter Harriet is in jeopardy of losing credit in several of her classes. It is imperative she doesn't have any more unexcused absences. Please contact her counselor, Miss Caddish, to set up an appointment.

My thoughts spun back to last year, when Harriet hadn't turned in her homework for six whole weeks. Forcing her to complete her missing assignments had been almost as agonizing as having my husband dump me. But I thought the girl was back on track. Her latest report card displayed a sturdy row of Cs, and an A in Art, although I had yet to see any of the work she'd produced.

My mind skipped ahead to contemplate her future. If she didn't earn the necessary credits, she'd have to redo this semester and live at home for an extra six months before college. Who was I trying to kid? Harriet wasn't even interested in community college. She'd be lucky to graduate from high school.

I placed the letter on the kitchen table where Harriet would see it when she got home. As I showered and dressed, I imagined the explosion that was sure to ignite when she read it. I remembered Mom assuring me my younger daughter would settle down, and not to worry, after Harriet, age eight, toppled Nichole's birthday cake to the floor just before the guests arrived. But no such luck—Harriet only grew more resistant to my rules. And to me. I'd read parenting books like *Positive Discipline* and *The Strong-Willed Child*, but the more I tried to influence her, the further she pushed me away. Any desire for closeness only served to fuel hostility toward me. I'd wondered more than once if it would be better for both of us if I gave up.

I pulled on jeans and a T-shirt and didn't bother with makeup. The skin on my face was beginning to peel, making me look like I'd been blistered by the sun. As far as I could tell, the cortisone cream Dr. Kirschbaum prescribed hadn't made the slightest difference. Maybe it was a placebo.

The doorbell rang several times in rapid succession. I descended the stairs to see Bonnie rushing into the front hall. Her triangular ears pricked up and her stub of a tail wagging, she barked fiercely, the way she did when strangers arrived. I looked through the peephole and was surprised to see Gloria's beautiful face. When she lived down the block, we got together often, but in the four years since she and her husband moved, I couldn't remember her ever stopping by without calling first. And usually it was I who set up our meetings.

"Ta-da," Gloria said when I opened the door. Looking svelte as usual, she wore a charcoal-colored suit, the skirt's hem hitting her mid-knee to show off muscled legs and slim ankles. Her dark hair was wisped into a French roll and her earlobes hid behind pave diamond earrings.

As I hugged her, she kissed the air. "You poor thing." She leaned back and gave my face an appraisal. It had to be a shock seeing me like this.

"Don't worry, I feel better than I look," I said. "And it's not contagious."

"Glad to hear it." She glanced over my shoulder. "Are we alone?"

"Yes, Drew and the girls left hours ago."

Her back arched. "Drew, here?"

"Yup. Welcome to the *Twilight Zone*."

I beckoned her to enter, but she said, "I'm here to take you out to lunch. I've got an hour to grab something to eat and get back to the office."

I couldn't go out in public looking like this. "I'd better not. People will think I was mangled by a gorilla."

"Wear dark glasses and no one will know the difference."

"I don't think that would help and, anyway, people might think I'm a movie star and hound me for my autograph. Ha, ha." No chance of that. "Come in the kitchen and I'll fix you something. A tuna sandwich."

"Thanks, but we need to get you out of this dungeon. I know, bundle up and we'll go to Ivar's takeout and eat outside on their deck."

Fifteen minutes later, she and I were sitting at a picnic table at the north end of Lake Union. Except for a young couple, who didn't seem to notice our arrival, we had the place to ourselves. Bundled in my fleece jacket, I inhaled the breeze fluttering off the water. A cabin cruiser glided by, its driver sitting up top and wearing a captain's hat. To the south, I could see the Space Needle and downtown's buildings standing tall against a hazy sky.

"This was a good idea. It feels good to get out of the house." I mopped a chunk of cod through the creamy tartar sauce, then plunked it in my mouth. It felt marvelous to sink my teeth into the fish. So what if it was deep-fried, I told myself, it was also teemed with Omega 3s.

The collar of Gloria's mohair coat framed her oval face. "This is good for me, too," she said from across the table. "It's the first time I've been outside in weeks. I've been buried at work and attended a seminar last weekend."

I realized I was taking up time she could be spending with her daughter. "Do you ever drop by day care and have lunch with Shelby?" I asked.

"No, they say it's too confusing for the kids having parents come in and out like that. The children think it's time to go home. It's hard enough saying goodbye to Shelby in the morning. She always starts crying."

I'd hated leaving the girls with babysitters when Drew and I went to a show. How could Gloria stand it? "I bet she's happy when you come get her at the end of the day," I said.

She swallowed a fork-full of coleslaw. "I've been working so late, Jonathon's the one to pick her up. I barely make it home before she's in bed."

Taking another bite, I watched a tugboat guiding a barge on its way to the locks and Puget Sound. I remained grateful Drew had insisted I stay home and raise our children. "I'd rather drive an old car and skip the vacations," he'd said. In spite of everything, that was one gift I could thank him for.

"So, your hubby's been hanging around?" She seemed to be reading my thoughts.

I figured he'd been on her mind since we left the house. Gloria and Drew only tolerated each other for my sake. He'd never cared for her brassy independence and she'd always thought he wasn't nice enough to me.

"Last night he pulled out the barbecue and fixed us tender-loin steaks, and tossed a Caesar salad," I said. "I didn't know he could cook so well. Then he even cleaned up after." I couldn't bring myself to tell her he'd spent the night in the guestroom.

She pulled a small mirror out of her purse, checked her smile. "Sounds like the creep's trying to win you back."

"No way, he'll be in his lover's arms tonight." I could hear my voice sharpening, and I tried to mellow it. "But the kids were happy. Neither one has stuck around the dinner table like that for years." Refusing to lock eyes with Drew, I'd lapsed into laughter several times. Over dessert, I'd even experienced short-lived moments of hope. But I wouldn't share those thoughts with Gloria.

She applied mauve lipstick and smooshed her lips together. "I don't suppose anything else happened?"

"We didn't end up in a passionate embrace, if that's what you're fishing for." I would have said no to any romantic advance, but how satisfying to have him try, and me shut him down.

"I'm glad to hear it." She slipped the lipstick back in her handbag. "That man doesn't deserve to shine your shoes."

I don't know why I still felt like defending Drew when others spoke badly of him. It was a ridiculous reaction, and I needed to get over it. "Thanks for your support. Now tell me, how's it going?" I thought I'd hear about her husband, Jonathon.

"Fabulous." She sipped her Diet soda, leaving lipstick on the straw. "I've got a hot new client. I can't reveal his name yet, but he's six-foot-six, wears a helmet, and looks good in blue-and-white."

"Sounds like a football player?"

"Yup, and what an Adonis. Obviously, I can't put the moves on him, but you could."

I coughed in protest. "I'm only five-foot-three. He'd give me a crook in my neck."

"Well, then, let's find someone shorter, like Tony Daneli at my office. I've told you about him. He's a bachelor and as cute as they come."

As I watched seagulls circling overhead scavenging for dropped food or dead fish, I remembered Gloria's description of Tony's romantic escapades. The women in her firm nicknamed him. "The Heartbreak Kid."

I screwed up my mouth. "I thought you said he was a macho flirt who likes partying every night."

"So? You deserve a little fun. I'll set up a blind date in a few weeks when your face is all pretty again. Meet him for lunch and see what you think. You should be out there circulating if you want to meet someone."

Replacing Drew was the last thing on my mind. "Hold on, I'm still married."

"Haven't you signed those papers yet?"

I forked into my coleslaw instead of answering. She knew I'd been dragging my heels. For months, she'd pressured me to cut the cord.

"What are you waiting for?" she asked.

I took my time chewing, then said, "Sue told me not to hurry." But it was more than my attorney's advice; I wasn't ready. I'd heard of graveside mourners throwing themselves onto a casket and refusing to let the dead person be buried. Maybe that was me, an inconsolable widow?

"I'm sure Sue doesn't want you waiting this long." Two men seated themselves near us. She tipped her head at them in a flirtatious manner and then returned her attention back to me. "You should get on with your life, Ruthie."

"I can't. I have two children and parents who need me."

Her head shaking, she tossed me a look of disbelief. "Your girls don't need to be burped or require diaper changing anymore, and your folks don't want you moping around by yourself for the rest of your life."

There was no way I was ready to dive into the dating scene. Maybe that was another reason I chose to stay married. "Even when the divorce goes through, it wouldn't be fair for me to get involved with anyone. My life's in transition."

"Every person over the age of twenty-one could say the same thing. Adults come with strings attached."

I thought of cantankerous Harriet and of my father's befuddled state of mind, and my shoulders slumped.

"Sometimes my strings feel more like chains."

"THAT EVIL EYE hasn't worked on me since the third grade," Harriet said, her words garbled. She spun around to grab a can of Diet Coke out of the refrigerator door.

"Open up," I demanded. "Come on, I'm going to see it eventually."

Finally, she thrust out her tongue like a gargoyle. On the fleshy tip sat a silver ball the size of a pea.

I felt my body recoil.

She sucked her tongue back in. "Are you satisfied? Now you have something else to gripe about."

Barefooted, she and I stood almost the same height, but her platform shoes gave her an extra four inches, so she towered over me.

"Who did this?" I felt like screaming or breaking something. "How dare they without parental consent?"

She wrenched on the tab and opened the aluminum can. "I told the man I was nineteen and he bought it."

"But, when?"

"On the way home from school. Some friends and I took the bus to the U-District. Alicia had her ears pierced and Shandra got a ring in her navel."

"I don't care what those other girls did. I want you to take that thing out of your mouth this minute. You could get an infection." I was afraid to ask if the instruments had been sterilized. Hepatitis was a death too horrible to contemplate.

"You can stop worrying." She chugged her drink like a truck driver tapping into a beer. "I'm almost sixteen. A woman, not a little girl anymore."

I kept the corners of my mouth from quirking up. I knew a smile would send her into a rage.

"I'll call your father," I said, out of habit. "He'll set you straight."

"Daddy won't care." She reached into the cupboard, seized a box of saltine crackers and wrestled one out. "He loves me the way I am."

"I love you, too, but I can't allow this." I took a step closer, but she swerved out of my reach. She broke off a corner of the cracker and threw it to Bonnie, who caught it midair. Then Harriet chomped into the rest of it, her mouth sloppy.

I needed a strategy, a game plan. Was she after power or revenge, or was she begging for attention? "What are you trying to prove?" I asked. "Why are you so mad at me?"

"Because you've ruined my life."

The kitchen resounded with her harshness.

Her ears back, Bonnie retreated to her bed and curled into a ball. Poor dog must have thought she was in trouble.

I put out my hand to take Harriet's, but she snapped it away.

"Please, I don't want to fight," I sat at the kitchen table and patted a place for her. "Can we start this conversation over?"

She stood tall, her shoulders flung back. "If you want to talk to someone, call Daddy and ask him to move home."

She thought he'd listen to me? In the past, my begging and pleading had backfired, driving him further away. If anything, my pitiful weakness made him despise me.

"I can't do that," I said, "but maybe he'll make dinner for us again sometime." Although I doubted he'd stop by any more often than he had before my accident.

"No, he'll never come back." A tear escaped from one of her eyes. I hadn't seen her cry for years; I couldn't remember the last time. She blinked hard, then wiped the moisture away with a finger, smudging her black eye-liner.

I heard Nichole exiting her bedroom, then descending the stairs. I pointed to the note from school. "I got a letter from your counselor today. We can wait until after dinner to discuss this, if you don't want your sister hearing."

"School is too boring to talk about."

"Boring or not, I want an explanation for your unexcused absences."

"Oh, that? When I'm only a minute or two late in the morning, my homeroom teacher marks me absent. That old hag has it in for me."

The silver ball winked at me from behind her teeth. I averted my eyes. "I'll have to call your counselor to set up an appointment."

"Relax, I'll handle it." She whipped up the letter, folded it into a square and jammed it into her pants pocket. When Nichole entered the room, Harriet said, "When's dinner? Is there anything decent to eat?"

"We could order pizza," Nichole said.

"You know I'm on a diet." Harriet's hands clamped her narrow waist; her fingers almost met in the center. "I can't eat carbohydrates or anything high in fat."

Nichole eyed Harriet's wiry figure. "If you ask me, you're ten pounds underweight."

"I didn't, so mind your own business."

I had to hand it to Nichole for not reacting. She went to the refrigerator and brought out a head of romaine lettuce.

"You can eat salad, right?"

"Miss Perfect to the rescue again. Never mind, I've lost my appetite." Harriet flung open the glass-paned kitchen door and tromped outside.

I could see raindrops spitting from the clouds. "Wear your jacket," I said, to no avail.

She slammed the door so hard the windows shimmied. I clenched my jaw; my molars fit together like a mortar and pestle.

"She's probably just going to Annie's, only a block away." Nichole set the alarm. "Don't let her get to you."

I didn't think Harriet and Annie were friends anymore, but I nodded. "Okay, you're right. It's better to let Harriet cool off by herself."

From the table, I watched Nichole dice tomatoes and left-over chicken, combine them with lettuce leaves, then sprinkle olive oil and balsamic vinegar over the top. Tall and athletic, she resembled her father. Her physical attributes were the opposite of mine, but our minds lived in sync.

"How are your applications going?" I still couldn't believe she was old enough to be thinking about college.

"Great." She delivered the salad, plates, and flatware to the table. "I may apply to a couple of California colleges too." She kept busy serving, her gaze not meeting mine.

"Really? I thought you wanted to stay close to home."

She sank into her seat. "I do, but I thought it would be interesting to see what happened. Out-of-state colleges can be expensive, but Dad said sometimes they're worth the money."

"Of course, a good education is invaluable. But we have excellent schools in the area." I couldn't imagine how lonely I'd be when Nichole moved away. Just having her live in the dorms across town at the University of Washington would be like losing a piece of myself. "We both want what's best for you. Your father and I agree there."

"Dad said he might take me to California to check things out. Do you mind?" She aimed her stare at the pepper mill in the center of the table as she chewed a mouthful of salad.

"No, although I can't see much point in it." Drew must have put these notions in her head, I thought as I plunged a piece of chicken into my mouth. The next time I spoke to him, I'd put an end to it.

5

"I NEED TO WARN you, your father's changed." Mom reduced her volume as if Pop sitting out in the car could overhear us.

"Three weeks ago, he looked fine." I caught sight of my reflection in the front hall mirror. I'd applied two layers of foundation and a good dousing of rouge, but my face still wore a yellowish-green cast. "If anyone's different, it's me."

"Honey, he thinks Drew's still living with you as your husband."

I found her words too improbable to believe. Pop had been furious with Drew's infidelity. He'd called Drew a lowlife and a reprobate. Fathers didn't forget those things.

"Mom, are you sure?" I realized I was looking down at her; she used to be an inch taller than I. "Maybe he's pulling your leg." I glanced through the doorway to see my father waiting in the front passenger seat of his fifteen-year-old white Lincoln Town Car. I assessed his dignified profile, with its patriarchal nose and strong jaw. He'd always been the pillar supporting our family. Sure, he acted opinionated sometimes, even domineering. Anything but dim-witted. Could it be that Mom, bless her heart, was blowing the situation out of proportion? It would be difficult having your spouse under foot twenty-four hours a day.

"I'll bet the doctor figures out what's wrong," I babied my bad arm into my jacket sleeve.

"I hope so." Mom's lipstick had bled into the tiny crevices on her upper lip. "Dr. Huff said memory loss can be caused by a number of things, such as LBD—something to do with protein lumps in the brain—or dehydration or even depression. I don't think your father's been happy since his last day of work. He never should have retired."

"But he deserves time off after working all those years." I buttoned my jacket with difficulty. "The stock market opens so early, and now he can sleep in."

"Men like your father want to be in charge. They like making the decisions. He never knew what to do with himself around the house. He reorganized my kitchen several times, puttered in the yard off and on, but now he just vegetates in front of the TV watching whatever happens to be on." She moved across the threshold without glancing down. "I have the hardest time getting him out of the house. Today, I said you needed a ride, that you can't drive with your injured arm, and you still don't have a car."

"The part about the car's true. The insurance company finally decided mine's totaled. I'm waiting for their check."

"That's good news. Isn't it?"

"Yes, but I don't look forward to shopping for a new one. My Honda had low miles and was in such good shape." I intended to drive it another ten years. The money from the insurance company wouldn't buy one half as nice.

I still had no idea how I'd wrecked it. Had I dozed off behind the wheel? A rogue case of narcolepsy? Maybe I should go to a sleep-disorder clinic instead of a neurologist.

"I could kick myself," I said.

"No use thinking that way, dear. What's done is done."

Out on the porch, I shut the door, then wiggled the handle to make sure it latched properly. Pop wasn't the only forgetful person in this family. Since home from the hospital, I'd been absent-minded, myself. Last night, I'd neglected to watch my favorite TV program on the Home and Garden channel, and this morning I forgot to feed Bonnie until the poor dog began whimpering with hunger. Or had one of the girls fed her as promised.

My mother proceeded down the steps; I was relieved to see her using the handrail.

"Wait for me." I tried to catch up with her, but she increased her speed. As we approached the car, a crow cackled as it hopped between the bare branches of the maple tree.

My father glanced our way and I waved, but he stared back blankly, as if examining a fleck on the glass.

I glided into the back seat. "Hi, Pop." I leaned forward to kiss his cheek, and felt bristly unshaven whiskers pricking my lips. Was he growing a beard? I'd never known him to be without a smooth chin. I glanced through the corner of his glasses and saw greasy fingerprints.

"There you are." His voice sounded gruff. "What took you so long?"

"Sorry." I strapped on my seatbelt and felt it pinch my waist.

Mom slid into the man-sized driver's seat and started the engine. Did she not realize she could adjust the seat height and lower the steering wheel? I'd have to show her later.

"Ruth Ann's moving a little slower these days," Mom said. "Remember, she just got out of the hospital."

"Another baby?"

I stared at the back of his grizzled head. Maybe he was getting scatterbrained, after all; he was repeating his jokes.

Without checking her blind spot, Mom steered the car away from the curb. "Now, Ed, we went all through that." She rolled through a stop sign to take a right. "Ruth Ann was in a car accident."

"I know, I know. Don't talk down to me." My father craned his neck to speak to me. "Bring the family over for dinner this week. I want to talk to Drew about his portfolio."

I didn't know what to say. Drew and I sold our measly stock holdings years ago to invest in his voice recognition software business. Pop had admired my husband's desire to create software for the disabled, arthritic, and the blind. Pop must remember the transaction—he handled it and then helped Drew take out a small business loan.

"I don't think dinner will work," I said.

"Nonsense."

"Pop, we don't own any stocks, and Drew and I are getting a divorce."

"That's impossible. No one in our family's ever gotten a divorce."

If he was serious, he was worse off than Mom had described. I recalled the last few times I'd stopped by my parents' home. On two occasions this last month Pop had been napping, and I hadn't given it a second thought. I'd assumed men his age needed afternoon snoozes. One Sunday I'd found him planted in front of the TV set, its volume blaring as the Sea Hawks fumbled the ball. I'd called hello, but my father hadn't answered, which was typical of him when engrossed in a football game. Unless it was halftime, my mother and I were used to chatting in the kitchen while he sat riveted to the screen.

Mom's eyes found mine in the rearview mirror. She gave me an exaggerated wink and said, "No use arguing with him. Right, Father?" She swerved around a corner, and I grasped onto the armrest.

"There's nothing to argue about." He spit out his words. "I told her to bring the family over. Why does everyone have to make things so difficult?" His hand raking through his hair left spiky tufts in its wake. "Where are we going, anyway?"

AFTER THE NURSE took my blood pressure, pulse, and temperature, Dr Kirshbaum shambled into the exam room. Now that I was out of bed and standing at his level, I realized he was a wiry, small-boned man.

"How are you doing?" he asked. As I lowered myself into a straight-back chair, he landed on the wheeled stool and opened a computer screen. He scanned the data—I assumed all about me. "Any more headaches?" He scooted over to me.

"I had one this morning when my fifteen-year-old locked her sister out of the bathroom." I chuckled although I hadn't found Harriet's behavior amusing at the time. "But I feel okay now."

Watching me with probing eyes, he smiled. "Anything else?"

"I've been tired." I glanced at the computer screen and wondered what was written in it. "And my brain feels clogged, like it's full of Jell-O."

"You still don't remember what happened the day of your accident?"

I shut my eyes and saw a snapshot of myself as a young girl. Over the last few days, splotches of memories—things I hadn't thought of for years—had scuttled through my mind. While flossing my teeth yesterday, I'd remembered bringing home my report card in second grade, and my father's lowered brow as he read aloud, "Ruth Ann is helpful and courteous, but she seems easily distracted." I'd relived the feelings of shame and my decision to earn straight As in an effort to please him, although he never seemed to notice—not like when my brother hit a homer or caught a fly from the outfield.

Later, while swabbing the kitchen counter, I recalled my first kiss at age thirteen, exchanged with a neighbor boy three years my senior. Out in the alley, he pressed his drooling lips against mine and fumbled to undo my blouse. When I shoved him away, he said, "Ruth Ann's a chicken." He later laughed about me with his friends, no doubt, because one of them clucked whenever he saw me. I wanted to forget that wretched incident, and thought I had.

Then, drifting into slumber last night, I remembered how, in high school, I'd flitted like a moth around the periphery of the popular girls' clique. Always an onlooker, never dancing in the center of the flame.

But like bubbles on the tide floating just out of reach, other recollections eluded me.

I opened my eyes. "It's not only the accident I can't remember. I'll get stuck on a word, a simple word like *security*." This morning my mind struggled for ten minutes trying to recall it. "It seems the harder I try, the further the word slips away."

His head bobbed as he spoke. "Memory loss can be exacerbated by stress."

"I doubt stress is my problem." My voice sounded taut, like a stretched rubber band. "My car crashed. I was knocked unconscious."

"Yes, of course. But I don't believe you sustained a concussion."

"That's good news." So, when would my clear thinking and energy level return to normal?

Minutes later he wrapped up his examination. "I see Dr. Garcia is your general practitioner. She should be able to look after you from now on."

A uniformed assistant moved me to a nearby room to speak to Pop's neurologist, Dr. Huff. As I waited in the windowless cubicle, a computer in the corner and a VCR and TV set up on a low table, I perused the printed articles tacked to the bulletin board. One piece urged bicyclists to wear helmets to prevent head injuries, something I didn't need to worry about since Harriet wouldn't be caught dead riding a bike and Nichole would naturally use a helmet. Another spoke of the perils of ingesting certain drugs together, none of which I had ever heard of. I shifted my gaze to a rack filled with pamphlets, then pulled one out to see the words *Alzheimer's Disease*. I knew practically nothing about the condition, only that victims' minds ripened like bananas, their brains turning mushy before the rest of their bodies showed decay. I opened the pamphlet and read: "Alzheimer's disease is characterized by the progressive decline and eventual loss of multiple cognitive functions, the loss of ability to plan and execute daily activities, and the loss of word comprehension and ability to perform complex tasks."

I asked myself if these symptoms described my father and decided they didn't. And Alzheimer's was hereditary, wasn't it? As far as I knew, neither of Pop's parents suffered from dementia. Grandpa Len died at sixty-five of a stroke and Grandma Tessa, outliving him twenty years, enjoyed cooking and quilting until she fell off a stepping stool and broke her hip, then died of pneumonia.

I did the math and calculated Pop was eighty-two. He had always been Type A, a man on the go. Growing up, I rarely saw him at the breakfast table. He jetted off to work before my brother and I woke up, and on weekends my father rose early to play tennis or swim laps at the community pool, then work out in the weight room. I recalled he'd stuck to his exercise routine until about five years ago, when his elbow began aching too much for tennis. Soon after, he announced swimming bothered his knees, and he didn't know anyone at the pool anymore.

I refolded the pamphlet and slipped it back in the rack as if it had never been opened. Just because Pop was turning into an old fogey didn't mean he had Alzheimer's. Yet something was wrong.

Rapping on the door startled me, then a tallish man with dark wavy hair and a wide moustache entered. He was handsome in a rugged sort of way, his features uneven but attractive. He carried with him an air of superiority—his chin held high—that kept me from automatically reaching out my hand to shake his.

"Mrs. Templeton?" His gaze rested on the front of my jacket. I looked down to see I'd fastened the buttons into the wrong holes. Yikes. How long had I looked like this?

"May I call you Ruth Ann?" he asked, his expression deadpan. I got the feeling he was containing a smirk at my expense. As I undid my buttons, then wriggled out of my jacket, I imagined myself through his eyes. Between my battered face and lop-sided clothing, I must look like a bag lady.

"Call me Ruthie." I tried to regain my composure as I hung my jacket on a hook near the door. "And what's your first name?" I don't know why I asked; I didn't care what it was.

"Victor." He laced his fingers, holding his hands against his abdomen; I couldn't help but notice he wasn't wearing a ring. "If you'd prefer calling me Victor, I suppose you could."

Had I offended him? I wanted to concentrate on Pop, not get in a verbal tussle with his doctor.

"Thank you for talking to me in private." I spoke with respect. "What's going on with my father?"

"I'm not sure."

"Do you think he has Alzheimer's?" The words felt like broken glass in my mouth.

"It's too early to tell." He had yet to smile, although laugh lines framed his mouth.

Staring into his face, I tried to see behind his hazel eyes to where the truth lay. Maybe he wanted to keep doctor-patient confidentiality, even if my parents had given him the okay to speak to me. Or maybe he was trying to protect me from the harsh facts. Or perhaps he didn't think I was intelligent enough to understand.

"In other words, he could have it," I said.

"It's possible."

His evasiveness nettled me. I had a right to know if my own father was ill. Why had Victor—Dr. Huff—agreed to speak to me if he wasn't going to be honest?

I said, "He either does or he doesn't."

"Things aren't that clear-cut. A diagnosis can be difficult."

"Then how do we find out?"

"First, we'll need to rule out other possibilities." He shifted his stance toward the door, as if his mind had already exited. But I wanted to prolong our conversation.

"Just a few years ago Pop was as strong as a man half his age." I folded my arms. "Today he could barely climb out of the car when we got here, then acted nervous in the elevator. When he worked, his office was on the thirty-second floor and it never worried him one bit."

"Your mother mentioned he was tops in his field, and at one time president of Rotary." He faced me, his hands dropping to his side. "How's your mother holding up?"

"It's hard to tell. She's a Pollyanna. She believes there's going to be a happy ending to every story. She even thinks my husband's coming back to me." The words blathered out before I could stop them. I felt exposed, standing in a hailstorm, unprotected as the stones pelted me. I had no intention of admitting my husband tossed me aside for another woman to anyone. Or maybe Mom had already filled him in.

"We're separated," I said. "Soon to be divorced."

"Sorry." He spoke without a trace of sympathy in his voice.

The white rut where my wedding band used to reside had long since disappeared. Once Drew's business took off, he'd wanted to replace my quarter-carat diamond with something showier that would shout out that the Templetons were moving up. But I'd adored my sparkly stone. When I slipped my ring on my finger the first time, I'd vowed never to remove it.

"That's got to be difficult," he offered, when I didn't speak. Did I hear a scant display of sympathy or did he have indigestion?

"Thanks, but I'm fine, really." I tried to make the words ring true. "In the end, getting divorced may be for the best." My thoughts bumbled out of my mouth; I didn't believe a word of it.

I scanned his grim expression. "Are you married?" I asked.

"I find it best not to speak about my personal affairs with patients." He proceeded toward the door.

"Sorry." Why had I apologized? I'd heard about arrogant doctors and their feelings of superiority. He'd rooted around in my marital graveyard but acted offended when I asked him a simple question.

His thin-lipped smile seemed artificial. "Now if you don't mind, I have patients waiting."

"All right." I felt like a miscreant child being dismissed for early bedtime, but I reminded myself we were the ones paying his salary, not the other way around.

Good riddance, I thought, and sent him my iciest glare.

6

As Drew cracked open the door to Harriet's counselor's office, I read the name *Janet Caddish* inscribed on the frosted glass.

Drew entered ahead of me. "Hey there, we're the Templetons, Harriet's parents," he said. I followed him to see a woman in her mid-thirties positioned behind a desk the same era as this refurbished 1920s building.

"Come in, I'll be with you in a moment." She pounded the tip of her ballpoint pen as she scrawled a note, then pushed it aside and said, "Please, have a seat."

I waited for Drew to claim a chair, then I took the other. Keeping my weight forward, I wondered how many times Harriet had sat in this spot. An exemplary student, I'd never been sent to the principal's office for poor behavior. I'd spoken to my high school counselor about accelerated classes and college opportunities and had assumed that's what counselors were for. I would have done anything to avoid a scene like this. Anything.

"I'm Janet Caddish." She peered over the rim of her reading glasses and sent Drew a smile, then her expression turned serious as she noticed my face.

My hand moved to my cheek. "I was in an accident," I said, leaning back in my chair.

She glanced over to Drew, and he cleared his throat. "A car accident," he said.

"That's too bad." She took a moment to reflect. Was she sizing Drew up as a wife-beater? I enjoyed the thought of him squirming under her unwavering gaze.

"I'm sorry to keep you folks waiting," she said. "We're having an assembly tomorrow morning. A kickoff for Career Week. It's never too early to get these kids motivated."

"I agree," Drew said, trying to take control of the conversation. "I grew up with nothing. I had to build my business from scratch. Kids today need to figure out what they're interested in and stick to it."

Janet removed her glasses, holding onto one bow. "Do you think your daughter has any special interests?"

"Sure, she's a very smart girl," he said. "We had, or at least I had, no idea she was falling behind in her studies. If I'd only known."

The chair back was jabbing into my spine. I tried to remember how many open houses and teacher-parent conferences Drew had attended with me. Not many. According to him, there was always something more important demanding his attention.

"I've had occasion to speak to Harriet several times this month." Janet directed her stare at me, as if I were the source of Harriet's problems. "I agree she's bright, but she's not working up to her potential." I was hoping you could fill me in, help me understand why she seems determined to fail."

"My husband and I separated six months ago, which might have something to do with it," I said, then heard Drew drag a breath through his nostrils. "But Harriet has always been a willful child. That's not even her real name."

"Yes, I read in her school records her name is Natalie."

"It's a beautiful name. My aunt's." Truth be known, I admired the name more than the woman who bore it. My mother's older sister held a grudge against Mom—some dispute about my parents' marriage, and I'd wondered if they both had their sights on the same man, my father. "Why my daughter insisted on changing it is still beyond me, but then I've never understood her."

"She's just independent." Drew worried his fingers together.

I was glad to see him looking uncomfortable; he deserved a sampling of what he'd bestowed upon me.

"In any case, we have a serious situation on our hands." She folded her glasses into a rectangle. "Harriet must not continue missing classes or she won't earn credit in several of them. And her grades are barely passing. We have an excellent special ed program here, but I don't feel the work is too challenging for her. If she'd just show up and put in the effort she could pass."

"Of course, it's not too hard," Drew said. "She needs guidance, is all. Now that I know there's a problem, I'll make sure she gets her work done."

"Really?" I asked. "And how will you manage that?" I addressed Janet, woman to woman. "My husband lives on the other side of town, and Harriet won't listen to me."

Her telephone rang with insistence. "One moment, please." She put the receiver to her ear. "Caddish here." A pause ensued, during which time I looked straight ahead and counted to ten in my head. I could feel Drew's stare piercing the side of my face.

"All right, I'll be right there," she said, then got to her feet. "I'm sorry, this won't take long." Then she hustled out into the hall.

As soon as the door was shut, Drew walked his chair around to face mine. "I've never been so mortified in my life." He looked like a balloon ready to burst. "Why on earth did you tell her I moved out?"

"I didn't realize it was a secret. As soon as our divorce is official, the whole world will know." I should place an ad in the paper with our wedding photo just to spite him. Or on a billboard?

"Of course, it's not a secret." He kept his voice just above a whisper, like a snake hissing. "But you make it sound like Harriet's difficulties are my fault."

"I'm not the one who bailed out, and I refuse to let you spin things around to make me feel guilty. Harriet was doing much better when she had two parents living under one roof."

"She's in high school now. You know, boys and all kinds of things to distract her."

It figured the first thing to come to his mind would be the opposite sex.

"Distractions? Is that what Kristi is?" I couldn't help myself; whenever I saw Drew, I thought of his lover.

"This is hardly the time to talk about her."

Tapping my foot on the floor, I glanced around the office, with its low ceiling and cracked and peeling paint.

"Ruthie, our girl's just going through a rough spot," he said. "Give her time, she'll be fine."

"Time doesn't fix everything. How about me? You think I'm going to be good as new after an allotted period?" I bolted to my feet. "Why don't you talk to the counselor, since you're the expert on everything." I ripped open the door and the glass pane shuddered.

"For Pete's sake, you're overreacting." As he stood to follow me, I stalked out into the hall, then banged the door shut in his face. Pausing for a moment, I imagined his anger welling like a tidal wave in that small room. When Janet Caddish returned, how would he explain my disappearance? Would he call me hysterical, perimenopausal? Should I pull myself together and go back so she'd think I was a good mother? Or was I tired of caring what other people thought?

It felt like a lever was flipping in my brain, as if a river that had been flowing upstream suddenly started gushing in the opposite direction, allowing floodwaters to rush with the pull of gravity as they always should have. My fists balled as I realized how much I disliked Drew. He wasn't my friend and never had been. He was a self-centered opportunist, a hypocrite, and a liar. My eyes began to sting. I blinked but couldn't stop two tears from sliding down my cheeks. I spun on my heels and rushed down the hall.

Classes were in session, and I feared the bell would ring, spilling a throng of students across my path. I didn't want my daughters or their friends to see me like this; I didn't want to run into a teacher I knew.

As I lunged toward the school's front door, I heard someone say, "Ruth Ann?" I turned and noticed Jackie. In the hospital, she'd told me her son attended Roosevelt High School and that she volunteered in the health office one morning a week. Seattle's population was over half a million, but if you had kids, it remained a small town.

She pulled a square of Kleenex from her purse and handed it to me.

"Thanks." I blotted my cheeks and nose. "I was talking to Harriet's counselor."

"I've sat in that office a few times. With five kids, I've heard it all." She looked over my shoulder at the empty hallway. "Did you come alone?"

"Drew brought me, but he's still in there. I'd rather crawl home on all fours than wait for him."

Her mouth widened into a grin and she inclined her head toward the exit. "May I drive you? I'm on my way out."

"I could take the bus or walk."

"It's no trouble and I'd enjoy the company."

Minutes later, we were strolling down the sidewalk. We came to a cross street where I noticed three youths lingering on the opposite corner taking drags off cigarettes. Was this where Harriet hung out when she was supposed to be in class? I felt like scolding the boys and shooing them back into school, but I kept going. I didn't have surplus energy to expend on other people's children when my own was teetering on the edge of failure.

Jackie's legs swished under her ankle-length skirt as she led me to her aging Chevy sedan. I gave directions while she maneuvered the car through traffic.

"Feel like talking about it?" she finally asked.

I contemplated mentioning Drew, but decided it was a waste of time. Who cared what he said or did? "It's Harriet. I don't know which is worse, her skipping school or getting a tongue piercing."

"Goodness, that sounds painful." The bench seat shook with her laughter. "If it makes you feel any better, one of my sons used to have orange hair and he still wears an earring. He was eighteen at the time, and I decided to pick my battles. I figured hair grows out, and I'm still hoping he gets sick of the earring. But there are worse things, like alcohol and drugs and jail."

"I agree, but Harriet's only fifteen. She's not old enough to vote or make legal decisions for herself. Take a right. It's the two-story brick house with the dark-green shutters in the middle of the block."

"I remember back in high school," Jackie said, "we did some stupid things. Our parents must have thought we'd lost our minds."

"But it was nothing compared to this generation." I realized I was still clinging to the soggy Kleenex; I stuffed the wad into my pocket. "In high school, my wildest shenanigan was having a crush on Mick Jagger. I was afraid to give my parents any guff. My father would have sent me to my room. And, unlike Harriet, I would have gone."

"In my family, it was my mother who was the drill sergeant. I took on that role, too, but I've turned into a marshmallow and spoiled my last one, a fourteen-year-old boy."

We pulled up front of the house. "You and I don't live so far apart." She eased up on the gas. "Keep going straight three blocks, then left for one."

I figured I must have passed her house on one of my many neighborhood walks with Bonnie.

"Great, I hope we run into each other again. Thanks for the ride." A simple thank you didn't seem sufficient for a woman who'd shown me such kindness. "Jackie, you've seen me at my worst, but I want you to know until recently I led a boring, normal life."

"I'm sure you did and will again." Then she wrote her telephone number down on a scrap of paper and handed it to me.

7

THE NEXT AFTERNOON, I headed outside to the rental car Drew had picked up for me. I'd decided Gloria was right: moping around the house all day was doing me no good. All morning I'd found my body moving at snail-speed, while my mind whirled with projects that needed doing, none of which I could accomplish until my arm healed completely. Dr. Garcia had promised I could stop wearing the brace in another week if I continued to coddle my wrist.

With no destination in mind, I dropped into the Ford Taurus's velour seat and adjusted the mirrors and lowered the steering wheel—thus removing all traces of Drew, who stood just under six feet tall. The sky released a sprinkling of rain; the clouds seemed no higher than the top of the birch tree down the street. I cranked on the windshield wipers and listened to them sigh.

I decided to visit a discount store north of town for a pick-me-up, even if it did mean burdening my Visa debt. Over the past few months, I'd used shopping as therapy—to salve my wounds and elevate my mood. When I revealed my splurges to Gloria, she assured me I could always take the stuff back.

"After what you've been through, you deserve to indulge your-self," she'd said, although I wasn't sure I believed her.

Twenty minutes later, I was pushing a shopping cart between shelves laden with china and glassware and knick-knacks. My eyes rested on a ten-inch-tall wooden lighthouse. With its blue-and-white stripes, it would look perfect up at the island, as would the ceramic seagull lying next to it. But there was no point. Drew and I would sell the cabin soon. I couldn't afford to keep the place, and there was no way I'd allow him to hang on to it. The thought of his bringing another woman there made my scalp tighten. If he and I couldn't own it as man and wife, neither of us would.

Moving up the cooking aisle, I recalled the last weekend the family had spent there. I remembered with clarity waiting on the beach that August afternoon as Drew toured the bay in our ten-foot metal boat checking our crab pot. Behind him, snow-topped Mount Baker filled the sky. I'd listened to the hum of the motor and stared at the mountain's flat triangular shape. Big and powerful and steadfast, I'd thought, it had stood for thousands of years and would endure until the end of time.

I was wiser now. Nothing lasted forever.

At the register I paid for a couple of kitchen towels and a paring knife I didn't really need, then returned to the car. Tossing the bag into the backseat, I considered not going home, maybe taking in a movie, then having dinner wherever I happened to end up. But sitting alone in a theatre sounded gloomy, and I hated eating by myself. Didn't everyone?

I figured by the time I got home Drew would be there. At least he'd called first to announce he was planning to help Harriet with her homework. "Good luck," was all I could say to him. The girl went to extraordinary lengths to do the opposite of what I wanted. For Drew to accomplish anything, I'd have to hide out in the bedroom.

As I drove out of the parking lot, I pictured his swanky silver BMW 530i, which he'd purchased just weeks after our separation, lounging out front of the house. Apparently his seventeen-year-old Toyota Land Cruiser didn't fit his new carefree bachelor image. There had been several times when I'd considered ramming my car into his new toy, just for fun. I imagined his face whitening with rage, his mouth foaming like a rabid dog's. "Oops," I'd say. "Sorry, my mistake." That pleasurable moment might be worth the expense. Once, I'd coasted my car up behind his until the bumpers touched; five-mile-an-hour bumpers that weren't supposed to be damaged by low impact. Like me: on the exterior I looked fine, but my scars festered deep inside.

I reached the freeway entrance, but on a whim continued across the overpass, then got on, traveling north. I'd drive a few miles, I told myself. Anything would beat listening to Drew beg, then badger Harriet into doing her schoolwork. He'd offered to fix dinner after, and Harriet had requested barbecued spare ribs. I couldn't stomach the thought of sitting down to a meal with him. I didn't want to lick the sauce off my fingers, then have to thank him, as if he were some kindly neighbor who happened by on his way to his real life.

I merged over to the middle lane. All around me, traffic raced forward, but I was washed with a sense of calm, as if my car were being pulled along by the other vehicles. Twenty minutes later, I passed through the city of Everett. I flicked on the radio and heard the oldie "You Can't Hurry Love." I sang the last few bars along with Diana Ross. I hadn't felt like singing for ages, not even in the shower. When that song ended, a woman began crooning a sad melody of love lost.

Determined to keep up my spirits, I switched stations until a Rolling Stones tune began to vibrate the car. Drumming my fingers on the steering wheel, I felt like a teenager—wild and a little reckless.

In what seemed like moments, I saw the Stanwood exit sign leading to the island. I hadn't thought about Drew or Harriet's bad grades or even my parents for an hour, and I regretted it was time to return to reality. As I descended the exit ramp, I told myself going home was the only sensible option. But it was 5:30, and the traffic from Everett south would be clogged solid. I decided to mosey into Stanwood to snoop in the antique mall. In the old days, while Drew browsed in the hardware store, I'd pick out a mystery or romance novel, then wander through the antique mall looking for embroidered pillowcases, vintage tablecloths, or whatever captured my fancy. I liked old things and the history they carried with them.

When I reached the village of Stanwood, I drove along the lazy main street to find a *Closed* sign hanging in the antique store's window. Without a second thought, I got back on the main road and headed toward the cabin. I'd never driven there by myself, and now my former timidity seemed silly. Drew had always sat behind the wheel. He'd made all the decisions: when we'd leave Seattle, where we'd stop along the way, and when we'd return home. I must have liked it that way, or thought he knew best. But he'd proven beyond a doubt he didn't know what was best for me.

Over the last half-year, I'd started making decisions for myself. I learned manly skills, like how to run a power lawnmower, how to record on our TIVO, and where to take the car to get its oil changed. And, I'd been able to handle each task without much effort. Maybe I didn't need a man at all.

Proceeding over the elevated bridge, I could see the tide standing high in the narrow channel that separated the island from the mainland. To the north, the crowns of other islands floated on Puget Sound; to the south stretched placid Port Susan Bay and our side of the island. The closer I got to the cabin the happier I felt. My eyes scanned the farm with the three horses I always admired, then the white church with the lofty spire, and finally dazzling views of the water through the evergreens. I hadn't realized how much I'd missed being here or how much I loved this place.

Twenty minutes later, I reached the familiar cross street and took a left. My foot pressed hard on the brake pedal as the car descended the asphalt road lined with fir trees. Passing several cabins perched on high-bank property, I was surprised to see a car parked next to an A-frame, which I didn't think belonged to a year-round dweller. In spring few city folks came here to risk the island's unpredictable weather that sometimes turned downright nasty.

I reached our always-empty mailbox and the path leading to our cabin. I figured by now Drew would be making wise-cracks about my tardiness and Nichole might be worrying. I could come back some other time, I told myself. Earlier in the day, maybe with Nichole or Gloria, although I knew she'd have difficulty leaving her family and job. And Nichole's weekends usually revolved around homework and friends, which is how it should be.

I cut the engine. While I was here, I might as well check the place over and make sure no pipes had burst during January's freeze. I hadn't thought to winterize the cabin and didn't even know what that entailed; another of Drew's chores. I opened my car door to find the air much cooler than in the city. The buttermilk-colored sun was sinking behind the trees growing on the hill to the west, leaving the forested area shadowed and mysterious. With purse in hand, I headed down the path toward the water's edge. In my haste, my foot skidded across a mossy spot, then I heard rustling in the bushes. New growth threatened at face-level and brambles crossed the trail like arms stretching out to hinder my progress. But I kicked them away, then continued until I caught sight of the cabin, with its aging shingled walls and mismatched windows. The glass-paned door smiled at me. I lengthened my strides until my hand touched its smoothness. I remembered the day I'd carefully sanded and then repainted the door's wooden frame cherry red to echo my jovial mood.

I rattled the doorknob even though I knew the cabin was locked tight, although there wasn't much fear of intruders. Few people ventured down our road even in the summer. I didn't carry a key; Drew always opened the door for me. I went around the side to peer in the kitchen window. How many wonderful times had the family enjoyed around that oval table? The room had brimmed with laughter, conversation, and love.

I vaguely remembered Drew's hiding a key somewhere, but that was fifteen years ago. Feeling as if I were on an adventure, I searched under various slabs of driftwood lying at the side of the house, then looked behind the sliding bench, my favorite spot on a summer's day. Finally, I stood on a stool to reach up under the rafters. The key, hanging from a nail, felt like ice in my hands. I lifted it off, then worked it into the lock and opened the door.

Stepping inside, I inhaled mildewed air, reminding me of my parents' basement. In the past, we would come up several times during the winter to dry out the place. Each fall I'd purchase a thousand-piece puzzle to bring along, then over the course of the winter we'd fit the pieces together as we sipped hot chocolate and shared stories.

I glanced out the window toward the east at the pewter gray water. Darkness was surrounding the cabin and I felt goose bumps on my arms. The cabin's only heat source was the fireplace and electric baseboard heaters in the two small bedrooms. As I stepped to the hearth, I tried to remember if I'd ever assembled a fire by myself. No, and it was time to learn. Reenacting Drew's ritual, I reached in and opened the damper. Then I crumpled sheets of year-old newspaper, stuffed them in, and arranged kindling on top. I dragged a wooden match across the fireplace's stone face, then heard a snap and smelled a blast of sulfur. As the newspaper, then the kindling took off, the glow of warmth comforted me. I sank down on the couch, its worn cushions conforming to my shape.

I brought out my cell phone and tapped in Drew's number.

After one ring he answered, "Hi, there," in a provocative tone he hadn't used with me since we were dating.

"It's me," I said.

"Oh. Hello." He sounded like he was speaking to a telemarketer.

"I wanted to let you know I won't be home for dinner. I'm up at the beach."

"You mean on the island?" His words gathered velocity. "What on earth are you doing there?"

With my free hand, I fed the fire a larger chunk of wood and watched the flames embrace it.

"I needed space."

"It's only an hour-and-a-half drive," he informed me. "If you start now, you'll be home in time to eat with us."

"I don't think so."

"Look, if you want me to leave, I will." He was using his irritated father voice, the one he aimed at the girls on the few occasions he took charge of discipline. "Is that what you're after?"

The pinnacle of responsibility, I'd never not come home; I'd always panicked that something would go wrong in my absence. "I'm after solitude." I didn't understand my motives, only that I needed to be here. "I'd like to stay the night if you could watch the girls."

"I can't drop everything. I have plans."

"I'm sure you do." In the past I'd be doubting myself and caving in to his demands. But not today, "Nichole and Harriet are your children too."

"Of course, they're my children, but they live with you."

"The other day you reminded me the house is still half yours."

"Fine. You win."

"Thank you." Although it seemed ridiculous to thank a man for spending time with his own children.

I said goodbye, then put on a jacket chosen from the assortment we kept there that were too old for city wear. I strolled out onto the porch to sit on the wide high-backed patio swing. Ten yards away, the water lapping against the beach sounded like a strumming harp. I rested my head back, let my lids droop shut, and rocked with my feet.

Breathing in the salty fragrance, I caught a glimpse of peace.

8

RAIN PLINKING ON the cabin's metal roof and the bed-room's wall heater clicking at irregular intervals woke me. I opened my eyes to check the clock on the bed table and read 3:00, which was impossible judging by the morning's light filtering through the curtains. The electricity must have gone out during a storm earlier in the winter and I hadn't thought to reset the clock last night.

Clad in my flannel nightgown, I pulled the comforter up around my neck and stretched my legs. It was impossible to forget the many mornings Drew and I had nestled in this bed so close to each other we were like one being. That's how I'd felt, anyway.

With no TV and nothing to read, I'd retired early last night. My supper of tuna and stale crackers hadn't filled my stomach, and it growled with hunger. I kicked off the covers, wrapped myself in my bathrobe, then padded into the living room to see raindrops skating down the windowpanes. A mattress of threatening clouds hunched over the foothills across the bay and hands of wind whipped up the water's surface.

As I shredded newspaper and fashioned a fire, I reminded myself it was Saturday morning. The girls would be sleeping in; they didn't need me for anything this morning. And Drew? He'd do what he pleased, as always.

I made coffee and devoured more crackers with hardened peanut butter from the refrigerator. I didn't want to leave the island until I'd spent some time on the beach. Not more than a few minutes, I assured myself, as I changed into sweats from the dresser stuffed with clothes—again, too old for the city. I zipped on a waterproof jacket, then stuffed my feet into rubber boots. I tugged my hair back into a ponytail and covered my head with one of Drew's baseball caps. If he were here, I wouldn't have worn it—as a statement.

I found the tide far enough out for me to walk on the beach. It seemed to be receding, but this time of year the extremely low tides, exposing the two hundred yards of muddy sand residing below the band of rocky shoreline, tended to occur in the middle of the night.

Under a smattering of raindrops, I moved slowly over the seaweed-covered rocks, heading south into the wind. As I trekked past sandy cliffs that towered almost a hundred feet above me, I listened to the slapping of the water, the dripping of rain on the bill of my cap, and the grinding of stones under my feet. The wind picked up, wailing in my ears like distant sirens. I pushed against it with defiance and was soon on the marshy spit where the girls, when younger, loved to spend afternoons building forts and pretending to be shipwrecked on a desert island. Each winter, high tides, coupled with blasting storms out of the north, would uproot their creations, then leave a fresh medley of driftwood. Sometimes Nichole and Harriet would find a buoy or an oar, and once a dinghy with a hole in its side. They had been crushed when the current carried the boat away, leaving a dead seal in its place.

That afternoon, Drew had disappeared with the car and later returned towing our new metal skiff with a seven-horsepower motor.

"You're the best daddy in the whole world," Nichole had said, and I'd agreed with her.

"You're our knight in shining armor."

I stood looking south to where my home was—what used to be my refuge, my security, everything I believed in. When would the memories die? When would Drew be banished from my mind?

I began to sob. How could I have any tears left? This was ridiculous. I'd had enough of wallowing in the past. Was I obsessed? Stuck circling around and around like a mouse in a never-ending maze? I'd heard of children venting their rage at punching bags. Maybe that's what I needed to do: beat a pillow with a stick or buy a voodoo doll and stab its belly with needles. No, I'd told my daughters that young ladies didn't behave like ruffians. But I wasn't young anymore and couldn't go on like this. It wasn't working. I decided to shriek as loudly as I could. The sound took root in my abdomen—a guttural animal-like howl that vibrated my vocal cords. After my outburst I felt liberated, almost happy, so I yelled again, this time waving my arms like a heron. I stomped my feet, uprooting rocks, one the size of a golf ball rolling down the slope and kerplunking into the water. That got me laughing so hard I had to bend at the waist to catch my breath.

My tirade left me feeling energized. How unlike the old me, who always trod between the lines of conformity. Maybe this was why Harriet, as a little girl, acted her most cheerful after a tantrum.

I turned around, now feeling the rush of air on my back as I retraced my steps. In a whoosh, my cap sailed off my head like a seagull in flight. I charged forward to capture it, only to have it scamper several feet further. I took another giant leap and ran right into a tower of a man, the force of him knocking me back several steps. I craned my neck to see his somewhat familiar face.

"Doctor Huff?" What was Pop's neurologist doing here? I must be hallucinating. I'd permanently injured my thinking capacity. I imagined myself soon to be incarcerated in a mental ward.

He stared at me for a long moment. "Ed Templeton's daughter, Ruth Ann?" he finally said, his mouth severe. "Are you all right?" He must have heard my screaming and thought I'd lost my mind.

"Yes, I'm fine." I pulled a hankie from my jacket pocket and glanced away to wipe my face, which must be blotched and puffy. When I looked back, I expected he'd be gone. But there he stood in 3-D, all six feet of him, like a junkyard dog regarding an intruder, when in fact I had every right to be here.

"I'm surprised to see anyone on the beach this time of year," I said. Was he stalking me? No, he couldn't have followed me here yesterday. And why would he? It was obvious in his office he didn't find me the least bit attractive.

He retrieved my hat and handed it to me. "Your mother mentioned you owned a cabin somewhere on the island."

How much had Mom told him? Pop, once in the navy, would remind her, *Loose lips sink ships*. Sometimes her gossiping could swamp a whole fleet.

"Is your place close by?" He spoke slowly, as if I were a lost child who couldn't find her way home.

"Yes, not far." Drew's cap in hand, I motioned down the beach. "And you?"

"A friend has been loaning me his cabin." Dressed in a windbreaker, he looked more at ease than the uptight doctor I'd met. His head was bare. Beads of water gathered at the ends of his dark curling hair and his chin showed a trace of stubble.

I pushed my hat back on. "Well, goodbye." I hoped he'd continue south to the spit, but as I marched toward the cabin, I could hear his shoes kicking up gravel next to me. His long legs had no trouble keeping my hurried pace. Although we moved within feet of each other for ten minutes neither of us said a word.

He finally touched my arm and spoke. "Have you eaten breakfast?"

I came to a halt. "Yes." Although my stomach was complaining with hunger.

"You don't look well. You'd better come along with me." When I started walking again, he added, "Please, you'd be doing me a favor. I tend to worry about my patients—and their children."

Maybe he thought mental illness ran in my family. He was the last person I wanted to spend my morning with, but I supposed he looked safe enough—unless he bored me to death.

"I'll come for a minute." He'd recognize I wasn't loony after all. Then I could flee this awkward encounter. A relief for both of us.

About a quarter of a mile before reaching my cabin, we left the beach and began our assent up to high-bank property. I followed Victor on a path cut between cedar trees and hemlocks. Already drenched, I pushed past knee-high Oregon grape, salal, and ferns. As we ascended a dozen steps crafted from railroad ties I considered turning around and creeping back down the trail. He probably wouldn't notice my retreat but running away would be silly. Victor was pompous, yes, but my parents knew and respected him. And maybe he'd fill me in on Pop's health. My chance to speak to an expert.

He turned his head and smiled at me for the first time since we'd met. "Don't worry," he said. "I've never poisoned anyone yet."

Ahead, I spotted the A-frame house I'd previously only seen from the road. Small and sturdy, it reminded me of a chalet one might find in the Alps. And I realized it was Victor's car I'd noticed the day before: a five-year-old or so Lexus—not the show-offy vehicle I expected him to drive. Maybe his ego was already so inflated he didn't need a hotshot car.

The rain beating down into the forest sounded like Snoqualmie Falls from a distance. As we neared the house, I felt a shiver run through me. Victor opened the unlocked front door and a cloud of warm air billowed out, beckoning me to enter.

"I'm too wet to come in," I said. Time for a hot shower.

"Nonsense."

As I crossed the threshold water dribbled off my jacket onto the mottled brown shag carpet.

"That doesn't matter." My friend says the rug needs to be replaced." His hands took hold of the shoulders of my jacket and he helped me remove it. He slung it on a peg, then took off his own jacket. "Come in, have a seat."

I left my hat on another peg and stepped out of my boots. Entering the high-ceilinged room, I situated myself on a worn leather couch, positioned before a hearth glowing with embers. Victor changed into moccasins; I noted he wore what looked to be hand-knit wool socks. He moved to the fire and tossed in several logs, which smoked for a moment, then produced a bustle of flames. The air grew toastier, causing my fingers to sting.

"Are you comfortable?" he asked.

Hearing those words helped me relax. There was no reason to be nervous, I assured myself. He viewed me as his patient's zany daughter who needed counseling.

Even if I looked like a drowned cat with her hair plastered flat, I didn't even bother fluffing it. "Yes, thank you. Although you needn't go to any bother. As you can see, I'm perfectly okay."

"No trouble. I already have coffee in a thermos." He entered the kitchen, an open area visible from where I sat, and came back with a mug of syrupy liquid. I took a sip and enjoyed its nutty taste—better than anything Drew had ever brewed.

He returned to the kitchen and removed eggs and sausage from the refrigerator. Soon the aroma of sizzling meat filled the room. Standing at the counter, he cracked eggs with proficiency and whipped them with a fork. As I waited, I thought how the old me would feel lazy for letting him cater to me. *Don't let others do for you what you can do yourself,* Pop had told me. But I was ravenous. And Victor had insisted. Why not take advantage of his generosity? Or was it his controlling temperament— even out of his office—that insisted I behave a certain way?

I looked around the living room with its sloped rough-cedar walls and saw a small desk, its surface buried under papers, a laptop computer, and a dozen books. Out the sliding glass doors leading to a deck, I spotted a bald eagle traversing the bay in search of fish.

"Voilà." Victor presented me with a plate of scrambled eggs, sausage, and buttered toast. Like a chef coming to my table in a restaurant, he watched me take the first bite.

"Very good." I was pleasantly surprised at the eggs' buttery taste, and also by his attempts to make me feel at home. If I didn't know better, I'd think he was a regular human being. "Aren't you going to eat?" I asked.

"I already had something earlier." He settled on the over-stuffed chair sitting at right angles to the couch. "I wasn't expecting guests. But I'm glad I ran into you."

He was? I coughed a laugh. "As I recall, I'm the one who ran into you."

"I was playing hooky." He glanced over to his laptop. "I was supposed to be working on my project."

"What kind?"

"A book. A compilation of my research."

"This would be a wonderful place to write. Few distractions." Not that I'd ever tried my hand at writing. But like our cabin, I hadn't noticed a TV set—only a battery-operated radio sitting on the kitchen windowsill.

His eyes turned sober. "Staying here usually clears my mind and I can get in eight, even ten hours of writing. But I haven't been able to concentrate." He leaned forward, his elbows resting on his knees. "The truth is, I'm wondering if I should scrap the whole project. Press the delete button and be done with it."

I was taken aback by his candor. Wasn't this the offensive character who'd refused to speak about his personal affairs?

"That sounds a bit drastic." I flattened my napkin in my lap. "I'm sure whatever you're writing will help your patients."

"If anything, they've helped me."

That, too, surprised me. He'd come across as a self-sufficient man who accepted assistance from no one.

"What's the book's theme?" I asked.

"It follows ten patients, from their first symptoms of dementia until—" He stopped mid-sentence, but I wouldn't let this opportunity to learn about Pop slip by.

"That's okay, you can say it." I swallowed a bite of sausage and waited for him to go on, but he didn't. "Men like my father?" I asked.

"As I mentioned, it's too early to come to any conclusions about him."

"But did they start out with the same symptoms?"

"Yes."

"And they all died?"

"The last one passed away a week ago." He seemed genuinely pained at the loss. "But, of course, we're all going to die eventually."

"That's the truth." I still couldn't believe how close I'd come to death, myself. Here I sat, inhaling the fragrance of burning wood, listening to it hiss and flutter, tasting the peppered sausage—all my senses alive. I wasn't worrying about my heart beating its steady rhythm or my lungs drawing in enough air, then expelling it. My organs functioned on autopilot; death seemed a million miles away.

"How old is your own father?" I assumed he must be about Pop's age.

"Mine?" His voice hardened. "He ran out on my mother and me when I was a kid."

"Don't you ever hear from him?"

"Never. He took his own life."

He got to his feet and reached for the poker, stabbed it into the fire to prod the logs together.

"I'm sorry." Not just for bringing up the subject, but for Victor's terrible loss. "I shouldn't ask so many questions."

When he turned back to me, he was wearing his doctor's office demeanor—not an ounce of friendliness left. He looked older, his skin parched.

"Yes, that seems to be your habit," he said, distantly. "If you'll excuse me, I need to get back to town."

I was being dismissed again, but it didn't get my goat this time. "Sure, okay." I finished my eggs in haste and carried my plate into the kitchen. "Thanks for breakfast. It was very kind of you."

"You were in obvious distress." He held up my jacket as if he couldn't wait for my departure.

"I wasn't in distress." I stepped into my boots. "In fact, for the first time in a long time, I was enjoying myself."

AS I LOOKED around our cabin it occurred to me the place needed to be cleaned and straightened before it could be put on the market. When we sold, the new owners might purchase the furniture, although it had little monetary value. But that left a truckload of personal items; the room verged on clutter.

My gaze rested on the lamp: a glass jug I'd filled with shells and stones, and paired with a lampshade I'd picked up at the thrift store. I'd been proud of my creation and the golden light it produced but couldn't think of a place in the city I would use it. Next to the lamp stood a driftwood knot the size of a tennis ball with several eagle's feathers stuffed into the center crack. Again, a thing of beauty here, that would look out of place in my Seattle living room. I glanced down to the multi-hued rag rug I'd considered a treasure when found at the antique mall, but it suffered from frayed corners and a worn spot in the center. Like oil floating on pasta water, this way of life and the city's didn't mix.

On the mantle rested nine or ten framed snapshots capturing the family's special moments on the island. Drew's grinning face dominated most of them. In one picture, he looked a proud father as he carried baby Nichole in a backpack. In another, he was the loving husband, his arm around my shoulder as we lounged on the sliding chair. In another, he appeared utterly satisfied as he napped on the hammock. I couldn't help wondering if he'd been dreaming of Kristi that afternoon last summer, but decided I was wasting valuable braincells thinking about him. What good would it do to know?

I was tempted to toss his photos into Puget Sound and let the tide drag them away. I could imagine the waves smacking and grinding them into the rocky beach. But he was still the girls' father; they missed him and might want his pictures in their bedrooms. In an act of what I considered unselfish charity, I decided to take them to town.

In need of cardboard boxes for packing, I drove to the grocery store five miles away. While there, I purchased a fried chicken breast and potato salad from the deli counter for lunch. Then I stood in the checkout line behind a pregnant woman who was writing a check for a cartload of food and beverages.

"How's it going, Ruth Ann?" a man behind me said. I turned and recognized Hal Vandervate, the realtor who'd sold us our cabin fourteen years ago. Nearing retirement age, with sloping shoulders and a scruff of thinning hair, he was carrying a ten-pound bag of flour. His wife must have run out in the middle of a cooking project.

"Not bad." I was glad I'd taken the time to smooth on concealer and foundation. Inspecting myself in the mirror twenty minutes ago, I'd noticed I was beginning to look my old self again—not all that terrible. In fact, pretty good.

"And the family?" He set the flour on the belt. We'd run into Hal several times over the last few years, and he'd met both girls.

"We're all fine, thanks," I lied. "And you?"

"Couldn't be better. Business is booming. I have more buyers than I know what to do with."

"Great." It meant we'd have little trouble selling our cabin. Hal would be the obvious person to list it, but I couldn't bring myself to say the words. Drew should make the arrangements. Let him explain why we four would never come here again.

I paid my money and made my departure. By the time I got back to the cabin most of the clouds had parted to reveal a canvas of azure sky. Although the air remained chilly, sunshine greeted me as I carried my food and cartons down the path. I dropped the boxes by the kitchen door, then headed around to the porch and sat on the patio swing to eat my lunch. I wasn't used to being by myself. Always, there were people to care for, to watch over, or entertain, and a sink-load of dishes to be washed. I wondered how single women filled their days without children. Did they adopt or wait patiently for grandchildren to be born? I tried to embrace the stillness, telling myself relaxing was an acceptable pastime, in spite of what Pop might say.

As I finished my last bite of chicken, my cell phone rang. Taking it from my purse, I glanced at the screen and saw Drew's name. I answered with reluctance but reasoned that maybe Nichole or Harriet needed me.

"Where are you?" Drew asked without saying hello first.

"Still at the beach."

"Do you want me to come up there?" His voice blasted into my ear; I held the phone away and could still hear him clearly.

"I mean, are you all right? Can you drive home okay?" He sounded upset. Did he still care about me or was he only concerned about the automobile rented out in his name?

"I'm fine and I promise to take good care of the car." I was beginning to feel cold. I stood but needed both hands to gather my things. "I'd better go, unless the girls want me for something."

"No, Harriet spent the night with some friend named Alicia, and Nichole said she'd be gone most the day, then has a date this evening."

I had to ask, "Why are you still there?" I presumed he'd rendezvous with Kristi the moment the girls left the house.

"I thought I'd wait around until you showed up." His sentence went up in the end, like a question. "I've got to tell you I think it's weird the way you took off. You're usually not so irresponsible."

So, he only called to scold me? "Let me get this straight." I felt defensive. "The man who ran off with a floozy thinks I'm irresponsible."

"Why must our conversations always revert back to that?"

"You're right." I was impatient to hang up. "I don't want to fight. Goodbye."

Preparing to leave, I fastened the cabin key onto my key chain. Then I filled a box with photos, lay it on the ground outside, and locked the door. With Drew handling the sale, this could be my final visit. I hated that thought, but it beat selling the Seattle house, which might be a possibility if I didn't get back to work in the near future.

I walked down to the beach for one last look. Standing at the water's edge, I faced north. The sun washing across my back sank in through my jacket and sweater. The tide had receded further and the breeze skipping across the sandy flats sent the moist smell of seaweed to my nose. Further out, the wind toyed with the water, sending one-million diamonds dancing across its surface. A flock of terns wove tight circles and a king-fisher hovered high, ready to dive.

As I turned to leave, I spotted something glowing at my feet. I stooped to pick up an agate, reddish-gold in color, with a glossy surface. I rubbed it between my fingers, then slipped it into my pocket.

9

"YOU'RE BACK." HARRIET watched me walk through the front door carrying the cardboard box. The silver ball buoyed in her mouth as Harriet spoke. Drew hadn't found her tongue piercing as repulsive as I had. "It's just a fad, she'll grow tired of it," he'd insisted. I still couldn't imagine why anyone would wear such a thing. What was the point?

"Hi, sweetie." I tipped the carton of photos for her to see the contents. "I brought these back from the island for you and Nichole. Why don't you take a look through them?"

"I don't want any of that junk."

"Not even a picture of your dad?"

"Trust me, I don't need reminders of when we were all happy. Santa Claus is dead."

At least Bonnie was happy to see me. She sniffed my shoes no doubt detecting the aromas of the island. I scratched between her ears, and she licked my fingers. "Your sister might want a couple."

"I wouldn't doubt it. She's still living in a make-believe world."

It bothered me no end when Harriet made snide comments about Nichole. Drew and I had done everything in our power to treat them fairly, but Harriet always viewed her portion as half empty.

"Someday you'll appreciate having such a nice sister." I set the box and my phone on the dining room table. "My big brother either ignored or tortured me." I'd exaggerated, although it had sometimes seemed that way to a girl with few friends aching for his approval.

"Are you still hoping we'll be best friends?" she said. "That's never going to happen. The thought of us acting buddy-buddy makes me want to retch." She pointed a finger to her opened mouth. "We're opposites in every way—music, clothes, friends, men. Which is fine with me. I wouldn't want to be like her."

We stood eye-to-eye like two cocks poised to fight. I refused to look away first. I was still her mother and deserved respect.

Harriet leaned an inch closer. "I got stuck with your looks, and thanks a lot. Couldn't you have given me Dad's tall, blond genes instead of your short, pudgy ones?"

I felt my eyeballs bulging as I continued to stare into her face. I could think of a thousand biting words I wanted to sling her way. Like, "Shut up, you little brat. You're not getting any allowance for a year. Go live with your father if you don't like it here." But I knew she'd embrace my tirade as proof I didn't love her. She'd never forget what was said; the girl's brain was a steel trap; too bad she didn't take advantage of her good memory at school.

I decided to try a different tactic, one that might catch her off guard and deflate her hostility.

"Harriet, I think you're beautiful."

Her laughter cut like a razor. "Yeah, right. You think I'm ugly."

"Why would I think that if we look alike?"

"Because we're both ugly."

I don't think anyone had ever called me ugly before, although I'd certainly thought it several times since the accident. I tried to disregard her brutal assessment, but it wounded me to my core. That's how vulnerable I was. And if she really thought she was ugly I had failed her as a mother.

My phone rang, but neither of us made a move. I felt my pulse pounding against my temples, vibrating my head. A couple of months ago, during my annual checkup, Dr. Garcia noted my blood pressure was elevated, and I'd said I could always tell when it was on the rise. She'd said a person can't detect their own hypertension, but she was wrong. Right now, my blood was distending my veins to their limits.

As the phone rang again, I tried to remember the breathing exercise I'd read about in a self-help book everyone was touting a few years back. Breathe in through your nose for four counts, I told myself. Hold it for seven, then breathe out through your mouth for eight.

Finally, on the fourth ring Harriet reached for my phone and flung it to her ear.

"What?" she said. Then her voice turned cuddly. "Oh, hi, Grandma. Yeah, she's right here." She pushed the phone toward me. "It's Grandma Millie."

"Hi, Mom." I was glad for contact with the outside world.

She sounded frantic. "Ruth Ann, your father's gone."

He'd died? I envisioned Pop on his recliner in the living room, his jaw unhinged and his eyes rolled back. A heart attack? A stroke?

"What happened?" I asked, dreading her answer.

"I was in the kitchen peeling potatoes." Her words tumbled together, slurring themselves. "Ed was watching TV, some game show I couldn't stand listening to. I didn't check on him for over thirty minutes."

Waiting for her to finish, I forgot about Harriet's impudence. About Drew's infidelity. About uppity Dr. Huff and his eggs. I wished Mom would hurry up and spit it out, but knew I wasn't ready for what she was going to say.

"When I finally went into the living room," she said, all breathy, "he wasn't there, and the front door was ajar. He must have gone out while I was running water, because I didn't hear a thing."

Relief swept through me. Pop was alive. "You mean he's outside?" Why had she scared me to death? "Maybe he's in the backyard putting out garbage."

"No, I checked, and in the alley, too. And he didn't answer when I called his name."

"Maybe he's on a walk." Not that I could recall his taking one before.

"But he could get lost or hit by a car. In his state of mind, he may never come back."

"It's going to be okay, Mom. I'll come right over." I dashed to my car and sped to my parents' home, about ten minutes away. As I drove, my mind wrestled with the absurdity of my father getting lost in his own neighborhood. Yet I remembered reading a newspaper article about an old gentleman in eastern Oregon who'd wandered off and was found days later, dead. The whole scenario had seemed implausible, and I'd surmised foul play was involved. But the authorities declared his death resulted from exposure to the elements.

I spotted Mom coming down from a neighbor's front porch. She rushed over to my car.

"I checked the yard, the alley, talked to several neighbors" She paused to catch her breath. "Shall I call the police? Would they even respond to something like this?"

"You'd better. If there's a patrol car in the area, they might keep an eye open for him. I'll drive around while you wait at home."

I knew the neighborhood well; I'd grown up in this two-story craftsman-style house. I remembered my father teaching me to ride a bike on the level sidewalk out front. "Don't let go, Poppy," I'd squealed. But when I glanced around, he stood far behind, laughing, his hands on his hips. Those were precious moments I clung to, occasions when he had stepped out of his busy downtown work life to spend time with me. As I took a right, I realized on that day Pop had been younger than I was now—the top of his head covered with thick brown hair and his body limber.

I drove past my old grade school, a Queen Ann style structure. My heart heaved a melancholy sigh each time I saw its mustard-yellow exterior. Time spent there passed for the most part carefree. It wasn't until I hit my teens that my self-confidence took a nosedive.

I spotted a mailman walking ahead and I stopped to ask him if he'd come across my father. I felt like a traitor describing Pop as a confused old man wearing a pair of mismatched sweats and bedroom slippers. But the man shook his head. "Sorry, no. Good luck." On the next block I spoke to a woman walking a sleek greyhound, then some teens throwing a Frisbee, but no one had seen him.

After twenty-five minutes of zig-zagging around the area, I returned home. No squad car or ambulance out front. A good sign, I hoped.

Entering the front door, I found my father in his easy chair gnawing into a Milky Way, its paper torn back haphazardly.

"Hey, Pop," I said. "What's up?"

He raised the hand clutching the candy bar but didn't reply. Then he bit into it again with zest, smearing chocolate on his lips.

"Mom?" I called.

"In here." Her voice sounded weak.

I continued into the kitchen and found her leaning against the sink. Her pink eyes looked like open wounds against her pale complexion. "I was just going to call you," she said. "Thought I'd better let the police department know I found him first."

"Where was he?"

"The Mini Quick."

The small store with its four gas pumps was located several blocks away. I scolded myself for not looking there, although Pop considered their petrol substandard. He was very particular how he fueled and maintained his Lincoln. To my knowledge, he'd never set foot in the place.

"He was at the cash register wanting that candy bar," she said. "No wallet, no money." Her head shook, but it looked more like a tremor than a statement. "Thank the Lord a woman we know came in to pay for her gas and realized what was going on. She drove your father home, although she said it wasn't easy getting him to come with her."

"And I see she bought him the candy, too."

"Yes, she was very kind." Mom drooped into a chair by the table. "Ed didn't seem to recognize her, nor did he say thank you."

"Really?" My father had always possessed impeccable manners. He'd drilled *please* and *thank you* into my childhood speech until I said the words even when there was no call for them. It was hard imagining his not acknowledging the woman, but, then, it was difficult picturing him leaving the house without his prized alligator wallet, or even eating a candy bar. He'd always been a health-food eater and avoided sugary foods calling them empty calories.

My hand stroking her back I attempted to comfort her as best I could. I wished I could tell her everything was going to be all right, but that wasn't true, unless Dr. Huff knew of some magic potion. When Mom calmed down, I would ask her to call his office to insist we try every medication out there.

"Thanks." She attempted a show of confidence. "We're okay now."

"But what about next time?" I couldn't help thinking out loud.

"I'll have to keep a better eye on him is all."

I sat in the chair adjacent to her. Glancing around the room, I assessed the 1970s appliances and the same yellow cupboards I'd known since childhood and tried to tally up what the house needed in repairs. The sink disposal didn't function, and I bet the washer and dryer in the basement stood on their last leg, not to mention the shake roof that needed replacing. I'd always assumed my parents would live right here until they passed away peacefully in their sleep, but all of a sudden this beloved home loomed like a ravenous pit.

Maybe it was time to think about moving my folks into a retirement home.

10

I WATCHED NICHOLE LUG a midsize canvas suitcase down the stairs to the front hall and set it by Drew's feet. I'd never seen the suitcase before. Had he purchased it especially for their trip while I was waylaid in the hospital?

"I'll be ready in a minute, Dad," Nichole said, then darted back upstairs.

Drew wheeled the suitcase toward the partially-open front door. "Ruthie, I don't see why you're making this into such a big deal," he said, as if I were the one out of line.

My mouth opened in anger, but I kept my voice tempered so Nichole wouldn't hear my outrage. "How long have you two been planning this little excursion?"

"We've been tossing the idea around for a month or so." He gave me a shrug. "Honestly, I thought you knew."

I racked my brain and recalled Nichole and my conversation over dinner. "She mentioned she was considering a couple schools in California. Once. Are you sure this isn't all your idea?"

"No, she brought it up. Maybe she didn't think you were well enough to travel. Or maybe you forgot?"

The word *covert* came to mind. I wondered if the dialogue between these two had initiated during my hospital stay.

"I wouldn't forget something like that," I said, and he shrugged again.

Nichole jogged down the stairs wearing her jean jacket. "We're just looking, Mom," she said. "Nothing has been decided yet. I might not even get in."

Her GPA stood at 3.9 and her SAT scores were top-notch. I couldn't imagine any colleges wouldn't accept her. "I thought we agreed it would be best if you stayed in the area," I said. "We even had the dorm picked out at the university. Unless you'd prefer living in a sorority."

"I'll probably end up at the U, but I want to see what Scripps is like. Candace said it has a wonderful psychology department. She and her parents are going down this weekend, too."

This was news to me; I thought Nichole wanted to teach high school French. "The University of Washington must have a fine psychology department, too," I said. "At a quarter of the price. Not to mention the cost of airfare every time you come home for the weekend." Who was I kidding? If I wanted to see her other than Thanksgiving and Christmas, I'd have to fly down there myself.

"Let me worry about the money." Drew sounded like a radio announcer promoting cut-rate financing.

"And it takes so long to get there." I understood I was delaying, not stopping, their departure.

"No longer than driving to Washington State, my alma mater," Drew countered. "We want our girl to have the best, right?"

I resented his tactics. What was I supposed to say, that I preferred Nichole go to a second-rate school? "When I was a girl, I did what my parents suggested," I said. Which wasn't entirely true. Pop had urged me to wait a few years before getting married, but I'd rushed right into matrimony as if Drew where the only eligible bachelor on earth. Of course, if I hadn't married him, I wouldn't have my two daughters.

Drew inched toward the door. "I don't believe in forcing kids to follow in their parents' footsteps." True, his father hadn't bagged out of the marriage.

"They didn't force me," I said.

"Okay, you've given Nichole your recommendation. Who gets the final say?" He tilted his head in her direction. "I assume she does."

"Sure, of course, she should go where she wants. But I stayed near my parents, and it was for the best."

"I didn't, and my folks were fine with it."

Drew grew up in Montana. What did he know about staying close to home? He saw his parents maybe once or twice a year. Not that I blamed him for not wanting to spend time with people who hardly ever asked about their grandchildren and criticized Drew's choice of vocation and my housekeeping.

"You ended up marrying a woman from another state, and never moving back," I said, not wanting to concede the point. "You hardly ever see your parents. You don't want that happening to us, do you?" My brother and his family had moved to Massachusetts ten years ago. If I had followed suit, how would Mom have handled Pop's jaunt today?

"Is this about Nichole going to California or the fact that I'm the one taking her?" Drew sent me a stilted smile. "You're welcome to come along, if that would help ease your anxieties. Go pack a bag while I call the airline and purchase another ticket."

"Who'd look after Harriet?" I asked. Someone had to be responsible around here.

"She could stay with a friend."

"Harriet's hanging out with a new crowd at school this year. I barely know her new friend, Alicia, and have never spoken to the girl's mother. There isn't time to find their telephone number, arrange an overnight, pack my stuff and make the house secure, and you know it." If he'd really wanted me along, he would have asked me weeks ago. And that would have given me time to put the kibosh on the whole trip.

"I'll help you," he offered half-heartedly.

"It won't work." I scoured my mind for more excuses. "We have Bonnie to think of. I can't let her starve to death." Although the Wongs, the twenty-something couple next door, would probably feed her the way I looked after their calico cat when they went on vacations.

Drew checked his iPhone. "There's our Uber. We'd better run."

I figured Drew didn't want to leave his pristine BMW down at the airport parking garage collecting door dings. I could have given them a ride if they'd only asked, but it was too late now.

"Fine, fine, have a good time." I couldn't fathom spending forty-eight hours with Drew, anyway. Our idle chitchat would be used up after thirty minutes, then what would we talk about? As Harriet would say, *Gag me.*

Drew hoisted up the suitcase and opened the door. Nichole strode out as if she were late for school. No goodbye hug. No, "See you in a couple of days."

A moment later, I stood at the front window watching the Uber disappear down the street. I felt adrift, like an island floating in the middle of an ocean. I wrapped my arms around myself. I'd love to be held like a little child again, to have someone else in charge of my life. If only there were a way to bring back those moments of security. I went to the phone and started to call Mom, but she had enough on her plate without worrying about me. As I set my phone aside the sound of the back door jiggling open, then closing, reached my ears. Bonnie trotted into the kitchen and gave a welcoming yap. I recognized Harriet's giggle, then I heard the deep mumble—a man's voice?—followed by a block of silence.

I walked into the kitchen and found Harriet in a lip-lock with a tall scraggly kid with hair so black it must have come out of a bottle. Harriet had never shown interest in the opposite sex. In fact, she'd called the boys in her class immature idiots. But apparently, she'd changed her mind, and I was about to meet her first boyfriend.

I cleared my throat and the boy jerked back, staring at me with a mixture of embarrassment and fear.

"My mother," Harriet told him, not releasing one arm from its hold.

I moved closer and the young man shrank away from Harriet. A scarlet blaze flushed across his acne-riddled face. "Hi, Mrs. Templeton."

"Have we met?" I asked.

"Alex and I have been going to school together since second grade," Harriet informed me as if I were a dimwit for not remembering him.

Finally, it clicked; I marveled at his transformation. "Sure, hello, Alex." Just last year he'd stood shorter than Harriet and wore his light-brown hair extra short.

Harriet riddled me with her glare. "Do you have a problem?"

"You mean with Alex being here?"

He grimaced at the sound of his name and sidestepped toward the door.

"Not at all," I said. "In fact, why doesn't he stay for dinner?" I pulled out a kitchen chair to show the sincerity of my invitation. "Nichole is out of town with your father and there's plenty to eat."

"Uh, I'd better go." Alex's hand wrestled with the doorknob. "I'm supposed to be home...that big history project." He managed to escape before either Harriet or I could reply.

She shut the door behind him, then gyrated around in her usual theatrical style. "You scared him away. Now he'll never come back."

"Sorry." Not entirely. I didn't appreciate his using my kitchen for a make-out center.

"You never like my friends."

"That's not true," I said. I hardly knew any of them. "He looks like a nice boy, just mixed the black shoe polish up with the shampoo." Her frown told me I'd said the wrong thing again. Now I was in for it.

She raked her fingers through her bangs. "Think you're funny? As if you'd know anything about hair."

"Sorry." Apologizing further would only lengthen the discussion and give her more ammunition to thrash me with. I decided to change the subject. "So, you have a history project?" I wondered if I could coax her into completing it without Drew's presence.

"No, Alex and I have different teachers. Since when do you care so much about my homework?"

"I've always cared, but I've been stepping back to let you be responsible, and so we don't butt heads."

"You've got to be kidding. You've been on my case worse than ever."

"Only when the school writes me. If you'd arrive at your classes on time—"

Her hands flew up to plug her ears. "I can't hear you!" she shouted. "I can't hear you!"

The front doorbell rang. Bonnie sprinted to the door, then barked. I was glad for an excuse to escape the room. I opened the door to see my neighbor, Jim Wong, holding a cardboard box crammed with men's clothes. I figured he was collecting articles for a clothing drive.

"I think this is meant for you," he said, wearing a nervous smile. "As I was getting out of my car a minute ago, a woman drove up and asked me to put this on your front porch. She looked angry enough to eat nails, so I said, 'Okay.'"

He transferred the box into my arms. I recognized one of Drew's favorite ties tangled up with a pair of his slacks and the golf shirt I'd picked out for him a couple years back.

"What did she look like?" Not that I'd recognize her.

"Cute, strawberry-blonde hair, average height." He wiggled his eyebrows Groucho Marx style. "The other woman?"

I don't know why I was surprised he knew about my personal affairs. Of course, he and his wife would have noticed Drew's absence. Juicy news whipped around neighborhoods like a flock of sparrows.

"I guess so. We've never met."

Kristi had the gall to come to my home? Why was she returning Drew's stuff? Was she prowling around the neighborhood looking for his car the way I used to right after he left me? Pathetic behavior. For half a second I felt sorry for her, then I reminded myself she was a home-wrecker who cared nothing about me or my children.

11

T HE FIRST THING I saw when I entered the architectural firm where I'd worked for five years was a san-
dy-haired woman in her twenties sitting comfortably at my
desk, typing at my computer like a pro.

One hand resting on the mouse, she glanced up and said,
"May I help you, Ma'am?"

I hated being called ma'am; it sounded old. Well, next to
her I was.

I felt a mite shy, like the morning I returned to third grade
after my weeklong absence following my appendectomy—
that tense moment of rejoining the fold, trying to go unnoticed, wishing my awkwardness would pass. But in elementary
school no one had taken over my desk, while this trim receptionist, in a silk blouse and sepia-brown suit, looked like she
belonged in this modern downtown office more than I did.
Sure, I was thin, but there was nothing chic about me—not
with my fluffy hair that never obeyed and my casual clothes
that bordered on sloppy. I admonished myself for wearing
slacks and a turtleneck sweater.

"Hello," I said, "I'm Ruthie Templeton." When her blem-
ish-free face showed no recognition, I added, "I work here."

"Nice to meet you." She gave a faint smile. "I'm Brittany."

I glanced around the familiar room: oak-wooden floors and off-white walls adorned with framed ink drawings of homes my boss, William Dunning III, had designed, and several of his awards. I admired easygoing Bill, with his paunchy tummy and robust laugh. His passion lay in designing mega-homes, the kind erected for the Street-of-Dreams, an annual event attracting buyers with incomes in the upper one percent.

Bill emerged from his glassed-in office that overlooked Elliot Bay. "Terrific, I wasn't expecting you for another week," He came across the room to greet me with a one-armed hug.

I showed him my brace. "I stopped by to thank you for the beautiful flowers." Yesterday my wrist had felt back to normal, but this morning, after dusting and vacuuming the living room, it started aching again. "Sorry, I make a terrible left-hander."

He didn't hide his disappointment. "Well, hurry up and get better. We're swamped. Remember the McMannus project on Bainbridge Island? It's all ours."

"That's wonderful, congratulations."

"You know how people are," he said. "Now that they've decided to use my design, they want their home built yesterday."

I nodded. It took some of our clients years to commit to a project, but once they did it was full throttle ahead. And I loved being part of the process. Bill often came to me for advice, saying he wanted a woman's perspective. But I liked to think it was because of my innovative ideas. I'd spent my childhood admiring different styles of architecture, planning and dissecting, then putting my pencil to paper. "Our girl's going to be an architect," Mom had said more than once. And until my senior year in college, I'd thought so too. With visions of designing affordable homes with European flavor, I had intended to continue in the school of architecture to earn my master's degree, then get licensed. But I turned myopic the day I met Andrew Templeton. I'd jumped on his ship and sailed away without a compass.

"Have you met Brittany?" Bill sounded more like a proud father than a boss. "She was sent over from the temp agency. She's been a lifesaver." Obviously pleased at his declaration, Brittany beamed back at him.

"I hope I'm not working her too hard," he said, giving her a wink. "I don't want to wear her out."

"You won't, I love it here," she said. "It's ten times more interesting than my last few jobs where all I did was file records."

The phone jangled. My first impulse was to answer, but Brittany beat me to it, saying, "Good afternoon, Dunning Architect and Design, Brittany speaking," with exuberance. "Sure, that will be fine. Thanks for calling." Her words were politely assertive, professional. After hanging up she turned to Bill and said, "Mr. Kashiba can't make it in today. He rescheduled for tomorrow at 2:30."

"That helps," he said. "I still need to check his property's zoning for height restrictions."

"I can do that online," Brittany said. "I have the web address right here."

"Great, you're an angel."

I didn't recognize the name Kashiba, nor did I have a clue how to look up zoning on the internet. I realized I'd need to take more initiative when I got back to work or be replaced.

As Bill walked me to the door he said, "We like Brittany so much, we may find a permanent spot for her."

"That's nice." I wasn't sure there was enough work for the both of us. Bill's firm was a small operation. Marianne, the bookkeeper, came in three mornings a week, and I answered the phone, made appointments, and brought Bill his coffee.

"I'll let you get back to work." I turned to leave. "See you next week."

"The sooner the better. We're installing Apples tomorrow and I want you up to speed on the operating system and new software before next month's invoices go out."

My face must have revealed confusion, because he said, "Computers. We're switching to Apple."

It had taken me years to become proficient on the PC. I'd even bought one for the girls and me to use at home. "Are you sure that's necessary?"

"Yes, I want to hook up to my brother-in-law's network in Los Angeles, not to mention my laptop at home."

I knew his wife's brother was an architect too. But couldn't they send emails and talk on the phone?

"Should I take a manual home to study?" I asked.

"I'm sure you'll pick it right up."

"Okay, thanks." I wished I had his confidence.

When I got home Harriet was lurking in the front hall—a rare occurrence. After school she usually hid behind her closed bedroom door with the music turned up loud enough to drown out my pestering voice.

"I need money," she said.

I should have known. "What for?" I wasn't about to pay for body another piercing or tattoo.

"A dress for a school dance. It's formal."

"Really? Sounds fun." I was glad she wanted to join in on school activities, get herself prettied up, and enjoy being feminine. Was she going with Alex? I couldn't imagine him in a tuxedo. When he picked her up—one of his parents driving because he was too young to have his license—I'd insist on photos.

"And don't suggest I wear one of Nichole's old rags."

"I didn't say a thing."

"You didn't have to. It's the way you look at me, like I'm some kind of freak."

"I'm looking at you because we're talking." Determined not to argue, I painted a smile on my face and tried to lighten my voice. "I understand you want a new dress, and I think that's fine. Why don't I take you shopping right now?"

"You don't have to come with me. I'm capable of choosing my own clothes. All I need is cash or a charge card."

There was no way I'd entrust this girl with my wallet. "I'd like to go," I said. "It'll be fun for me. Anyway, how else would you get there?"

Her arms locked across her chest. "Okay, but I don't want to go to one of those department stores where they have hundreds of the same dress."

"Okay, then, where?"

"There's a place I like on Fremont. Can I drive?"

"I'm afraid not. The rental company doesn't allow girls with learner's permits to drive their vehicles." I was grateful for avoiding the hair-raising ordeal. The good news was that Drew had agreed to take her out for driving lessons twice a week. I had to hand it to him, when it came to Harriet, he possessed twice my patience and three times my courage.

The ten-minute ride to the Fremont District stretched long and silent. If Nichole had been in the car, the air would have glittered with laughter and easy conversation. I glanced over to see Harriet staring straight ahead. She was my own daughter, I thought, sitting right next to me, but we had nothing to talk about.

The moment I pulled the car into a spot, Harriet thrust open her door and bopped out. Swaying atop her platform sneakers, she clomped across the street without looking for oncoming traffic. She zeroed in on a shop I'd never noticed before. As I followed her, I scanned the front window to see mannequins clad in skimpy halter-tops and belly-exposing slacks; the pants sat so low on the hips I couldn't tell what held them up.

Once inside, blaring music assaulted my eardrums. I passed two high-school aged girls standing at the counter speaking to a salesperson. Harriet roamed to the far end of the room where she started sifting through a rack of clothes. She pulled out a dress made of a lavender sequined fabric. I strolled nearer to see that the bodice was nothing but a flimsy square of cloth with a string to tie around the neck. The wearer's back would be completely exposed.

"No way." I expanded my volume to be heard over the blaring music. I remembered my first formal, a dusty-pink velveteen floor-length dress trimmed with flowered ribbon. Yes, I know, that sweet innocent look went out years ago.

"You're right," she said, "that's a little-old-lady color." Harriet jammed the dress back onto the rack, then she selected several black numbers and marched into a fitting room.

"I want to see what I'm buying," I said. I stood outside her door, watched under it to see her jeans drop to the carpet, then her knit top. As a girl, I'd loved shopping downtown with my mother—our special time, usually followed by a lunch of chicken salad at our favorite restaurant. As I contemplated sharing those memories with Harriet, the dressing room door blew open and she strutted out wearing a clingy dress with a floor-to-waist slit exposing one leg. My mouth dropped open as I surveyed her ivory thigh, then her round breasts under the flimsy fabric. When had she grown so shapely?

"You aren't supposed to wear a bra with this." She glanced at herself in the mirror.

I pursed my lips long enough to keep a negative comment from spouting out of my mouth. I took a cleansing breath, then said, "By the way, who's the lucky guy?"

"I don't know. But if I don't buy something early, the good dresses will be gone."

"Wouldn't it be a good idea to have a date first?"

"Nah. If someone doesn't ask me, I'll go alone. Things have changed, Mother. Women don't sit around waiting for some Prince Charming to show up." She returned to the fitting room and a minute later emerged wearing a dress with a plunging neckline that barely covered her breasts. At least the hem flowed to her ankles, and the sleeves were long enough to conceal her tattoo. But it revealed way too much cleavage.

Harriet eyed herself in the mirror and frowned. "Boring. I want something that makes a statement." She glared at me in the mirror and shook her head. "You're making me nervous staring like that. This isn't working." In a minute she was back in her jeans.

"Want a latte?" I asked her as she exited the fitting room.

"I guess." She scanned herself in the mirror and tugged down on the waist of her jeans until her navel peeked out. "I thought you said buying lattes was a waste of money."

"I save them for special occasions. And this is one." She sent me a you've-got-to-be-kidding look, but I smiled back.

"Come on, they have scones, too."

"No, I'm on a diet."

"Then we'll ask for fat-free milk." I was beginning to wonder if the girl had an eating disorder and was intentionally starving herself. But I didn't dare say anything. Not here.

I led her to the coffee shop several doors down and purchased two double-tall decaf mochas. I felt like a robot going through the motions, but I was determined to find a way to spend quality time with her. There had to be something we both liked.

I looked over the cluster of round tables and saw they were all full.

"I'm leaving in just a minute," an older voice said.

"Hi, there." I noticed my mother's friend Lillian McConkey, whom I'd known most of my life.

"Come sit with me." She removed a shopping bag from one of three chairs and placed it at her feet. "It's good to see you."

"Same here," I said, thinking Lillian looked the picture of vitality. With her silver hair brushed away from her face to show off high cheekbones and her makeup smartly applied, she appeared ten years younger than Mom, although I was pretty sure they were the same age. "Do you remember my daughter Harriet?" I asked, pulling out a chair.

When Lillian shook her head, I added, "Her name used to be Natalie and she had brown hair."

"Yes, of course." She smiled up at Harriet. "What a lovely young woman you've turned into."

Harriet couldn't resist grinning back. Then she sobered her expression as she turned to me. "Maybe while you two are yakking, I'll check out another store."

Couldn't she humor me for five seconds?

"It's not like I can buy anything without your money," she said.

"All right but come back in twenty minutes."

Lillian chuckled as Harriet, clutching her latte, disappeared out the door. "She reminds me of the old days, when I used to follow my kids around."

"Harriet's a slippery one." I sat.

"Very pretty. She looks like you."

"We both inherited my father's Italian genes," I said, "but that's as far as it goes."

"Are you sure?" Her small eyes were merry. "Sometimes similarities are hard to see from close up."

"In other words, I'm headstrong and spoiled?"

She chuckled. "Not at all. But I'll bet there were a few times when your parents wanted to tear their hair out. Am I right?"

I laughed, assuming Mom had filled her in on some of my childhood antics. "Okay, I was a pill. But it never seemed to bug Mom all that much, sort of the way my older daughter is with me. I just think, Nichole's having a bad day and tomorrow she'll be back to normal." I watched a woman and two giggling preteen girls stroll past us. The trio looked like they were having the time of their lives. "But my younger daughter was born stubborn and has been a challenge ever since."

"I bet she turns out fine."

"Last year she got a tattoo, even though I forbade it, and last month she dyed her hair that hideous red." I was hoping Lilian hadn't noticed the tongue piercing.

She patted the back of my hand the way Mom might. "I know those things are difficult, but it could be worse. My grand-daughter's about to become a mother at nineteen. After much turmoil, she married the young man and says she loves him, but things sure didn't turn out as her parents planned."

At least Harriet wasn't messing around with the opposite sex, except for adolescent smooching in my kitchen. That was something to be thankful for. "Congratulations," I said. "A baby's arrival is always a joyful event."

"Thanks, and I am looking forward to being a great-grandma, although I thought it wouldn't occur for a few more years. Maybe a decade. Now, my daughter—she's not thrilled about becoming a grandmother, not one bit. And she worries her daughter's marriage won't last a year since the young man is at junior college and has no income. But I bet it will all work out."

For as long as it took me to sip my latte and replace the cup on the table, I wished I owned a kernel of Lillian's blind faith. It would be a relief to believe that all things would work out, the way Mom did.

But then I saw Harriet coming my way shlepping a shopping bag, and the moment passed.

12

MOM AND I sat in Pop's Lincoln outside the Emerald City Senior Home. She'd insisted I drive my father's hulk of a sedan until I purchased a new car, an ordeal I'd been avoiding. "It's been wasting away in the garage for months," she'd told me. "That's not good on the engine and I sure don't want Ed taking it out for a spin. If it's at your house, I won't have to hide the keys anymore."

I needed a set of wheels, that was the truth. My insurance company had sent me a meager check to replace my vehicle, then promptly informed me I needed to return my rental or start paying for it myself, which I couldn't afford. I knew nothing about automobiles and had avoided looking in the classified ads. Was it safe for women to contact strangers, then go to their homes to test-drive their cars? But I couldn't see myself kicking tires at a used car lot either. Did people really kick tires? What I needed was a man's assistance but couldn't ask Pop or Drew to come to my rescue anymore.

"Your father would be miserable here." Mom craned her neck to view the six-story stucco structure.

She was right, and I hated being the bad guy. "But Mom, you said you have to watch after him day and night. That you worry he'll wander off again and hurt himself. How long can you live like that?" It hadn't been an easy task finding one of Mom's friends to pay a visit to Pop while we came here. He'd been less than cordial to Mom's friend when she sat down in the living room and brought out her knitting.

"It's not so bad." Mom sounded like she was trying to convince herself. "I need to be more diligent. When you and your brother were kids, I managed to keep an eye on you just fine."

"That was over thirty years ago, when you had twice the energy. If I were in your shoes, I'd be exhausted." I opened my door. "Come on, we're here. We might as well go in and see what it's like."

Mom expelled a lengthy sigh, but I knew I was doing the right thing. I led the way up the circular drive and into the foyer, a grand room with twenty-foot ceilings, the biggest chandelier I'd ever seen, and a forest of potted palms.

"We're here to see Cynthia O'Dell," I told the receptionist, and she picked up her phone to announce our arrival. Yesterday I'd called Cynthia, Sales and Placement Coordinator, and she'd assured me most of their residents moved to Emerald City when young enough to enjoy the many amenities offered. "Once you see it, you'll want to move here yourself."

Cynthia, a statuesque brunette about my age, emerged from the office carrying a key ring. Clad in a long-sleeved tunic and palazzo pants, a chunky beaded choker, and matching earrings, she looked as though she'd glided out of a Chico's catalogue.

We exchanged names and shook hands. "You caught us on the right day." She amplified her words with precision, maybe from speaking to so many seniors. "There's usually a two to three month wait, but we have a studio available on the second floor conveniently near the elevator."

I wondered how rooms became available. After the resident died or entered hospice? But I didn't want to ask in front of Mom. I was trying to keep this meeting upbeat, an adventure. But it reminded me of taking one of the girls to the doctor's office for an annual checkup when they were younger.

Cynthia led us up a wide staircase that curved around a glassed-in elevator shaft and took a left at the top. "It's just been painted." She opened the door to a cubicle not much bigger than my bedroom with a kitchenette scrunched off to one side and a sliding door opening to a balcony with barely enough space for two chaise lounges.

My heart sank when I scanned the tiny room. I looked around for a door leading to a bedroom, but there wasn't one. "Kind of small, isn't it?"

"It's a studio," Cynthia said. "If it's not large enough we could put your mother's name on the waiting list and move her to a larger space when one opens."

Mom stepped over to the kitchenette, really just a nook with a pint-size refrigerator and a two-burner stove.

"Most of our residents eat their meals in our dining room." Cynthia was all smiles. "Wonderful food, and a great place to meet people."

"Mom, having someone cook dinner for you would be nice." I wondered how to engage my mother in the conversation. She hadn't opened her mouth since we set foot in the room.

"There's plenty to keep you busy," Cynthia said. "I'll give you an activity schedule to look over."

"Pop loves cards," I said, although it had been years since I'd seen him play. "Maybe there'll be a pinochle table."

Cynthia spun around to address Mom. "You're married?"

"Yes."

I had intentionally neglected to mention Pop while on the phone. Until recently I'd always been proud of him.

"I didn't realize," Cynthia said. "Tell me about your husband. What does he think about the move?"

"We haven't discussed the details with him yet," I said, when Mom didn't answer.

"When will he be able to come for a visit?" Cynthia asked. "Mildred, you look fit and alert. Is your husband equally as healthy?"

Mom's hand moved to her collarbone. "Not exactly."

"My father's been moving a little slower these days," I said.

"And his memory's getting rusty." Mom's words trailed off at the end of the sentence.

"I see." Cynthia's demeanor changed noticeably. If anything, she looked pleased by Mom's declaration. "We also have a marvelous nursing facility on the fourth floor and a Memory Care unit on the lower level. Of course, it's locked at all times for the patients' safety, but it's very convenient for spousal visitations."

I imagined a rat and spider-infested dungeon in the basement but I assured myself it was against the law to cage human beings like animals. Or did old people with failing memories lose their rights?

As we stepped back out into the hall, Cynthia asked, "Would you like a tour of the rest of the facility?"

"Sure," I said, even though I could tell from Mom's fidgeting she couldn't wait to leave. We rode the elevator to the third floor and entered a dining room with two dozen or so tables and picture windows offering views of the Cascade Mountains. Not a bad place to be, but I couldn't imagine my parents coming here to make small talk with complete strangers. Not that my parents weren't friendly. Mom, anyway, was outgoing with people she didn't know. And the elderly folks sitting here eating their lunch seemed nice enough. Eventually my parents would overcome their shyness and initiate new friendships, I reasoned, and maybe even run into old acquaintances.

The three of us continued up to the fourth floor. As the doors swept open, I inhaled the bleachy, antiseptic hospital smell I got to know all too well after my accident. My ears searched for familiar sounds, but quiet blanketed the hallway. As we walked past the rooms, I glanced in to see shriveled-up men and women lying prostrate on railed hospital beds. Visitors sitting by several of the beds spoke in hushed voices. Even the lighting was subdued, as if ready to be extinguished.

A stocky nurse pushing an ancient woman in a wheel chair smiled at us, but her bird-like passenger, who couldn't have weighed more than ninety-five pounds, stared blindly into nothingness. I envisioned my father being carted up and down the hall while his muscle mass atrophied. I felt like weeping.

Back at the front desk, the receptionist advised Cynthia her next appointment was waiting in her office.

"That unit won't be available very long," Cynthia told Mom and me as she shook our hands. "Keep in mind, we normally have a waiting list."

"Maybe we should leave a deposit." I realized we hadn't even discussed the cost. I had no idea if my parents could afford living here. At one time my father was a shrewd businessman, but he had lost out when the market plummeted and he hadn't reinvested before it took off again. He'd complained he never should have bought into high tech stocks and should have diversified. My folks owned their home, which was good news—or had they taken out a second mortgage without telling me?

"You may leave a deposit, but we'll want to interview your father." Cynthia spoke in a no-nonsense voice. "It's crucial our new residents are capable of living here safely."

"Is there some information we could take home?" I asked.

"Of course." Cynthia presented us with a glossy brochure, its cover photo taken using a wide-angle lens that expanded the foyer to palatial dimensions. "There's an application in the back. And one online. You may return it with a deposit, but as I said we'll need to have your father evaluated by our staff. We do have beds available in the Memory Care unit."

Back in the car, I said, "Gee, they don't make it easy to move in there, do they?" I drove us through the U-shaped drive past the glass front doors and paused for a moment to give Mom one more look inside. "I'll bet Pop could pass their dumb old test."

"I don't know, dear. Your father fell the other day."

And she was just mentioning it now? "Where did it happen?" I asked. "How?"

"He caught his foot on the hall rug."

"Was he hurt?" Their navy blue and maroon oriental carpet had lay in the same spot for as long as I could remember. Maybe the corner got turned up from Mom's vacuuming. "Did you take him to the doctor?"

"He wouldn't let me. He was all confused and didn't know where he was."

"Not know his own home, where he raised a family and after thirty years celebrated a mortgage-burning party? You should have called 911."

In the rearview mirror I saw the driver of an empty white van nudging my rear bumper, wanting our spot. I rolled the Lincoln forward to make room for it to stop by the front door. Several nicely dressed women Mom's age exited the building and climbed into the back seats—on their way to a museum, a matinee, or downtown shopping? I could envision my mother taking an outing with them, but what would Pop do? Of course, what did he do now?

"It wasn't that serious," she said, pooh-poohing me. "Your father insisted he was fine."

I felt like I was stepping from a dock into a tippy canoe—an out-of-control, dizzying sensation. I was becoming my parents' parent. I hated to admit the resentment spiking through me; the last thing I needed was two more unruly teenagers to look after. Not now—I didn't possess the strength to manage my parents' affairs. But I realized I needed to readjust my attitude and lower my weight to the center of gravity, until I regained balance. Getting your sea legs, I'd heard it called.

"Mom," I said, taking us back onto the main street, "Pop isn't rational enough to make those choices for himself anymore."

"You could be right. But when you've been married to a take-charge man like him as many years as I have, you learn to compromise. He's not a child, after all."

"No, but he's beginning to act like one." They both were.

13

I HOVERED AT THE top of the escalator at Sea-Tac Airport's baggage claim area waiting for Drew and Nichole's plane to disembark. I'd contacted the airline to find out their flight number and arrival time and assumed they'd be pleased to avoid another Uber ride. What could possibly go wrong? Why did I feel so antsy?

Several limousine service drivers wearing bored expressions lingered nearby holding up placards with names written on them. Finally, a throng of people exited the underground tram and began trailing up the slow-moving stairway. I watched a boy not old enough to be flying by himself step off and be swept up in his mother's arms; I figured his parents were divorced and his father lived in California. At least Drew hadn't moved to another state.

A couple strode off the escalator, followed by a young man with a military-style haircut who was met by a young woman, perhaps his wife or fiancée, the way they kissed and hugged each other with such fierce tenderness—how Drew and I used to embrace each other many years ago.

After thirty or forty more individuals I finally spotted Nichole and Drew. I expected the two to be tired from their trip, subdued even, but they looked like best buddies coming home from attending a winning football game.

"Nichole, sweetheart," I said, and her eyes turned serious.

I waited for them to reach me, all the while pretending it hadn't irked me that neither had called home for three days. I could have reached Drew on his cell phone, but I thought he should have had the decency to check in with me.

"This is a nice surprise." Drew probably wished I were Kristi. I'd wager they had a spat and were back together again. "Thanks for coming, Ruthie." His voice lacked conviction.

"How did the trip go?" I asked, and his face opened into a smile. I figured he wanted to fill me in but was waiting for Nichole to speak.

"Very well," she finally said, her gaze scanning the area and landing on the blinking United Flight 396 sign. She seemed to be containing a wide grin, undoubtedly keeping her spirits reigned in for my benefit. But her sparkling blue eyes revealed her excitement.

"Good, I'm glad." Half of me believed it. After all, I'd spent the last seventeen years helping her build a foundation for happiness and success. But threads of jealousy and resentment controlled my other half, choking my good intentions.

Drew wrapped an arm around Nichole's shoulder as we made our way across the linoleum floor to the baggage carousel. "Scripps College had our girl's name written all over the campus. There wasn't one thing she didn't like about it."

"It's beautiful down there, and warm. She gave me a sideways glance. "I didn't even have to wear my jacket. And everyone was friendly." Her voice bubbled like she'd just opened a birthday present to find exactly what she was hoping for. "I've always wanted to live in California." Her lips remained parted as if caught in mid-sentence.

"Really?" I said. "Since when?"

"Since I was little, I've dreamed of living by the ocean. Not for the rest of my life. Just a few years."

I imagined her on the beach playing volleyball, a game she loved, with all sorts of young men ogling her slim figure. I'd always appreciated that in the Northwest little emphasis was placed on Hollywood glamour. Our only celebrities were people who'd proved brains and persistence triumphed over slick good looks. But maybe Nichole didn't share my beliefs.

"There are so many distractions in California," I said. "Beach parties and suntans. How would you get any studying done?"

"There are plenty of distractions here too, Ruthie," Drew said. "You remember what it was like."

After enjoying Nichole to himself all weekend, couldn't he let me speak my piece without butting in? "I lived at home my first year in college and it didn't hurt me one bit," I said. "It seems like all my studies started to decline about the time I moved out."

"You were practically a straight-A student when we met," he said, in a way that cheapened my accomplishments.

An obnoxious alarm sounded and the carousel started revolving. I moved to the nearest spot only to discover Nichole and Drew were choosing to stand yards away. I knew I was reacting immaturely, but I felt like I'd lost my best friend.

I joined Nichole and Drew and watched the countless black suitcases parade by on the carousel. A moment later Nichole wandered to the other side of the carousel to speak to a girl I recognized from her soccer team. Was she also visiting Scripps?

Drew tipped his head to speak in my ear. "You're squashing our girl," he said in a biting tone.

I swung my head around to face him. "I'm doing nothing of the sort."

"Yes, you are, you're trying to control her and it'll backfire, I assure you."

In the midst of many a verbal battle, Drew had used the word *controlling* to describe me. The conversations always spun in the same tight circle with me defending myself and his being surer than ever that I was attempting to bend him into a pretzel.

Instead of answering with my usual rebuttal, I put on a remorseful mask and said, "Sorry I'm so miserable to be around," not meaning it. If anything, I'd glossed over too many problems during our marriage instead of facing our challenges head-on. I'd thought difficulties would always right themselves like capsized sailboats. Drew and I would do a little bailing and life would float back on course.

He seemed to be letting down his guard. "Neither of us is perfect, right?"

"I didn't say I was perfect, and I've never asked for perfection from you."

"Sure, you have. You're like your father."

How dare he drag Pop onto his muddy playing field? "My father's a fine man. The best. It wouldn't hurt others to try to be more like him."

"Yes, yes, I know, I'm Ed's opposite, never quite as good as he is."

I didn't want the strangers surrounding us to be privy to our dirty laundry. I lessened my volume and said, "He stuck around. He never would have left Mom, no matter what." Then I went off to assist Nichole, who was lifting her suitcase from the carousel.

Keeping myself quiet as I drove the three of us back to town, I listened to Nichole describe the dorm she liked best, then rave about the food. Thirty minutes later we walked through the front door of the house.

"Thank you, Dad." Nichole gave Drew a lingering hug. When they parted, they exchanged a glance that told me they belonged to a secret society, one from which I was excluded.

"Glad to help, kiddo." He winked at her and she grinned.

She hauled up her suitcase and climbed the stairs. When she was behind her bedroom door, Drew said, "Ruthie, I'm sorry I mentioned your father. It wasn't fair or necessary. But haven't you ever wondered what it was like for your mother to be married to an inflexible man like Edward Jacobi? Fifty years of kowtowing obedience."

"Mom's one of the happiest women I know. And I don't think you're in any position to criticize anyone." I noticed the cardboard box crammed with his clothes still hunkered by the front door. I walked over to it and tapped it with my foot. "Your girlfriend dropped off some of your stuff."

I enjoyed watching his face blanch. He probably thought Kristi and I had met face-to-face for a screaming match, or maybe that she and I had formed an alliance—his worst nightmare.

"Sorry, I'll tell her not to come here again." He glanced at the box but kept his distance from it. Did he expect me to launder and put his things away?

"Won't you be needing these clothes back at the love nest?" I asked.

"I told you, we don't live together."

Which meant he kept these spare clothes at her place. How terribly convenient.

"Anyway," he said, "I'm not sure we'll be seeing each other anymore. She insisted I attend some big wedding this weekend and said if I went to California not to bother calling her again."

His statement should have pumped me with renewed hope for the two of us, but it didn't.

14

"MILLIE, GET IN here." My father spoke in a stern voice that still reduced me to a five-year-old. "Mildred!"

I trotted into my parents' living room from the kitchen where I'd been fixing myself a cup of tea. Pop sat in his chair facing the muted TV, the clicker in his hand. With dried oatmeal dribbled on the front of his shirt and his chin unshaven, he reminded me of the panhandler I'd recently seen on a freeway entrance.

I stood in his field of vision. "She's at the grocery store," I said. "I'm taking care of you."

"I don't need anyone taking care of me."

I'd said the wrong thing again. Ever since I'd arrived an hour ago, I'd done nothing but offend him. "Of course you don't." I tried to imitate the lilting voice my mother used. "Mom asked me to keep you company, to help if you needed anything."

"There is something." His features began to melt and he suddenly looked on the verge of tears. Something he'd never done before. "I can't remember where the bathroom is."

At first, I thought he was joking but he stared back at me in earnest.

"I'll show you." I took his hand and tugged him to his feet—no easy chore, believe me—then led him into the front hall and toward the pint-sized powder room, with its tulip-print wallpaper. He teetered beside me, his grasp weak. Who was this man?

"Wait," he said as I turned to leave him in the bathroom. He stood for a moment before the toilet; his fingers grappled with the belt buckle as if he'd never worked it before. Could he not remove his own pants?

"May I help you?" I asked, and he nodded. Trying not to look—what woman wants to see her father naked?—I unzipped his slacks, worked them and his boxers down over his hips, and guided him to the seat, where he landed with a thud.

I closed the door, then leaned against the wall just outside the bathroom. I'd grown up in this house but had never waited in this spot. There was no reason to. My chest ached with so much sadness I was tempted to run out the front door, to escape, but I couldn't leave Pop by himself.

The toilet flushed, but minutes later he still hadn't come out.

"Are you okay?" I asked through the door but got no answer. Finally I entered the bathroom to find him standing with his underwear and trousers bunched around his ankles. Again I looked away as I tugged up his pants and refastened them. Nothing in life had prepared me for this moment. Not raising two children, not dressing them, or changing their diapers. It took all my might to hold in the sob that rumbled from deep inside my guts.

I escorted him back to the living room. We sat like strangers in front of the TV set watching a golf tournament, something I couldn't care less about. Pop's face angled toward the set, but he didn't seem to notice what happened on the screen: the fifty-yard chip or the two under par, which in the past would have aroused enthusiastic comments.

After what seemed like an eternity Mom opened the kitchen door and called, "I'm home." She sped into the living room. "How is everyone?"

Getting to my feet, I couldn't manufacture a smile. "We're fine."

She kissed my father on the cheek. In a flash his face veered around, rage boiling in his eyes, and he clenched his fist.

"Be quiet!" He was using his bad dog voice, sounding like he did when scaring the neighbor's German shepherd off their lawn. "I told you never to interrupt me."

Mom leaned out of his reach. "All right, dear. I'll go put the groceries away."

I had never heard Pop growl at Mom like that in all my years. It felt as though he'd pitched the tirade straight at me.

"How can you let him treat you like that?" I asked as soon as she and I were in the kitchen.

"He didn't mean anything." She reached into a paper bag and removed several cans of Ensure. "Your father doesn't have his former self-control when he gets annoyed."

I couldn't believe she was acting so blasé. "Annoyed? He looked ready to hit you."

She put one finger up to her lips to hush me. "He's doing the best he can."

Had Pop lost all self-control? Was he reverting into a two-year-old? Didn't he love Mom and me anymore?

"Why didn't you tell me things were so bad?" I asked. "I could have helped." Although I wasn't sure how.

She stacked the cans in the cupboard with precise motions. "I didn't want to burden you, dear. You've had problems of your own."

"I guess I have been a basket case these last six months." My world had revolved around my sorrow, my brokenness. And Drew. I needed to stop obsessing over him. A waste of time when I could have been supporting my parents. An idea sprouted like a seed in the back of my mind. "When the divorce goes through, I may start using my maiden name again." I wondered what Drew would think of the idea and figured he'd go ballistic. But too bad for him.

"Ruth Ann, why would you want to go and do that?" She ripped the cellophane wrap off a box of Red Rose tea and placed the bags in the flowered canister she'd used my whole life. "What about your girls? They'd have a different last name."

"Lots of women keep their maiden names when they get married these days. Gloria did." I knew Mom didn't approve of women like her. "And both my girls can't wait to be out on their own. They probably wouldn't care one way or the other. Eventually they'll get married and have new last names."

"But changing your name seems so final."

"Mom, divorce is final." I took the empty grocery bag off the counter and refolded it, bearing down hard on the creases. "I may even start dating again. Why should Drew have all the fun?"

"Is there someone you have in mind?"

The question caught me off guard. Entering into a new relationship had been the furthest thing from my mind, so I said the first name I thought of. "Victor Huff? He might be a good candidate." If he weren't such an oddball.

"Better think again." Mom took the bag off the table and jimmied it into her bursting bag drawer. "As a matter of fact, Dr. Huff is married."

If she'd wanted to shock me, she'd succeeded. "Are you sure?" If he was, he certainly wasn't proud of the fact.

"Mildred," my father yelled. "Get in here this minute."

Mom and I rushed into the living room to find the front of his trousers soaked with urine.

I CRIED ALL the way home. In the front hall Bonnie greeted me but I didn't have the stamina to respond. I found a tissue and blew my nose so hard I honked like a Canada goose. Then I headed to the stairs. Before I reached the first step, I heard someone unlocking the front door. As it eased open I turned to see Drew strolling in wearing the powder blue shirt I'd given him last summer. I remembered when purchasing it thinking the color would echo his irises, which it did beautifully. If I had to do it over again, I would have given him ugly clothes. Then Kristi would have thought he was a dork, as Harriet would say.

"You're supposed to ring the bell before you enter," I said.

"I did."

As I considered the possibility that my nose-blowing had drowned out the sound of the buzzer, his phone chimed. "Aren't you going to get that?" I asked.

He made no move to answer it. "It must be your girlfriend," I said to Drew, who'd followed me into the room. In my dower mood I was looking for an altercation.

"She wouldn't call me," He was an expert on his darling Kristi's personal foibles.

"Why not? She delivered your clothes in person. I'll hand it to her. She's got more nerve than I do."

The cell phone in his pocket began chirping again. He found it, silenced the ringer, and stuffed it back in his pocket.

It had to be Kristi. "You're going to be in trouble," I said in the singsong voice I used as a child to entice my brother into taking a swing at me when Mom was looking.

"Whoever it is can wait," he said.

I wondered how many times he'd ignored my phone calls while he was playing kissy-face with Kristi. Over the last few years, I'd found it odd when he didn't answer his cell phone, but assumed he'd been in meetings or speaking on his phone at work. How could I have been so dense? In my mind the Scarecrow from the *Wizard of Oz* sang, "If I only had a brain." No, I needed to stop ridiculing myself. Why was I putting myself down? I hadn't done anything wrong. Husbands and wives were supposed to be soulmates. I should have been able to trust Drew with my life.

I marched over to the oak desk I'd inherited from Pop's mother. I slid open the top drawer and removed the file marked *Divorce*, which had been hiding in the darkness for over a month. I'd avoided opening this drawer so I wouldn't have to see that cursed word, but suddenly *divorce* spelled freedom to me. I felt like a butterfly struggling out of its cocoon.

I opened the file and spread the papers my attorney, Sue Donaldson, had sent me on the coffee table. "Have a seat" I selected a pen from the chipped coffee mug that served as a pencil holder. "I'm going to sign this and you can be my witness."

"What are you talking about?"

"I'm going to put an end to this fiasco."

"Hey, wait a minute. I don't think we should do anything until you're all better."

His show of concern made me think he belonged in Hollywood where someone would pay for his acting abilities.

"I am all better." I tossed him a reckless smile. "This is as good as I get."

As I sat on the couch the pen flipped out of my hand and rolled across the table. Before I could grab it, Drew scooped it up, then seated himself on the chair across from me.

"I didn't mean your face," he said. "And by the way, you look almost as good as new. Except your eyes are a little puffy today. I meant some kind of therapy, to help you sort things out."

I refused to admit I was distressed about Pop, how he'd resisted Mom and my efforts to change him into fresh slacks until she bribed him with a cookie. Mom said she was going to start insisting he wear Depends—diapers, really—telling me this wasn't Pop's first mishap.

"What things need sorting?" I asked Drew, figuring he didn't mean my sock drawer. "Are you referring to my accident?"

"Yes, if that's what it was. When you disappeared, I was worried sick, ready to call the hospital."

"You've always claimed worrying is a waste of time. Now, give me my pen, then I want you to leave." I restrained myself from calling him a bozo, but my bold thought made me smirk.

"Listen," he said, "I moved back to help you out. You're the one who took off without notice." He twirled the pen with his fingers. "Now that I'm here I think I should stick around for a while."

"You mean move back home?" Was this one more passive aggressive ploy to drive me insane? Leaning forward, I put my palm out to receive the pen, but he kept hold of it.

"Yeah. The last couple of days, I've been thinking. I've decided we should wait on the divorce."

Again, he was calling the shots and all I could do was react. I sprang to my feet. "What do you want from me, a pound of flesh?"

I spun around and wrenched a Bic pen out of the cup on the table. Then I signed my name with exaggerated flare in the space Susan had marked with an X.

15

"THAT WAS MICHELLE," Nichole said, hanging up her phone the next morning. She glanced at the clock on our microwave. "It's 7:30 and her car won't start. And Dad already took Harriet on his way to work."

I was glad I'd dressed minutes earlier. "I'm happy to give you a ride to school, darling."

"I could always take the bus." Ever since her trip to California, she'd avoided me. I hated the distance between us.

"No, I'm free, and you'd be late to school. Besides, it'll give us a chance to touch base."

I tugged on my raincoat, grabbed a cup of coffee, then led the way to the Lincoln, a luxury I was finally getting used to. Sure, the car consumed too much gas, but I liked its cushy leather seats, power windows, and cruise control. And best of all, no monthly payments. And the money from the insurance settlement lay safely in my new savings account gathering interest.

Rain slapping against the walkway splattered my ankles, but I didn't care. I would have waded through a river to spend time with Nichole.

"Thanks for the ride," she said as we got in.

I smiled at my beloved daughter. "I'm delighted to do it." I knew after a ten-minute ride she and I would be back on track.

"Actually, Mom, I've been wanting to speak to you."

I turned on the ignition and windshield wipers then pulled away from the curb. "I'm glad, I've missed our daily chats."

She pressed her knees together, folded her hands in her lap. "I applied to Scripps College."

I tried to retain the buoyancy in my voice. "Sorry, sweetheart, but I believe you missed the deadline. Maybe you can think about transferring in your sophomore year." By then she'd most likely change her mind.

"I sent the application in early January."

"Behind my back? In secret?"

"My college counselor told me I should shoot for the stars."

I heard a honk, and realized I'd slowed to a crawl. I glanced in the rearview mirror to see a UPS truck's headlamps practically resting against my bumper. I sped up to thirty and the truck dropped back.

"What's going on?" I said. "Just two weeks ago we had things all settled."

As I slowed to take a left at the next intersection, the UPS truck passed on my right, sending an arc of water across my windshield and blinding me. I flicked the wiper speed up a notch, and my vision returned, but now the blade thwacking across the window sounded frantic, out of control.

"Isn't Scripps a woman's college?" I'd read that girls often excelled in all-female classrooms and were twice as likely to go on to earn their doctorates. I could imagine a women's college might offer the same benefits, and I knew it stood next to several co-ed campuses. But I asked, "Why would you want to go there?"

"Kristi said—" Her hand flew up to cover her mouth.

"What was that?"

"Kristi went there and loved it."

"You're letting that tramp influence where you go to college instead of your own mother?"

"Mom, I didn't want to like her. But she's actually very nice. She taught me how to crochet."

The image of them sitting tête-à-tête, knitting matching scarves made me grip the steering wheel—mad enough to pull it off the column. "You're asking her to teach you things? She dates married men. She's evil."

"I know what Dad did was wrong, but he's still my father. If I want to see him, I may have to see her too. Anyway, she's always been polite to Harriet and me. Maybe because she doesn't have her own children."

"She wants kids?"

"I don't know. But if Dad marries her and they have some, they'll be my half-sisters or brothers."

Why hadn't this scenario entered my consciousness before? The truth was most women wanted children. No matter what they told their girlfriends or parents, when a single woman met Mr. Right she'd start dreaming of wedding ceremonies to be followed by baby showers. Why would Kristi be any different? I hated the idea of Drew's fathering another child. I pictured him with digital camera in hand, coo-cooing into a baby bassinet with a blue blanket. I knew Drew longed for a son, someone to carry on the Templeton family name, although he'd never admitted it. Kristi's little darling would edge my two children into second-rate status. Plus—plus, I hated that I was powerless to influence Drew's tomfooleries. Give up, I told myself, but then I felt defeated, powerless.

The school stood less than a block away. I followed the procession of cars up to the building's front entrance. As the bell clanged Nichole leapt out and dashed up the steps. A moment later I watched a tall black youth exit the sedan in front of me. The car rolled forward and I trailed it around the corner to the stoplight. As its driver turned her head to the left to check for traffic, I recognized Jackie's profile. The light changed and I followed her for a dozen blocks as we wove our way back to our neighborhood.

My thoughts flipped back to Nichole's college application. I brooded over the verbal missiles I'd sling at Drew when I saw him next. As I rolled through an intersection, I glanced in both directions to check for oncoming cars. My neck felt glued to my shoulders and a moment later my head began vibrating with waves of a rhythmic pain. I never used to have migraine headaches. Not until recently. I reviewed the last year and guessed they started before the accident. Even before the most recent miserable Christmas season. Did I experience the first one the night Drew said he didn't love me anymore?

I fished through my purse with my free hand until I located the travel-size vial of ibuprofen. I popped two discs into my mouth and gulped them down with cold coffee.

Jackie pulled over as we neared the crest of the hill in front of the Sunlight Bakery and Café, an establishment well known for its excellent breads, soups and sandwiches, and warm atmosphere. As I drove up beside her, she caught sight of me and signaled me to stop. We both lowered our windows, then she invited me to join her for coffee. I parallel parked the Lincoln for the first time and managed not to dent the fender of the car in front or behind me. One small victory for a woman who went to great lengths to find angle-in parking.

"Nice to see you looking so well." Jackie held open the café's front door for me. I could feel my tension easing. I wondered how many of Jackie's other former patients continued receiving benefits from her caring spirit.

Stepping inside, I inhaled the yeasty aroma of rising dough; my eyes scanned the six-foot-high metal rack cradling loaves of bread and the glass case brimming with desserts and berry pies. We followed the hostess into the carpeted dining area to a table against the wall. Half of the twenty or so tables were filled with chatting patrons, their words mingling with the background music.

Once we were seated across from each other, Jackie asked the waitress, a tall gal with a ponytail, for a cup of decaf.

"Make mine a double tall mocha and a piece of coffee cake," I said. When the waitress returned to the kitchen, I said, "After the conversation I just had, I'll take all the help I can get, even if it means one thousand added calories."

Quit your bellyaching, Pop would say if he were here, but I pushed his voice out of my mind. I needed someone to talk to. Fresh ears. I supposed I should seek a professional counselor but didn't want to spend $150 an hour for a few nods from a man or woman who'd never met my family members. It would take weeks just to fill them in. And Jackie seemed a wise woman—non-judgmental and compassionate.

I rested my elbows on the table and dove in. "My daughter Harriet has continuously fought me tooth and nail. Like I'm some vile entity she can't get far enough away from. But I could always count on Nichole, until recently."

"You've told me about Harriet," she said. "But I didn't realize you were having problems with Nichole."

"She wants to move to California."

"And not finish high school?"

"No, she wants to attend college in southern California next fall." I sounded lame. Why would Jackie think there was anything wrong with that unless the four years of private college tuition would leave me broke?

"And you'd miss her," she said. "Of course, you would." She smiled up at the waitress as the young woman delivered our order.

Rather than continue expressing self-pity, I plunged my fork into my coffeecake, its crust thick with brown sugar and cinnamon, and swallowed a mouthful.

"After I dropped you off the other day," she said, "I had an idea that might help. A few years ago, when my world was falling apart at the seams, I found the perfect spot to plant my feet. I hope you won't think I'm being too pushy by making a suggestion."

"Not at all." I sipped froth off the top of my latte, then licked my upper lip. "At this point, I'm open to anything."

"Do you enjoy quilting?"

"Uh—I don't know how." Grandma Tessa had wanted to teach me years and years ago, but I'd always been too busy.

"Would you like to learn? I'd love to take you with me to my bi-monthly quilting group."

I adored quilts, but actually making them seemed like too much trouble. I couldn't take another disappointment. Yet hadn't I just stated I'd try anything? My mind scrambled for a polite way to backtrack. "I can't sew worth a hoot and I don't think I can afford the materials," were the only excuses I could think of.

"We were all beginners at some point. It's a fun group of women. We help each other—in a number of ways."

I had to get the truth over with even if it meant hurting her feelings and ending our friendship. "I'd better pass."

She gazed at me with doe-like eyes.

"I hope I haven't offended you," I said. "Guess I've run out of energy."

"Not at all. I used to think the same way. I almost gave up when I was a teenager, about the time my daddy took off. Strange that I didn't find my confidence again until my husband did the same thing."

Now I was the one doing the staring. Her husband ditched her, but she didn't hold a grudge. I would never let Drew off the hook. I hoped hell existed, so he'd have a place to sizzle in the fry pan for eternity.

A smile bloomed on Jackie's face, and she waved across the room at a gangly young woman carrying a briefcase striding in our direction.

"Sorry I'm late," The woman's teeth protruded behind a grin. She dragged a chair over from another table and scooted in next to me, the edge of her chair abutting mine, hemming me in against the wall. Removing her jacket and draping it over the back of her chair, she brought with her an effusive bustle of energy, the opposite of calm Jackie.

"Do you two remember each other?" Jackie asked.

I shook my head, but the other woman exclaimed, "You bet, how are you doing, Ruth Ann?"

"This is Isolda Browning," Jackie told me when I didn't reply. "She visited you in the hospital."

I leaned back to get a better look at her. "Are you the one who gave me the mirror?"

Isolda's cheeks flushed crimson. "Yes, I'm the culprit."

"Isolda is our newest pastor at church," Jackie said.

"Congregational care." Isolda removed her steamy glasses and dried them on her tartan skirt. "That was my first hospital visit." She positioned the glasses back on the hump of her nose. "I'm surprised they let me come back after what I pulled. I should have insisted a nurse or doctor help you."

"No harm done," Jackie said.

"Of course not." And I meant it. No point in Isolda's feeling responsible for my shaky mental status. "I insisted you give me the mirror. And you were right. My black-and-blue marks are almost completely gone."

"Thanks for being so understanding."

The waitress came to our table and Isolda asked for chamomile tea. I thought the caffeine-free beverage was a good choice for this overly energetic woman.

"In a few weeks Isolda will be teaching a class at church," Jackie told me.

"I'm afraid no one will show up when they see who's teaching." Isolda wove her fingers together. "But if I end up with a roomful of people I'd better be prepared. In the past I've only taught middle school kids in summer camp."

"If you can keep their attention, you can do anything." I shook my head once as I recalled how Harriet had refused to attend summer camp of any kind. I'd longed to get her out of the house.

"Ruthie's right," Jackie said. "You'll do fine."

"What kind of a class is it?" I asked.

"The general theme is forgiveness." Isolda brought a spiral notebook from her cloth briefcase. "I asked Jackie to give me some insights and direction. She's been my mentor since I was in high school."

I reached for my purse, lying wedged between our chairs. "Then I'll let you two discuss things in private."

"No, please don't rush off," Isolda said. "If you have the time, I'd appreciate your input."

I had nowhere else to be, so I resettled in my chair to finish my latte. "All right, but I'm not sure I'll be much help."

Isolda accepted her tea from a waitress and thanked her. "Well, I thought I'd break the class into segments. Forgiving those who have harmed us, forgiving ourselves, and asking others for forgiveness."

"There is nothing sweeter than forgiveness." Jackie's face filled with an attitude of joy, like she'd just sampled my mother's brown-sugar frosting.

"What also tastes good is revenge," I said. To illustrate my point, I forked into my coffee cake, then brought it to my mouth too quickly, jabbing my lower lip. Pretending not to notice the pain, I slipped the food into my mouth, then patted myself with my paper napkin to make sure I hadn't drawn blood. I hadn't, luckily.

"If we want forgiveness," Isolda said, "we must forgive others."

"I haven't done anything wrong," I said, "so I don't need forgiveness. And I see no reason to forgive people who hurt me and show no remorse." My ibuprofen was wearing off and my headache was repositioning itself, one temple plinking like a piano key hitting a dead string.

"But holding onto bitterness eats away at our insides." Isolda spoke like Glinda the Good Witch. Oh, brother.

I couldn't help sharing a lesson from the school of hard knocks. "Wait until you're my age. You might change your mind."

Isolda turned in her chair to face me, her gaze taking hold of mine. "I hope I don't," she said, sounding for the first time like my peer. "Choosing to forgive the man who killed my parents was the best decision I've ever made."

16

EVER SINCE SPEAKING with Isolda, my parents' well-being had gnawed on my mind. The moment I got home I dialed their number and counted as their phone rang four times.

Finally, just before their answering machine would kick in, my father murmured a weak, "Hello?"

"Hi, Pop. May I speak to Mom?"

"Who?"

"Mildred." I waited for a moment, hoping he was spoofing me, then added, "Your wife."

"She doesn't live here anymore." Then he hung up.

I called again, but the phone droned on until the answering machine started in. Maybe Mom was putting out the garbage or speaking to her neighbor over the fence, although it had started drizzling outside and it was unlikely she'd leave Pop for more than a moment. Something must be wrong, or was I turning paranoid?

My headache was intensifying, one side of my skull burning just below my scalp. I wanted to retreat into a darkened room and shut the world out. Isolda's story of her parents' needless deaths was the last thing I wanted to think about, but her haunting words had latched onto my brain and repeated themselves like aftershocks. Her mother and father had died in a car accident, but she'd forgiven the drunken slob who'd plowed into their Mazda. Why would she want to forgive him? He didn't deserve it and probably didn't even care.

As I lobbed a couple more ibuprofen in my mouth, my thoughts orbited back to my own dear parents, who might need my assistance. Ten minutes later, I drove up to the front of their house and saw Mom's car roosting snugly in the carport, just as it always did. False alarm, I told myself. But while I was here, I would give Mom a hug. From what I'd seen, she wasn't getting those from her husband anymore.

At the front door I gave the bell a tap and heard it chiming through the house. When no one answered, I rang the button again, then knocked, but still got no response. I peered through one of the tall windows flanking the door and spied the back of my father's craggy head over the top of his easy chair I could hear the TV blaring, but by now Mom should have answered.

I called through the window, then rapped on the glass. Finally, I saw Pop's silhouette shuffling to the door. He cracked it open several inches. Pushing it wider, I gasped as I saw his naked chest; he was wearing nothing but a pair of tattered boxer shorts.

I said, "Where's Mom?" but he was already on his way back to his chair. With saggy skin and spindly limbs his retreating body reminded me of a starving elephant. An ancient albino elephant—comical yet tragic.

My mother's voice drifted up from the basement. "Ruth Ann, is that you?"

She was downstairs doing laundry, I thought. The spin cycle of her twenty-five-year-old washer was raising such a racket she hadn't heard the phone or the doorbell. What a goof, for tearing over here at break-neck speed. I strolled through the kitchen and peered down the basement stairs to find Mom sitting on the bottom step. She craned her head to watch my descent but made no move to get to her feet.

"What are you doing down there?" I asked, now hurrying.

"Silly me, I missed the bottom step and twisted my ankle." Her complexion was gray, dull. "I feel so stupid." She was wearing sensible walking shoes. Still, she'd fallen.

"Are you okay?" I asked. "Do you need to see a doctor?"

"No, I'm fine." She rotated her foot in a slow circle but winced when she got midway through the movement. "I'm sure I didn't break anything." She grasped the railing for assistance but didn't possess the strength to pull herself erect. "Your father was in bed napping, so I came down to do a load of laundry."

Grasping her upper arm and feeling more bone than muscle, I helped her stand, but she was unable to put much weight on her injured leg.

"Pop came to the door practically naked." I was as shocked by that fact as I was by Mom's fall. Not long ago he was fastidious about his clothes: a pressed collared shirt and dark slacks or a polo shirt and khakis.

"Ed insists on sleeping that way. And once he's made up his mind about something, there's no changing it."

I supported her from behind as she hobbled up the stairs, then I assisted her to the couch.

"I still think I should take you to get x-rayed." I had to speak in her ear to be heard over the din of the TV.

"Who'd watch your father?"

"How about a neighbor?"

"Roberta next door came over when you and I went out. To put it mildly, she had a tough time managing Ed. I don't dare ask her again. And Sharon on the other side has a new baby. Most everyone else is at work this time of day."

"We could take him with us."

She propped herself up on one elbow. "Let me try resting my ankle until tomorrow morning. That's probably what the doctor would prescribe for me anyway."

"Then I'll spend the night here so I can look after things. Drew's at home. He can feed the girls."

In spite of her injury, Mom seemed pleased at the mention of Drew's name. Before she could comment about a possible reconciliation, I skedaddled into the kitchen, where I stuffed ice cubes into a plastic bag. Then I placed the cold pack on her elevated ankle.

I decided to risk aggravating Pop by lowering the TV's volume and was glad he didn't snarl at me. "I'll get him dressed," I told Mom. "Then I'll fix us a snack."

Last year, with Drew's help, my parents had moved their queen-size bed down to the first floor into what we used to call the TV room. The steep stairs to the second floor were proving too difficult for Pop to safely navigate with his bad knee.

In his bureau I selected a clean pair of boxers, a knit shirt, and sweat pants, and brought them to the living room.

"Here you go." I held the items out for him to take. "Time to get dressed."

He looked up at me without a show of understanding.

"He'll need help." Mom swung her good leg off the couch.

"Stay where you are, I'll do it." I steeled myself as I slipped off his boxers, then poked his feet into the clean underwear. Then I stood him up—not an easy undertaking.

"Leave me alone." He slapped me away.

"Now, Pop, what if company comes?" I tugged up the underwear. As I reached for his sweat pants he sat down again.

He looked me over. "Who are you, anyway?"

"That's Ruth Ann." Mom spoke in her merriest voice. "Our daughter."

I knew it wasn't his fault, but I felt wounded to my bones. I turned to Mom for help.

"He has some good days and some not-so-good days," she said. "Maybe it would be easier to let him wear his bathrobe."

I found his terry robe, then roused him to his feet again long enough for me to slip it on him.

"I'll fix us lunch," I said, but he stared past me at the TV set.

In the kitchen, I found the refrigerator gaping almost empty. Just a bag of carrots, some milk, a cube of cheddar cheese, and leftover broccoli chicken casserole enough for one. I wondered when Mom last purchased fresh food. When I was young, she'd insisted my brother and I eat vegetables and fruits every day, not to mention servings of protein.

I heated a can of tomato soup and grilled toasted cheese sandwiches. I brought Mom a dinner tray and set it on the ottoman.

"Thanks, I've never had anyone serve me in my own house before." She perked her mouth into a smile. "I could get used to this."

I figured she was putting on a show for my benefit. "Mom, you've always been there for me."

Next, I set Pop's meal in front of him on a TV tray. "Time to eat," I said, but his hands remained lifeless in his lap.

"He may need your help," Mom said.

Pop couldn't feed himself anymore? Or was he being stubborn? He was reminding me more and more of Harriet.

"All right." I scooped up a spoonful of soup then guided it to his mouth. "Open up."

He parted his lips, but when he closed them around the spoon, pinkish-orange liquid oozed out the sides of his mouth and down his chin. I could stand the sight of blood, no problem, but seeing this sent a wave of nausea through my stomach. I wondered if my coffee cake and latte would hurdle up my windpipe. But I couldn't fall apart. Mom needed me. They both did.

I grabbed a napkin and wiped the corners of his mouth and the spot on the front of his bathrobe. "There's a good boy," slid out of my mouth. I couldn't believe I'd spoken to my father as if he were a child, and that he hadn't rebuked me for my insolence. My heart ached for the man I once knew.

That evening I climbed the stairs to my childhood bedroom. My two favorite stuffed animals, an owl and a cocker spaniel, and my doll collection still decked the top shelves of the bookcase, and the paisley bedspread I'd picked out on my fourteenth birthday covered the single bed. I spent thirty minutes browsing through the bookcase housing my yearbooks and novels I hadn't read since college trying to find something to divert my mind. As I leafed through several Jane Austin hardbacks trying to remember their plots, fatigue clouded my head. I climbed into bed, its springs creaking, and turned off the light. The sheets felt as smooth as silk and the blanket's weight like a loving embrace.

How simple and easy life had been the last time I'd slept in this bed. My brother, five years my senior, had moved out when I was thirteen. I'd been an only child through high school, the hub of my parents' lives. It seemed like they would watch over me forever, that their *raison d'etre* was caring for my needs. Pop had been bigger than life; he'd reigned like a benevolent king. The thought of his emaciated flesh curdling like stale milk triggered a fresh round of melancholy. Someday I'd be that old, too, but unless I remarried, which seemed unlikely, I'd live alone.

I informed myself this was not the time to contemplate a lifetime of solitude. What I needed was a good night's sleep. As I listened to the faithful ticking of the clock on the bed table, I envisioned myself strolling the beach on a summer's day. Millions of colored pebbles lay at my feet and no two were alike. I felt myself drifting through the alpha zone and into slumber.

Glass clinked.

I woke with a start, sat up in bed. I was sure I'd heard something downstairs. Had a burglar broken in? My parents had talked about installing an alarm system but had never gotten around to it. Two sleeping old folks would be the perfect target for a prowler.

I dove into the robe Mom had lent me, then felt around the bed stand for my phone. I ascended the staircase with it clutched in hand ready to punch in 911 should I meet with an intruder. Entering the kitchen, I found Pop foraging through the freezer compartment of the refrigerator. I was thankful he was wearing his bathrobe and slippers. In fact, he looked quite his old self, and gave me a sheepish smile when he saw me.

"Having dessert this time of night?" I noticed he'd placed a glass dish on the counter.

"I was thinking about it, although your mother doesn't approve of my late-night snacks."

I glanced at the clock to see it was 11:30 but knew I wouldn't fall back asleep with him up and about. "I don't think she'll mind," I said. "In fact, I'll join you."

He removed a carton of caramel-swirl ice cream, his favorite, and set it on the counter, then pried off the cover while I fetched another bowl and two spoons. I dolloped out balls of ice cream and placed our booty on the table.

He sat down and began digging in. Swallowing a mouthful, he said, "All finished with your homework?"

I felt like I'd been flung back into the past; I hadn't heard those words for over twenty years. "Yes, Pop, I finished a long time ago."

"Good girl. By the way, I'd like you to work up some designs for the remodel."

I recalled my folks contemplating expanding and updating the kitchen when I was a teen, but they decided the project was too expensive. And once my brother and I moved out they wouldn't need the extra room.

"I can't help you, I didn't become an architect."

"You didn't?" He brushed his lips with his fingertips. "It's not too late. You're still a young woman."

My father's face was a roadmap of chiseled lines, but as I recalled he was about my age when we last had this conversation. He'd been dead-set against my cutting short my education before I earned my master's degree. "You've worked so hard, why quit now?" he'd asked, incredulous.

When had Andrew R. Templeton become the center of my universe? As I dipped into my ice cream and felt the smooth blob melting on my tongue, I remembered our first date, how nervous I was he wouldn't find me attractive with my hair all askew from riding on the back of his Harley. But at the end of our evening, his hands rose like two doves alighting on my shoulders, and he kissed me, then asked if I was free the next afternoon. I had plans to see a matinee with a girlfriend, but I told Drew my calendar was wide open. I gazed up into his handsome face sure I loved him already. Six months later, when he asked me to marry him, I'd been ecstatic. After telling my parents the blissful news, I drove to the drug store to purchase a copy of *Brides* magazine, and had never read *Architectural Digest* again.

The sound of Pop's spoon scraping the bottom of his dish brought me back to the present. "Did you know I used to play the violin?" he asked.

I contained a chuckle. "Are you sure about that?"

He dropped his spoon in his dish. "Of course, I'm sure." He closed his eyes for a moment and smiled to himself. Then his lids flapped open to reveal childlike enthusiasm. "My teacher said I could make a career as a musician if I wanted. But he warned me I'd never make any money, so I chose to go into business."

I knew Pop liked classical music. He admired Isaac Stern. But there was no way I could picture him carving his bow across a violin's strings to produce a delicate sliver of sound.

I didn't want to rile him, but said, "I've never seen your violin," then swallowed another bite.

"It's in the attic, somewhere. Your mother knows."

"Seriously?" I said, and he nodded with certainty. "Then why haven't I heard you play it?"

"I needed to make a living and feed the family. No time for fiddling on the roof." He grinned at his humor. "But I used to be darned good. My mother—your Grandma Teresa—would cry when she heard me playing *Ave Maria*."

This was a segment of my father's persona I'd never imagined. "Maybe we should find your violin tomorrow." I envisioned their attic stuffed with two steamer trunks and at least a dozen cardboard boxes. "You could play something for me."

"No, no, it's been too long." He held up a gnarled hand. "Too much arthritis. Anyway, I gave away my sheet music."

Minutes later I escorted him back to bed. As the mattress dipped beneath his weight, my mother rolled over. Her face contorted with fear.

"He's fine." I tugged up his covers. "We were in the kitchen having a snack."

"I can't believe I didn't hear him get up," she said, as I came around to her side of the bed. "He gets disoriented and could hurt himself or turn the stove on and burn the house down."

I placed a hand on her bony shoulder. "Go back to sleep," I said. "Everything's okay."

But for how long?

17

I FELT LIKE I'D just survived boot camp. Reclining on a foam mat barely cushioning my limbs from the exercise studio's wooden floor, I attempted to imitate the instructor's cool-down stretches. But why start now? I hadn't been able to follow her routine for the last grueling hour. When Gloria suggested I take this Zumba Latin dance workout with her she'd promised it was a beginning class. No sweat—a free trial for prospective members. "You like dancing, don't you? And Latin music? You'll love it."

Finally, the music ground to a halt. "You were fantastic," the instructor proclaimed in a voice broadcasting a profusion of reserved energy. The other people, mostly women in their twenties and thirties, glided to their feet and picked up their mats to return them to the back of the room. As I stood up, Gloria, who'd exercised front and center, walked to my side. Her face wore a rosy hue that divulged no sign she'd been in constant movement while waving her arms over her head for most of the hour.

"Well, what did you think?" she asked me, then swigged from her water bottle.

"That I'll be lucky to make it to my car." I ran my tongue across my lip and tasted salt. I'd never sweated so much in my life. "My legs are so stiff I'll have to ask someone to untie my shoelaces when I get home."

"Come on, I bet you'll be fine."

Several women strolled by talking at rapid-fire speed. I caught glimpses of their words to hear their toddlers were in the day care somewhere in the building.

"I'm usually not such a klutz," I said as Gloria and I followed them toward the locker room. It had been five years since I'd taken an aerobics class and was disappointed with my lack of coordination. "I'm glad I was in the back of the room where no one but the instructor could see me." Of course, my reflection in the mirror offered everyone a good shot. "The moment I thought I was onto her routine, she changed it."

"The dance steps take concentration, but keep coming and you'll catch on." Gloria swayed her hips. "We've been doing that routine for over a month."

"Now you tell me."

We reached the locker room to find half a dozen women in various stage of dress milling about the carpeted room with its two walls of lockers and a floor-to-ceiling mirror. Gloria had stowed both of our purses and jackets in her locker. She and I had agreed we'd shower at home later so she could get back to Saturday morning with her husband and daughter. And this way I wouldn't have to expose my body to these toned young women. Even when I was their age I didn't look like an Olympic athlete.

"Do you remember Stephen Harrick?" Gloria yanked her hair out of its ponytail. "You met him at my New Year's Eve party."

"The frog man?"

"He's a biologist." She wagged her index finger at me. "He teaches at Shoreline Community College and does consulting for Jonathon's firm."

New Year's Eve replayed itself in my mind like a rerun of a sitcom that never made it to prime time. Gloria had insisted I drop by her house for what she claimed would be a small gathering of friends. But I'd found a mob of her and her husband Jonathon's business associates, plus a couple dozen neighbors. My first impulse had been to turn tail and flee, but Gloria spotted me before I could escape. "Don't leave. You look darling." She'd latched on to my elbow and dragged me inside. "Come and mingle. You never know who you might meet."

It was true I'd gone to some trouble getting myself spruced up, but I was in no mood to party until the wee hours. I assured myself I'd make my exit as soon as I had something to eat.

Standing at the hors d'oeuvre table nibbling on skewered chicken with peanut sauce, I'd met tall and wiry Stephen, who'd seemed as uncomfortable as I was. After an exchange of names, he let slip he was single and not dating anyone. I had to admit he was attractive and intelligent as he entertained me with stories of his paddling the upper branches of the Amazon in search of horned frogs. Before I knew it, it was 11:55 and Gloria got the whole group crooning "Auld Lang Syne."

"Should old acquaintance be forgot"—I sang it like a funeral dirge, all the time wondering where Drew and Kristi were spending this auspicious moment. Probably somewhere festive, donning party hats and blasting noisemakers. Or worse, nestled somewhere private making love. As Gloria's clock announced midnight, Stephen wrapped an arm around my shoulder in a brotherly fashion and gave my cheek a peck. In an impulsive whim, I stood on tiptoes to kiss him lightly on the lips. I was instantly bombarded with embarrassment and regret. What had gotten into me? Was I so starved for attention I'd turn to a complete stranger? Fortunately, Gloria and Jonathon arrived to share hugs, then I made my getaway without speaking to Stephen again.

Gloria seemed to be stalling as she spun the dial on the combination lock. "I ran into Stephen the other day and he asked about you big time. I think he wants to take you out."

"First of all, I'm married. And even if I weren't, he's ten years younger than I am." I wouldn't mention my blunder on New Year's Eve.

"So? You look young. Age doesn't matter so much anymore." She finally opened the locker, handed me my purse. "How about the four of us doing something tonight? Jonathon and I are thinking about taking in a movie. I'll give Stephen a jingle and see if he's free. It'll be very casual, no strings attached."

"I'm busy." I reached into the locker for my jacket.

"Oh, yeah? What are you doing?" She watched my eyes like an attorney cross-examining her witness.

"I'll be up at the island," I decided as I spoke.

LATER IN THE day, a few miles from the cabin, I spotted the real estate office, a one-story building. Pulling into the gravel parking lot, I recalled Drew's and my conversation in the kitchen less than two hours ago.

"You're going again?" he'd asked. "For heaven's sakes, why?"

"None of your business." Who did he think he was probing for my motivation? The truth is, I needed to get out of the house. But Mom wouldn't let me spend another night with her and Pop. She'd said I should stay home and take care of my children and maybe rebuild my marriage. Plus, the island was the only place I could think of that wouldn't cost me any money. All week I'd felt like odd man out; Drew was turning the girls against me. He'd been a reasonable parent in the past, but now he acted like a wet noodle, bending to our daughters' every demand without consulting me first, and making me seem like an ogre.

"I just heard the weather report," he'd said. "It's supposed to rain. What will you do all by yourself? Maybe one of the girls should tag along." Where was his plethora of mock-concern coming from? I didn't trust his motives.

"They don't want to go," I'd informed him. "They have their friends and activities." I'd twisted the ice cube tray, causing an ear-wrenching sound, then shook the frozen squares into the cooler box. "By the way, while I'm there I'm going to tell Hal Vandervate to put the cabin on the market."

"Hey, not so fast, I want to go up there first."

As far as I knew Drew had never spent time on the island by himself. "You'd better not be planning to bring Kristi with you," I'd said. "I won't have that woman sleeping in my bed."

I entered the real estate office to find Hal behind his desk, parked before a picture window framing the Cascade Mountains and Port Susan. When he saw me, he got to his feet, moving slower than he used to. As he extended his long arm to shake my hand, he glanced over my shoulder, no doubt expecting to see Drew.

"Just me," I said, feeling tightness in my throat. This conversation was going to be harder than I thought. "Would you mind stopping by our cabin tomorrow to tell me how much you think it's worth?"

"Sure, I'd love to. Thinking of selling?"

"Yes, as soon as I— I mean, as soon as we can." I wondered how many homes Hal had listed as a result of divorce.

"Your place has been a great investment. It's probably tripled in value since you bought it."

"Wonderful." We hadn't purchased the cabin to make money. In fact, we'd toyed with the idea of enlarging it and retiring up here, then leaving the property to our daughters and their children. Drew and I had even saved the girls' plastic buckets and shovels so our future grandchildren could build sandcastles and dig for ghost shrimp to use for fishing bait.

"Yes, indeed," he said, his voice eager, "people are clamoring for low-bank waterfront like yours. It's a gem."

"I agree." The most beautiful place in the world, I thought, and turned to leave.

Fifteen minutes later, I steered the car down the lane to the cabin. Passing Victor's A-frame I was hoping to see some sign of him so I'd know another soul was nearby. But no smoke circled from the chimney, nor did a car wait outside. Maybe he'd given up his writing project and wouldn't return again.

I parked by our seldom-used mailbox. With my tote bag hanging from my shoulder, I lugged the cooler down the path. In the past Drew had carried the heavy items; I was glad I hadn't packed much. As I neared the front door raindrops began dampening my face. By the time I stowed my food in the refrigerator I could hear a steady blipping sound on the metal roof as the shower picked up.

Feeling my skin tingle from the cold, I flicked on a lamp, then knelt before the fireplace to rip newspaper and add kindling. A snap of the wooden match across the hearth produced a flame. I touched the match to the paper and the fire struggled to life.

I was hungry, but nothing from my cooler box—eggs, bread, a head of lettuce, and a tomato—sounded good. I opened the cupboard to find an assortment of canned goods, crackers, and cereal that needed to be eaten or taken back to the city. I chose chili con carne, a meal the girls had always enjoyed on cold wet evenings. I spooned the beans into a pot, turned on the stove, and watched the burner glow orange.

I remembered Drew's habit of sneaking up behind me in the kitchen as I prepared meals. Enveloping me in his arms, he'd nibble the nape of my neck until I wiggled out of his grasp. Often my reaction had been one of annoyance. What I needed was his assistance in cooking, I'd complain. Distracting me while I was chopping vegetables was downright dangerous, so would he please set the table instead of impeding my progress? And where was he when it came time to clean the kitchen after our meal? But in hindsight I wished I could take back my negative responses. Kristi probably relished his playful antics. I could picture them together, her encouraging his attention as his hands explored the curves of her hips.

I heard a spitting sound and glanced down to see bubbles erupting from the chili's surface like molten lava.

"Phooey!" As I pulled the pot off the burner a spatter of heat pierced the back of my hand. I licked my wound, then grabbed the spoon to stir the lumpy mass, and felt a burnt crust coagulated on the bottom. Frustration took hold of me. Trying to avoid the charred beans, I ladled off the top into a bowl, then sat myself down in front of the fire.

Shadows surrounded the cabin and the room turned gloomy. Outside, the cedar trees clustered near the cabin bent their shaggy heads as the wind blustered in erratic gusts. Low hanging branches scratched the side of the cabin sounding like animals wanting in.

This was my life as a single woman, I told myself. I needed to get used to it.

18

CLASPING A BRIDAL bouquet, I stood near a podium-like altar in the lobby of a tacky hotel lobby. Las Vegas? I saw a justice of the peace wearing a cheap suit and a narrow tie leading a couple through their wedding vows. I glanced around looking for my fiancé, but he hadn't arrived. Dejected, I waited and waited, then finally checked into the hotel, and in a split second I woke up the next day in my room. Then he arrived—a man I didn't recognize—and said he was ready to marry me. But I felt unsure. I asked myself if I truly loved him and realized I didn't anymore. I wanted to tell him I'd changed my mind, but when I tried to speak, I couldn't move my lips. Struggling for control, I opened my eyes to find myself alone, and the cabin's silhouettes still submerged in darkness.

Who was the man? I wondered, disconcerted by my thoughts. Not Drew, which pleased me. I was sick of his constant intrusion into my mind. Yet if not Drew, then who? I closed my eyes and tried to retrace the images, but the man had dissolved like a snowflake. Just a stupid dream, I told myself. Ridiculous. Anyway, the last thing I needed was another man in my life.

As I prepared my morning coffee, I glanced out the window to see the sun riding low in a pale blue sky. Annie's song "The Sun Will Come Out Tomorrow" started trilling in my ears and I felt somewhat energetic and hopeful. My calves and hamstrings, although stiff from the grueling Zumba dance class, were functioning better than I'd anticipated. Still, I had no intention of returning for another round of torture. I'd firm up my muscles walking and climbing stairs.

Soon after, I put on a jacket and headed to the beach with Bonnie following me. The tideland stretched out, exposing a twenty-foot-wide strip of pebbles and beyond that, twenty yards of sandy flats. Crisp air cooling my cheeks, I headed north. This was perfect agate light and few people combed the shore this early in the year. At that moment, I spotted something glowing like a moonstone on the beach several feet ahead. I reached down to lay claim of a nearly-transparent agate and polished it between my fingers to savor the rock's smooth hardness. Then I deposited my find in my pocket.

I ambled on, collecting more stones, a swirly shell, and a fist-sized piece of driftwood that looked like an eagle's head. As my gaze scanned the beach, my ears took in the cries of gulls as they skimmed and swooped over the water. Further out in the bay a flock of loons flew north; their wings beat just above the water's surface like helicopter blades. The tide was inching in and my path narrowing. Finally, I turned myself around and started back. By the time I neared the cabin I'd been traipsing for two hours. My fatigued legs began to complain and my stomach grumbled from hunger.

I spotted two people standing on the beach in front of our place. Instead of admiring the view, the pair stood face-to-face, both speaking at once. As I came closer, I recognized Victor Huff and a woman in her early seventies.

When I reached them, Victor tossed me what seemed to be a smile of relief. He said, "Ruthie, great. I'd like you to meet my mother, Constance Huff." He scratched Bonnie between the ears; she leaned against his leg.

I couldn't help wondering if his gladness to see me had to do with a conversation of a serious nature. "Nice to meet you." I put out a hand.

Constance, wearing a wool scarf wrapped twice around her neck, mittens, and a parka, shook my hand with a stiff gesture and said, "How do you do?" She ignored Bonnie, who soon lost interest in Constance.

"Fine, thank you." I extracted my hand from her viselike grip.

"Up here all alone?" he asked me. When I said yes, he said, "Why don't you come for lunch? My mother brought enough pasta salad and king salmon to feed an army."

Constance looked less than enthusiastic about his suggestion, but she said, "Certainly, please join us. If you're not busy."

I was grateful for their generosity and salmon sounded delicious. "I'd like that, but I'm expecting a visitor in an hour."

"We'll wait for you," he said. "No hurry."

When I returned to the cabin, I tried to view the interior as a prospective buyer might. It had been ages since I'd given the place a thorough cleaning. I gathered the throw rugs and shook them outside. Then I pushed all the furniture to the perimeter of the room and swept and scrubbed the linoleum floor. Instead of returning the pieces to their original positions, I decided to try something new. By scooting the couch nearer to the fireplace, the room felt cozier. In the trunk at the foot of the bed I found a blanket with a native American Indian motif to drape over the back of the sofa, then added two pillows from the girls' room.

An hour later, Hal still hadn't arrived. Bored, I took all the prints and paintings off the wall, sorted them by frame color, then rehung them. I placed chunks of driftwood by the fireplace and rearranged the books in the bookcase, using old bottles filled with sand as bookends.

At last Hal showed up with apologies. As he stepped across the threshold he said, "The place looks terrific. Did you hire an interior decorator?"

I wondered if he was being overly solicitous. "No, I did it myself."

"You should go into the business. Say, I need someone to fluff up homes when they go on the market. I'll bet you could work miracles. Need a job?"

This wasn't the first time someone had remarked favorably about my decorating talents. "You're very kind," I said, "but I have a job and I live too far away."

"Not if you buy another home on the island." He eyed the room again. "I was surprised when you said you were selling. Not that I don't want the listing, mind you, I'm thrilled to have it. But I thought you folks loved this property."

"We do. You have no idea how much I wish I didn't have to sell."

"I won't be nosy, and that's not like me." His sunny face turned serious. "I'll get working on a market analysis and give you a call."

"Better put it in the mail." I didn't trust Drew and wanted to intercept the letter before he saw it.

When Hal left, I felt like indulging myself in a crying spree, but I was too hungry to miss lunch.

"You'd better stay here and take a nap, girl." I decided to leave Bonnie behind. Constance was obviously not a dog lover.

I checked my face in the mirror—not that it mattered. Victor had seen me looking like I'd just crawled out of an inferno.

He answered the door on my first knock. "Good timing, the fish is almost done," he said. His expression was haggard. Apparently, his conversation with his mother had taken a turn for the worse. I hated to intrude, but the wonderful aroma of baking salmon wafting through the open door beckoned me to enter.

"I was just going to come get you." He took my jacket.

A bowl of pasta salad already sat on the table set for three. He pulled a chair out for Constance, who took great care getting herself situated. Then he seated me across from her.

After some talk about recent development on the island, Constance mentioned the name Juliet. "You know her, don't you?" she asked me. "Victor's wife."

So, Mom was right. "No, I haven't had the pleasure."

"Really." It was a statement rather than a question. She stood to locate her handbag and open her wallet. Sitting, she passed me a photo of Victor and a flaxen-haired woman. Both looked to be having the time of their lives. From their attire—Juliet clad in a strapless dress, something I'd never have the nerve to wear, and Victor in a short-sleeve shirt—I assumed they were on vacation somewhere warm. And judging from Victor's smiling face, I guessed the photo had been shot over five years ago, maybe ten.

"She's lovely." Ravishing was a better description. Long blonde hair. Flawless face. Seriously, I could imagine her on the cover of a fashion magazine.

"Juliet works for City Hall." Constance said. "An assistant to the mayor. Very busy." She cast her glance in Victor's direction. "I suppose she's out of town?"

"Your guess is as good as mine."

I found it peculiar he didn't know where his own wife was, but as he had declared in his office his personal affairs were none of my business. I occupied myself unfolding my napkin and spreading it across my lap.

A timer sounded and he got to his feet, then returned carrying a platter of steaming pink fish topped with lemon slices. As he placed it on the center of the table, I had good opportunity to observe his left hand again. No ring, but the man was obviously married.

"This is a real treat," I said after Constance had served herself and it was my turn. I cut a generous wedge of fish, transferred it to my plate.

"I see you're hungry." Victor appraised my portion.

"Oops, I guess I could have come back for seconds. My appetite got the better of me."

"I admire a woman with a good appetite." He served himself an even larger piece.

The corners of Constance's mouth angled down as she picked up on his humor and attempt to help me feel at ease. "How is it that you're up here today?" she asked me.

"Mother, please," Victor said, letting me know Constance made a habit of being nosy.

I pretended not to detect the tension between them. "My husband and I own a cabin not far away." I sampled the pasta salad, finding it bland. When I added salt, she frowned.

"I assumed you were single," she said to me. "Where's your wedding band?"

I slipped my hands into my lap.

"Mother," Victor said with severity. "Would you like some homemade tartar sauce?"

"Yes, thank you, dear." She spooned a serving onto her plate.

"Victor mentioned you live in Stanwood," I said, hoping to steer the subject to a neutral ground. "It must have been a wonderful place to raise a family."

She let out a weary sigh. "Yes, it was, but Victor chose to move away at age eighteen."

"Seattle's just down the road," he said. "It hardly takes any time to get there."

"You're right," she countered. "But I don't drive much anymore." Raising her brows, she looked to me for support and said, "Cataracts."

"I'm so sorry," I said. "That's got to be difficult." I wondered if Mom's vision was also dimming into gray tones. Is that what she was alluding to when she said she experienced problems with depth perception?

"Mother's ophthalmologist has been begging her to have surgery." Victor squeezed lemon onto his salmon. "He assures us the recovery time is short."

"I will, one of these days." She swallowed a dainty bite of fish. "Dear, what do you hear from Peter?"

Victor's features finally relaxed. "He's declared his major. Biology."

"Your son?" I knew little about Victor, and wished I'd pumped Mom for more information about him. It struck me that she wouldn't approve of my being here right now even though I had no designs on Victor.

"Yes, he's twenty. And almost six inches taller than I am."

"How wonderful." If he was anything like his father, I thought, he must be quite a young man. I'd misjudged Victor. Or was he a Dr. Jekyll and Mr. Hyde with conflicting personalities?

Later in the afternoon, I heard knocking at my cabin door and was surprised to see Victor through the glass panes. Again,

I imagined Mom's reaction to our being together. But I let him in.

"I'm afraid my mother was being overly helpful at lunch." He ran a hand through his hair. "Sorry about that."

"Not a problem. She was nice." Maybe once you got to know her. She'd treated me with suspicion, like I was going to steal the flatware. "I'd probably be protective of my son, too."

"I should have mentioned earlier that I'm married." He stared out the window at a commercial crabber dropping pots several hundred yards from shore. "My wife and I haven't lived together for several years. Rumor has it she's in the Bahamas with a gentleman friend. She and I lead separate lives."

"I'd guessed that." Now that he'd cracked the drawer where he kept his private thoughts hidden, would he retract into his shell or say something cutting? At least he couldn't dismiss me from my own house. "You don't owe me an explanation," I said. "But I have to ask, why do you stay married?"

"First, I stuck it out for our son, until he graduated from high school, which was over two years ago. Then, out of laziness, I suppose, or fear. I figured as long as I was married I wouldn't be drawn into another relationship. That's the last thing I want." He stopped abruptly and gave his head a small shake. "What got me telling you this? I came over to apologize for Mother's behavior."

"If it makes you feel any better, my mother's still loyal to her soon-to-be ex-son-in-law, even after he cheated on me. She's the queen of denial. Not that I couldn't claim that title, myself. I've hung onto Drew like a drowning woman to a life preserver, and all for naught."

In my periphery I noticed a spider web dangling from the ceiling. I batted at the silvery thread, and a speck of dust drifted down and lodged on my eyelash. As I attempted to blink it away searing pain assaulted my eye. I cupped it with my hand.

"Are you all right?" He sounded again like a physician.

"There's something in my eye." I tried to open it, but the burning increased.

"This isn't my area of expertise, but perhaps I can help." He took my elbow and guided me to the kitchen sink. "Let's try rinsing it out." He poured water into a small glass, handed it to me. I leaned over the sink to douse my eye; the cool liquid eased the stinging.

"My hero." I wiped my face with a paper towel.

At that moment the door flew open like a tornado sneaking up on us. I looked past Victor to see Drew, his hands on his narrow hips and his jaw squared like some he-man cartoon character. Bonnie pranced at his feet.

19

"WHAT ARE YOU doing here?" I asked Drew. "Spying on me?"

"I was worried," he said, his head pushed forward and his lips white. "But I can see you're being well cared for."

"It's not what you think." Not that it was any of his business.

Victor offered his right hand. "Hello, I'm Victor Huff." Drew finally extended his arm but said nothing as the two men shook hands.

"I was helping this young lady get something out of her eye," Victor said.

"I could see you were helping yourself, all right," Drew shot back with scorn.

Victor chuckled. "I think I'd best be on my way." He bent down to pet Bonnie, who relished the attention.

"Thanks again for the delicious lunch," I said as Victor straightened his back. "And for coming to my rescue."

"A boyfriend?" Drew asked as soon as Victor was out the door.

Did I detect a note of jealousy? More likely I was witnessing Drew's desire to be the alpha male, the leader of the pack. I decided not to answer.

Through the window, I could see Victor strolling to the water's edge. He selected a flat stone, which he turned over in his hand several times. Then he sent the disc flying; it skipped across the water's surface at least a dozen bounces before sinking. For a moment he stood watching the spot where the stone disappeared, then he moved out of sight. It occurred to me that without trying or putting on airs he was exactly what Drew wished he could be.

I turned to Drew and noticed his sports bag lying at his feet. I aimed my index finger at it and asked, "What is that?"

"Clothes. I'm spending the night. Hey, I like what you've done with this room."

"Then I'm leaving. No, I'm not. I was here first. You can't just barge in and take over."

"I have every right to be here, I'm the one who makes the mortgage payments." He plucked up the bag and took a step toward the bedroom.

"Where are you going?" I demanded. "I'm using the bed."

"Fine, I'll sleep out here." He dropped the bag on the floor by the couch, then proceeded to the bathroom. "I suppose I can't use this either?"

Staring at the closed bathroom door, I was mad enough to scream *I hate you*, but those words would only serve to feed his theory that I'd gone bonkers the day of the accident. It was true I still couldn't recollect the details of that afternoon—past my entering the grocery store. I hated the lapse of memory; it was like reading a novel to find a chapter missing. But it proved nothing, really. Only that I'd hit my head, which could happen to anyone. Of the two of us, Drew was the one suffering from midlife craziness and apt to traipse off onto another tangent at any moment.

When he emerged, I stood in his path with my legs firmly planted. "Who's watching the girls?" I demanded. "Isn't that the reason you moved home, to spend time with them?"

"Relax. Harriet got invited to Alicia's for the night and Nichole's at Fran's. And Bonnie's right here." He sauntered over to the refrigerator and peered inside.

"That's my stuff," I said.

"I'm just getting a Pepsi. As I recall I stocked this refrigerator with pop, myself." He opened a can, then seated himself on the couch. Before I could stop him, he was sorting through the unread newspaper I'd brought up from the city.

"Hal Vandervate was out here this morning," I said.

"Tell him we'll put the cabin on the market next year."

That was exactly what I wanted to do, but I said, "I will not." I was done taking orders from Sergeant Templeton.

"What's the hurry?"

"Don't you dare act like this is my idea. It's your fault we're selling this place."

He spread open the sports section. "I figure if we're going to live together until Harriet turns around, it makes sense to wait."

"For what? Does this mean you gave up your centerfold playmate?" I could think of more appropriate names for her but avoided using such words.

"Not exactly. Although she's not happy with my decision to live at home."

I needed to get out of here. If I spoke to him another second, I might seize the poker and take a swing. Not that I was the violent type. And I wouldn't like prison food. As I neared the door, I glanced out the window to see the rain had started up again. I didn't want to get wet, and why should I? I spun around, snatched up the rest of the paper, and marched into the bedroom.

"We can coexist," Drew said as I closed the door. "Isn't that what we've done for the last five years—live like roommates?"

Once alone, I was too rattled to concentrate on reading. As I collapsed onto the bed, I wondered when a headache would begin hammering into my skull. But I felt fine. I closed my eyes and before I knew it, I was asleep.

I must have napped for over an hour, because when I awoke, the sun had descended behind the hill above the cabin. I could feel a pressing on my bladder but didn't want to use the bathroom because it would mean walking by Drew. But there was no avoiding it. Feeling in a fog, I staggered to my feet and cracked open the bedroom door. Drew wasn't there, although his bag still lingered on the floor. Bonnie snoozed next to it.

As I came out of the bathroom, he entered the front door carrying a grocery bag. Bonnie scrambled to her feet and sniffed at his shoes, then his pantlegs, as if her master was returning from a long voyage. He dipped into his jeans pocket, brought out a doggie treat, fed it to Bonnie. No wonder she was so glad to see him. Was he trying to steal Bonnie's loyalty?

"Since you won't share, I picked up dinner." He set a grocery bag on the counter and extracted a package containing a couple of boned chicken breasts, a bag of mushrooms, an onion, and a head of lettuce, and spread them across the counter, no doubt to make me envious.

His cell phone began ringing. "It must be one of the girls." He answered it. "Hello?" Then his voice cooled. "Oh, hi." He rotated away from me as if trying to negate my existence. "I couldn't make it there on time even if I wanted to, which I don't." During a long pause he stepped over to the window. His voice soured. "Look, I told you I wasn't going." Another pause. "Yes, she's here, but we're not sleeping together."

I tried to appear busy as I eavesdropped. My ears straining to catch each word, I perused the cupboard and counted the cans of dog food.

"Is that a threat?" Drew said with the bark he usually saved for irritating motorists. He whisked the phone outside and stood under the eaves to finish the conversation, which dragged on for ten more minutes. When he returned, he shoved the phone into his bag.

"Was that her royal highness summoning you?" I asked. "Better jump when she throws your stick. You don't want to make her mad."

His face flamed beet red, not his best color. "Look, I don't need two harpies pecking at me." He strode to the kitchen counter and yanked the plastic wrap off the chicken.

I felt like I was tormenting my big brother as a kid. "If I'm so irritating, why don't you leave?"

"No way. I won't let you drive me out." He placed the onion on the cutting board, raised our largest knife, then sliced the orb in half like it was a victim of the guillotine.

Sure, I knew I was acting immaturely, but I inched closer. "Tell me, what did the princess want?"

Drew chopped the onion into miniscule pieces; the blade clacking against the wood almost drowned out his voice. "Her name is Kristi. She wants me to escort her to a party."

The onion's fumes stung my eyes, but I stood my ground. "And she has a fit when you don't obey her?" I savored the grimace on his face. "When did you lose your backbone?"

He removed an iron skillet from the rack above the stove, set it on a burner, and added olive oil, the onion, and the mushrooms. Then he turned to me. "Ruthie, let's call a truce for tonight, all right?" He reached out his hand and his fingertips grazed my arm. "I'll even share my dinner with you."

Fool me once, shame on you; fool me twice, shame on me, Pop would say. Well, Drew had bamboozled me five hundred times and I wasn't going to let him sucker me again.

I lurched back, out of his circumference. "How dare you? Don't ever touch me again."

His features warped as he spewed out the words, "Don't worry, I won't."

And I had no doubt he was speaking the truth.

I WOKE THE next morning with a crick in my neck. I sniffed the air the way Bonnie might, but caught no trace of coffee, not even smoke from a fire. Drew could sleep anywhere and had probably enjoyed a perfect night's rest, while I'd thrashed in a jungle of sheets and blankets. As I rolled over and tried to dive back into slumber, my mind revisited the prior evening. At dinnertime the aroma of simmering chicken had tantalized me, but I tried my best to appear satisfied as I fried two eggs for supper. He and I had moved through the room like choreographed swimmers. We'd floated within inches of each other several times, yet managed not to brush elbows or even exchange a glance. It reminded me of the icy forty-eight hours that used to follow our blowups. The battles would detonate from the most mundane incidents, like my asking Drew not to run the water when brushing his teeth followed by his opening the faucet wider just to spite me. Or our debates over which newspaper we should subscribe to. Those arguments seemed trivial once my husband revealed he'd been sleeping with the enemy.

I sniffed the air again, but still no hint of coffee. I finally got up and pulled on some sweats. I checked myself in the mirror and fluffed my hair. Opening the door a few inches, I peeked out to see the couch yawning empty.

"Drew?" As I strode into the living room my eyes canvassed the area to see every trace of him had vanished. No bag, and even the pillows on the couch were back in place and the sports page refolded. I checked the girls' small bedroom, with its bunk bed pushed against the wall, but he wasn't there either. And no Bonnie. How dare he take her with him?

I felt like I'd been stung by a hornet. His leaving without notice felt almost worse than his arrival. But after a few moments of reasoning with myself, I concluded his departure was a blessing. Of course it was. He was gone and good riddance.

I stepped outside for fresh air. A resounding clunk from the direction of Victor's cabin vibrated the quiet, and then another clunk followed. Curious, I walked down to the water's edge, then up his path. I caught a glimpse of him at the side of the cabin. He seemed deep in thought as he balanced a section of cedar on end atop a stump, lifted a splitting maul, then powered it down. Two pieces of wood flew out to the sides and landed like wounded ducks.

He didn't notice my arrival.

"Good morning," I said.

He turned his head, wiped sweat off his brow with his sleeve.

I inhaled the heady aroma of newly cut cedar. "It's my turn to apologize." I moved closer. "That was Drew, my husband."

"So I gathered." He leaned the maul against the side of the house. "I'm glad I saw you two together, it helped me come to grips with my own situation. I've decided to call Juliet tonight and give her the option of filing for divorce, or I will."

"Are you sure?" I regretted Drew's and my animosity affecting someone else's marriage negatively. It struck me—when Drew and I were together we metamorphosed into a malignant cancer.

"I thought about Juliet and my marriage all night." A muscle in his jaw twitched. "The charade we live. Only in our case, she's the one who's out with another..."

"I'm sorry." If anyone could empathize I could.

"How about you and Drew? Is there any hope you two will reconcile?"

"No." I cracked a smile. "And I hope he's miserable for the rest of his life. What a kick if he went bald overnight, broke out with blisters itching worse than poison ivy, and a hairy wart made its home on the end of his nose. That would teach him a little humility."

Victor laughed. "I remember those feelings...but wait long enough and your anger will fade to apathy." He gathered an armload of split wood and began stacking it against the side of the house.

I picked up a chunk and laid it on top. "How's your writing going?"

"I'm feeling indifferent about that too. Another decision I made last night." He set another cedar slab on end, lifted the maul over his head and let it drop with a whack. The wood fractured down the middle.

Again, he seemed lost in thought.

20

"I'M HOME." I shoved the front door of the house open with my hip and carted in two full grocery bags.

I heard the anchorwoman from the five o'clock news, then spotted Drew in front of the TV in the living room. Bonnie sat attentively at his feet, ignoring me and treating him like the dominant leader of the pack. Irritating as all get-out.

"How was work?" Drew smiled. I've got to say this for the man: he was an actor extraordinaire. And I would fake being equally magnanimous.

"It couldn't have been better," I said. No need to mention that my first day back had dragged on like a case of the flu.

"Brittany's with us permanently now," Will had exclaimed when I entered the office to find my work space shoved over several feet to accommodate a desk for Brittany, who stood at the copy machine. "She's a whiz with Apple computers." His voice sounded buoyant, like he'd just landed a major contract. "She'll show you how our new system works."

I knew the computers had been installed but seeing my new screen glaring at me like an angry schoolteacher brought me down another rung. "I'm not very computer savvy," I said, knowing he was well aware of that fact. I dreaded having to start all over. Did my brain work anymore?

Once Brittany and I were alone she said, "I grew up on Macs. They're a cinch once you get acquainted with them."

The day crawled along with Brittany sorting the mail, placing the letters and packages in the appropriate places. Then she typed several letters for Bill and brought them to his office for his signature. I'd wanted to go over accounts receivable but needed to wait for Brittany's instructions. There was no way I dared tackle a new computer system alone. By the time I fielded several telephone calls and ordered office supplies, it was time to go home.

Yawning, I carried brown paper bags containing ingredients for spaghetti sauce and other needed household items into the kitchen, where I found Harriet hunched over her homework at the table.

"Why are you studying in here?" I set the bags on the counter.

"Dad said I have to do my homework in the kitchen every day after school."

"That sounds like a good idea." I hoped I hadn't cursed the situation by making a positive remark.

The scrumptious aroma of stewing meat hung in the air. Beef stroganoff? I spied the casserole dish through the oven's glass door and rinsed broccoli waiting to be steamed on the stovetop. Apparently Drew had prepared dinner already. I opened the refrigerator door and was met by a wall of food. He must have gone shopping on his way home.

Drew moseyed in, placed his hands on Harriet's shoulders and gave them a massage. She showed her appreciation by dropping her pen and leaning back in her chair.

"How's my girl doing?" he asked.

"Fine." She gave me a sideways glance. "Daddy says if I pull my grade-point average up to 2.5, he'll give me a $100 gift certificate from Nordstrom's. And $200 for a 3 point."

I stuffed the ground beef I'd just purchased into the meat compartment and noticed Gouda and Camembert cheeses, which I loved but was too frugal to buy. I admit, I bordered on stingy.

"I don't believe in bribing children to get good grades," I said.

"I'm not a child."

"Sorry. But the sentiment still stands."

She thudded her book shut and handed the paper to Drew. "I'm almost done with my math. Can I watch TV for a while?"

"Sure, Kitten."

Harriet slipped out of the room before I could ask her to set the table for dinner. "Why didn't you make her finish her work while you had her?" I asked. "A bird in the hand."

"She'll be fine. Let me be in charge of her school work." His voice sounded lack-luster. "Your method hasn't worked."

"True." I should be thrilled to be out of Harriet's cat-and-mouse game, but I didn't trust Drew to follow through. I gave him a look over and noticed a tired face with gray lips.

"What's wrong?" I asked. "You don't look so good."

"It's been a rough day." He moved to the stove and tugged the oven door open, then reached in to lift the top off the pot.

Suddenly he snapped his hand back and shook it.

I gasped. "Did you burn yourself?"

In obvious pain, he sucked on his fingertips.

Remembering one of Mom's tried-and-true home remedies, I splashed tepid water into a basin and placed it on the kitchen table. "Here, soak your hand in this."

He landed on a chair, submerged his hand in the liquid. "I might as well tell you, Kristi and I broke up."

"That's a surprise." It wasn't easy hiding my delight. I felt like clicking my heels and dancing a jig. "You two had a spat?"

He lifted his hand out of the basin to examine his wounded fingers. "She gave me an ultimatum." The sides of his mouth yanked back, then he shoved his hand into the water again.

Their fight must have been a doozy. "What kind of an ultimatum?" I asked.

"Move out of here, or call it quits."

"I don't really blame her." Which was the truth. "I wouldn't date a married man who's living at home with his wife and kids."

"Yeah, she deserves better."

And I didn't? I felt my hackles rise on the back of my neck as I envisioned Kristi's farewell speech. "Did you beg her to reconsider? Did you promise her anything, the way I did?"

"Ruthie, please. I feel bad enough."

Good, I thought. He deserved it. I recalled my conversation with Isolda about forgiveness but expunged her questionable wisdom from my mind. I wanted Drew to suffer. I heard once that happiness was the best revenge. In that case, I'd pretend to be happy even if I wasn't.

"I think I'll fix dessert tonight." I pulled my Fannie Farmer cookbook down from above the refrigerator and turned to the dessert section. "Here's one we haven't had for a while: fruit cobbler." I sorted through the freezer compartment to find a bag of frozen blackberries. Then I combined the ingredients and drizzled melted butter over the crust.

"I'll take out the stroganoff and stick this in." I put on the broccoli. "The oven's even set to the right temperature."

Minutes later, I called the girls for dinner. Drew shuffled into the dining room cradling the bowl. As he neared the table, he took a jerky step and a pocket of water splashed against his shirt, leaving a dark splotch.

"What's wrong, Daddy?" Harriet asked, alighting onto her chair.

"Your father forgot to put on a hot-mitt and burned himself." Part of me felt sorry for him; I couldn't help it. But the rest wanted to laugh out loud. "He'll have to eat with his hand in the water until the pain goes away." I served everyone, giving Drew an extra-large portion.

I nibbled a piece of beef. "This is delicious and so tender. I should ask you to make dinner more often."

A right-hander, Drew picked at his food with his left hand. He tried without success to cut half a chunk of meat with the side of his fork, then set the fork on the rim of his plate.

I couldn't help comparing him to Pop. "Nichole," I said. "Would you cut your father's meat and help him eat?"

"That's okay," he said. "I'm not hungry."

Later, when the timer buzzed, I popped to my feet and brought the cobbler with its browned-to-perfection crust and a carton of vanilla ice cream to the table.

"That looks great." Nichole watched me slice into the steaming dessert, then noticed Drew staring across the room. "Are you okay, Dad?"

"Yes, anything you'd like to share?" I muscled a spoon through the ice cream.

"I'd rather not talk about it." Avoiding eye contact with us, he lifted his hand from the water and dried his fingers with his napkin. His skin had whitened and shriveled.

"The girls are old enough to know what's going on." I played the happy hostess passing around the plates.

"Fine, have it your way." He finally looked to Nichole, then Harriet. "Kristi and I aren't together anymore."

"You two split?" Harriet said. "Cool."

But Nichole busied herself tasting a blackberry. For once I appreciated Harriet's zeal.

"I'm afraid your father wouldn't agree," I said. "But I'm sure this is a temporary setback. There are lots of fish in the sea. Right?"

"That was uncalled for." Drew's voice gained hostility.

Shrugging, I brought a forkful of dessert to my lips and swallowed. But the sugary taste caught at the back of my throat, making me cough and souring my stomach.

21

THE NEXT MORNING at the office I pressed the Command Save key on my computer, then smiled over to Brittany.

"Good for you," she said from her chair. "I think you've got it licked."

"Maybe you can teach an old pooch new tricks." I was proud of myself; I'd only begged for her assistance twice in the last hour.

I pushed my chair away from my desk and stretched my arms back. I felt drowsy. During my ragged hours of sleep the night before I'd felt like a sailboat in a tempest, the wind tossing me this way and that, the waves breaking across my bow. Upon waking I'd found my pillow askew and my quilt halfway on the floor. It was Drew's fault, I thought. How could any woman relax with her husband across the hall pining for another? The sooner he was out of the house again the better.

Later as I'd dressed, my thoughts progressed to my father. According to Mom, his new medication to lessen memory loss had demonstrated no effect. I always figured there was a pill to cure or at least improve every malady, but Pop deteriorated further daily and there seemed no way to stop his decline. Maybe we needed to get a second opinion, not that I didn't have confidence in Victor. In fact, Dr Garcia said he was tops, the most sought-after neurologist in town.

I opened the telephone book, found Dr. Victor Huff's office number, and dialed. "This is Ruth Ann Templeton, Edward Jacobi's daughter," I told his receptionist. "Dr. Huff said someone would send me information on dementia if I left my address with you."

"Certainly, Mrs. Templeton," she said. "Would you please hold?"

I waited for several moments, then heard a clicking sound followed by Victor's husky voice. I thought doctors never came to the phone.

"Ruthie, I've got several articles that might interest you," he said. "I'll get those in the mail for you today." I thanked him and started to say goodbye.

"By the way," he interrupted, "I made that call to Juliet the other night." A woman spoke in the background and Victor's muffled voice answered her. Then he said to me, "I've got a patient waiting, but I'd like to finish our conversation. I'm planning to be downtown around noon today. Maybe we could have lunch together?"

Two hours later I minced my way down steep Cherry Street and entered a popular restaurant I'd heard of but never tried before. Tucked beneath a bank building, the cafeteria-style deli seemed to sport two personalities. Bright fluorescent bulbs illuminated Formica tables on one side of the room, while the other, with its brick wall, red lights, and vinyl booths, felt cave-like. I scanned the area to see an eclectic mix of people—men and women in business attire, two policemen, and several construction workers chatting over their lunches, but no Victor. Others stood glancing up to a board listing the menu items as they inched toward a cash register to place their orders.

I wanted to get back to work so Brittany could eat her lunch too, although she'd assured me she wasn't hungry yet. By this time, I understood why my boss liked her so much; she was a sweet and capable young woman.

I stood for a few minutes just inside the door, then I folded into line behind the last person. As I ordered a roast turkey sandwich with cranberry sauce on wheat, I heard Victor speaking behind me.

"Sorry to keep you waiting," he said, out of breath.

I turned to face him and felt an unexpected flutter in my stomach. "I almost gave up on you," I said.

"You want cheese on that?" the man behind the counter asked, and I shook my head. "You want dessert?"

"No, thank you." I brought out my billfold.

"Let me get this," Victor said. He asked for a meatloaf sandwich, then paid for both our lunches.

Two women sitting against the wall were standing. Victor led the way to their table, where we sat across from each other. Suddenly feeling shy, I glanced around. Anyone who knew me would know Drew had ditched me, not the other way around. But what would people think if they saw me out with a man?

"So, you have news about Juliet?" I hoped I hadn't blared out her name too loudly.

"Yes, but I'm tired of thinking about her. I'd rather talk about opera. Do you like it?"

I hated to reveal my ignorance. "I don't know, as I said I've never seen one."

"I have two tickets for Puccini's *Turandot* for tomorrow evening. Would I be out of line if I asked you to accompany me? Strictly as friends."

The opera part sounded all right. In the past, when listening to an aria accompanying a movie clip, I'd wondered if I'd enjoy a whole production, although I'd heard some dragged on for five or six hours. But I had nothing else to do in the evenings, I reminded myself. As I munched into my sandwich, I envisioned Victor's coming to the front door and Drew answering it brandishing the samurai sword he'd bought back when he thought karate movies were a big deal.

"We could meet there, if that would make you more comfortable," he said, as if sensing my apprehension. "And I promise to be a perfect gentleman. Just an evening at the opera, no strings attached."

Again, I hesitated. Running into each other on the beach was one thing, as was sharing this quick lunch. But spending the whole evening?

"Tell you what." He tidied his mouth with his napkin. "I'll leave your ticket at the will-call booth. If you come, you come. If you don't, I'll understand."

CLAD IN MY black knit dress, I appraised my figure in the mirror on the back of the closet door. The fabric loosely defined my waist and hips, and the hem just concealed my knees. Was this too fancy for a Wednesday night? I wondered. No, I was attending the Seattle Opera, not a movie at the Metro Cinema.

As I found my raincoat downstairs, Drew gave me a good looking over. His eyes followed my curves. "Where are you off to?" he asked, his gaze lingering on my ankles.

I was glad I looked so good. "The girls know where I'm going and how to reach me."

"Hey— have fun." He followed me to the door. "What time will you be home?"

I decided to keep him guessing. "Don't wait up for me." I used to tell Mom the same thing when I was in high school, although she always did. Now I regretted causing her to worry.

Forty-five minutes later, after gathering my ticket at will-call, I handed it to an usher, who directed me to the front row of the first balcony of McCaw Hall, home of the Seattle Opera.

Victor, already seated and reading a program, jumped to his feet when he saw me and gave me the nicest smile. I got the feeling he thought I wasn't coming and had resigned himself to sitting alone. He appeared striking in his midnight blue suit, white shirt, and red silk tie. A sharp dresser—yet another facet of his personality revealed.

"I'm glad you came," he said. "You look very nice."

"So do you."

He laughed. "Why, thank you."

"These must be the best seats in the house." I sat, then watched men and women clad in evening attire, which in Seattle wasn't all that dressed up, milling on the main floor below us, and the orchestra members in the pit tuning up their instruments. The room thrummed with excitement.

He handed me his opened program. "Here's the storyline, if you're not familiar with the opera."

"I'm not. As I said, I've never seen one, unless Bugs Bunny singing 'Figaro' on TV counts." As I stared down at two pages of tiny print, I opted not to bring out my reading glasses that made me look like a schoolmarm. "Will they be singing in Italian?" I asked.

"Yes, but you can read the English supra titles above the stage. Turandot by Giacomo Puccini is the story of a woman consumed by hatred and revenge."

"Sounds intriguing." I could relate.

"It's impossible to go wrong with Puccini,"

Moments later the lights dimmed and the maestro, a silver-haired gentleman, appeared and bowed. A swell of applause inflated the house until he turned to the orchestra and lifted his baton. When the room quieted, the orchestra wove a mesmerizing overture, then the velvet curtains parted.

I sat spellbound. The opera, a Chinese fable sizzling with drama, captivated ninety-percent of my attention. But never did I forget the man seated at my side. In the dark, I looked over to find him giving me a glance. I was sure he wished his wife was seated next to him. How odd it must feel to see me, Juliet's opposite, planted in her spot like a weed in a flower box. From what I gathered she was sophisticated and cultured. She probably appreciated opera, was familiar with every aria, and even recognized the singers by name.

At intermission, the house lights brightened again.

"What do you think so far?" Victor asked.

"It's like a symphony and a play all rolled into one. I love it." I wasn't exaggerating. The production surpassed every Oscar winner I'd seen.

"And that was only the beginning. Are you thirsty?" He guided me to a small lounge restricted from the general public by a Members Only sign at the entrance and purchased two Perrier waters.

"I propose a toast." He clanked his glass against mine. "To more evenings like this."

I couldn't grasp his meaning but tapped the edge of my glass against his. Did he hope I'd come back to the opera by myself or did he want to continue seeing me socially?

A woman about my age wearing a beige satin pantsuit matching her hair color approached us. "Victor, darling." She kissed his cheek. "Introduce me to your lady friend." Then she extended a bejeweled hand to grasp mine while I gawked at her diamond choker, which looked right out of a Tiffany's case.

"Ruthie Templeton, this is Genevieve Parker, a dear old friend," Victor said.

"Call me old again and our friendship is over." She eyed me head to foot. "She's lovely, Victor," she said as if I were a child too young to understand or speak for myself. "Where have you been hiding her?"

"Now, Gen, don't jump to conclusions."

"Humm." She set her gaze on Victor. "I don't remember the last time I saw you looking so well. Positively dapper."

A bell chimed several times. "We'd better get back to our seats," He slid a hand under my elbow and steered me to the exit.

"An old flame?" I asked.

"We dated in college, but I didn't show enough potential."

"She dropped you?" The woman must have been a fool was my only conclusion. "Who did she marry?"

"Gen's been to the altar three times, but unfortunately none of the marriages worked out."

"That's too bad." She struck me as a woman on the lookout for husband number four. "She's quite attractive." I looked back to see her sidling up to a man I recognized from newspaper articles as the opera's director.

Minutes later, Victor and I sat in the blackened auditorium. Immersed in the story, I lost all track of time. I'd heard Gloria complain that operas were tediously long, but the next hour or so jetted by. During the final scene, a tear rolled down my cheek as the heroine almost killed her suitor, the prince, because he had revealed his name.

"His name is love," she sang with glorious vibrato.

I dabbed under my eyes as the lights filled the spacious room. The curtain call began, and the chorus strode out in their marvelous far Eastern costumes to take a bow. The room thundered with applause. I clapped almost as vigorously as when Nichole made the winning goal in her soccer team's championship game. Next, the other characters strode out one by one: the mezzo-soprano, the portly bass, the dashing tenor. With each appearance, the applause grew in volume. Finally, the soprano stepped to center stage and bowed, and people in the audience yelled, "Brava!"

Victor leaned my way as the curtains closed for the final time. "Looks like you're a converted opera lover," he said. "There's one more production this season, if you're interested."

"Sure, I'd love to." Or would it be wrong? People like Genevieve might misconstrue it as a date. Well, I decided I didn't care. Victor and I knew we were friends, nothing more. And I was having fun, at last—out of my rut and on an adventure.

"What opera is it?" I asked, sure I wouldn't recognize the name.

"*Der Rosenkavalier*, by Richard Strauss."

I was right, I'd never heard of it. "If it's half as good as this one, I can't wait."

"It's quite opulent and upbeat. I think you'll like it."

He helped me with my coat, and moments later we followed the throng of people down a corridor and outside to the walkway traversing the street. A chilly gust of wind opened the front of my coat. I shivered, wishing I'd worn warmer clothing.

"Thanks so much for inviting me." I stuffed my hands in my pockets.

"You're welcome, I enjoyed the company."

People hurrying to their cars nudged us forward. As I picked up my speed, Victor said, "Just a moment. I can't let you walk to your car unescorted."

Once inside the garage, the crowd dispersed. Victor and I walked in silence; our footsteps echoed against the cement walls. I considered my first impression of him: an arrogant codfish. I'd heard that each of us wears a façade practically every waking moment to keep others from knowing how we feel or what we think. I was glad Victor was comfortable enough with me to lower his walls and act himself. I liked the real man.

22

THE NEXT MORNING, I found Drew in the kitchen bundled in his bathrobe, an article of clothing he rarely wore to the first floor. Usually, he stepped right into a jogging suit.

"You were out late last night." He yawned without covering his mouth, his tongue stretching out like a viper's.

I sniffed the bittersweet aroma of freshly brewed coffee. How nice, he'd made a full pot. I poured myself a cup and took a sip to find that along with his newfound cooking skills he'd also learned to brew decent java.

"Who were you with, anyway?" He sneezed twice, then staggered toward the kitchen sink and yanked off a couple of paper towels to mop his dripping nose.

"My affairs are none of your concern." I noticed his unshaven chin and bags sagging under his eyes. "Aren't you going to work?"

"I'm taking the day off." He coughed into the towels. "I'm sick."

In the old days I would have fussed over him: taken his temperature, made echinacea tea, and given him vitamin C and golden seal.

"I'd better keep my distance," I said, my hand out, fingertips up. "Whatever you've got, I don't want it. I've already missed enough work." Feeling only a smidgeon of guilt, never had I enjoyed another human's suffering more. "I've been thinking, I may cut back to half-time, since you agreed to pay for everything as long as you live here. Bill hired a new girl and frankly I don't think he has enough work to keep us both busy."

"Fine with me. That way you'll be here in the afternoons when Harriet gets home."

"Right. Although I may go back to school."

He screwed up his nose and another sneeze blasted through his nostrils. Burying his face in the paper towels, he snorted, then coughed. "You're finally going to take that computer class I suggested?"

"No, although I found I'm pretty good at computers. Maybe not compared to you, but I can hold my own." I poured myself more coffee. "I'm thinking about studying interior design." The idea had germinated in my mind on the way home from the opera. I was tired of pacing the sidelines watching others be creative.

"Since when have you been interested in that?" he asked.

"Since forever."

"You want to redecorate the house or something?" Once again, he was demonstrating how little he knew about me.

"I don't know why I bother telling you anything." Not that I had a handle on how I intended to use my talents.

Harriet sashayed into the room wearing a mini skirt and a suede vest I didn't remember seeing before. Maybe Drew bought them for her.

"Are you guys fighting again?" she asked.

"No, Kitten." He coughed to clear his throat. "Your mother was just telling me about her plans to redecorate."

Harriet's lip curled up on one side. "Don't you dare touch my room, it's just the way I want it." She filled a bowl with cereal, then splashed milk on top, dribbling on the counter. "Hey, get dressed, Daddy, you have to drive me in ten minutes."

"Sorry, I'm sick. I can't go anywhere."

"Then how will I get to school?"

I stowed the milk back in the refrigerator, then mopped the counter with a sponge. "The bus stops less than a block down the street." I tossed the sponge in the sink. "And it's free."

"Only losers ride the bus."

"Then hitch a ride with your sister and her friends."

"I hate Nichole's preppy friends. They treat me like I'm some kind of freak."

"I doubt that very much."

"Ruthie," Drew said. "Why don't you just drive her?"

"Yeah, Mom, when was the last time I asked you for anything?"

I pressed my lips together and held my retort that was sure to escalate into an argument.

As I placed myself in the driver's seat ten minutes later, I eyed Harriet's exposed thighs. I sat for a moment wondering whether to send my daughter back inside for a skirt with a modest hemline. But unable to face another confrontation, I pulled away from the house.

She reached over and punched on the radio, then jiggled the tuner knob until a rapper's caustic voice blasted out of the speakers, followed by a deafening bass guitar that shook the car's windows.

I slammed my hand on the power button to silence it.

"Hey, don't turn off my music."

"That's not music."

"Like, you'd know what good music is?"

"It just so happens I went to the opera last night."

"Opera?" She started hooting then attempted to yodel.

"Stop that," I said.

"Chill out. What is your problem?"

I wanted to scream that she was my problem. But spilling my thoughts would only make matters worse. It never paid to let her know she'd gotten under my skin. She would sharpen her nails and dig deeper.

I stared out the windshield until we were a block away from school. As I rolled to a halt at the final stoplight, she said, "Let me out here," and threw the door open. "I don't want anyone seeing me with you."

"A MAN JUST called you, but he didn't leave his name," Brittany told me as I arrived at the office. "He said he'd try to get back to you later."

"What did he sound like?"

"Sexy." Brittany covered her mouth and produced a giggle. "His voice was sexy."

It could have been Victor, I thought, although I didn't consider him in that light. He knew my work number, but I hadn't expected to hear from him. Not yet, anyway.

The opera's music had waltzed through my brain all night. Splendid voices, magnificent costumes, a bigger-than-life set—the story had unfolded like a fairytale. And I supposed being escorted by a man more handsome than the tenor hadn't hurt my ego one bit. As I thought of Victor, I couldn't help but wonder what a deeper relationship with him would be like. Some lucky woman was in for a treat, once he was single.

"You've got a call on line one," Brittany said, and I reached for my phone.

"It's your mother," Mom said. "Sorry to disturb you at work, but when I called last night Nichole said you were out on a date."

"I was out with a friend."

"Really?" She sounded unconvinced. "She said you were dressed to the nines."

"Mom, I'm right in the middle of something. What's up?"

"I want to invite the whole family over on Saturday for dinner. I'll fix a pot roast."

"Great." I opened my calendar and saw nothing planned for the weekend. "I'll check with the girls and let you know."

"I meant you, Nichole, Harriet, and Drew."

"Why would you want to invite him?" I glanced to Brittany's desk and was glad to see she'd walked into Bill's office.

"He's still my son-in-law and your father loves him," Mom said.

She was meddling again; I didn't hide my annoyance. "Then invite him over sometime, without me."

"Honey, this may be the last time we all sit down at a meal together."

The words jarred me. "Are you referring to Drew or Pop?"

"We'll talk about everything when you get here."

Not wanting to miss Victor's call—if he was the mysterious caller—I dashed out to buy a sandwich at lunchtime, then ate it at my desk. But at 4:00 he still hadn't gotten back to me. As I prepared to head home, I noticed a dull fog had taken over my limbs and was weighing me down. Often over the last half-year, my moods had roller-coastered like a bird flitting first to the top branch of a tree, then plunging to earth to hide behind a rock. But at work, before Brittany's arrival, I was too busy

or distracted to pay attention to these swings. There was no
time for self-pity. I remembered my appointment with Dr.
Garcia last week. She'd quizzed me about my sleep and appetite, asked if I felt blue most of the time, and if I considered
ending my life. I'd answered each question with an emphatic,
"No." I was fine, I told her, even though that statement didn't
entirely ring true. But no one feels happy all day every day;
to expect that would be unrealistic. I was determined not to
swallow a Prozac every time life got a little rough when in fact
my mood swings could be triggered by PMS or the first symptoms of the flu. Pop had called antidepressants a crutch for
people who were too lazy or cowardly to stand on their own
two feet. And I saw no reason not to agree with him.

I dialed Victor's office number. It was only good manners
to thank him for the opera, I told myself. I might not drive up
to the island again for ages and would miss the opportunity
of running into him on the beach to speak to him in person.
Anyway, according to Gloria, nowadays women didn't sit like
wallflowers waiting to be plucked. If they wanted something
to happen, they made it.

Finally, the receptionist answered.

23

MOM ASKED EVERYONE at the table to bow their heads. "We have much to be thankful for," she said.

This was the first time my mother had ever led a mealtime prayer with Pop present. It seemed all wrong, like the north and south poles had traded places.

I cracked an eye open and peeked around the room. Mom, her chin resting in her steepled fingers, sat at one end of the rectangular table. She appeared small, bird-like, but her words rang clear.

"Let us take this moment to remember all the glorious gifts you've given us."

I watched Pop slump like Raggedy Andy at his end of the table. Across from me, Harriet chewed at her fingernail. Next to her, Nichole sat motionless, her eyes shut.

I wished she'd get on with her prayer so we could eat. My mouth watered as I breathed in the aroma of her pot roast that had no doubt been simmering in her oven all afternoon. I turned my head enough to catch sight of Drew, whom Mom insisted sit next to me. He seemed to be praying, which was a laugh. Not that he hadn't attended church when we met, a characteristic indicating stability in my motorcycle-riding boyfriend.

When was the last time I prayed for real? My mind searched back to my childhood days in Sunday school, then sifted through my high school years. Had my belief in God vanished in one fell swoop when I moved away from home? Or had it eroded slowly, like a melting snowman? Whichever the case, religion couldn't have held much importance or I would have stuck with it.

"Amen," I finally muttered while grabbing the wicker breadbasket and selecting a warm biscuit. I broke it in half and smeared it with butter, watched the yellow blob melt into the spongy surface. My mother had been making the same biscuits in exactly the same way since forever.

Mom carved the roast, also a first. She positioned an end slice on a dinner plate, sculpted mashed potatoes next to it, then dribbled gravy as thick and brown as molasses over the top. "This is such a treat," she said, passing the feast to Drew as if he were the guest of honor. "We haven't had the whole clan together for ages."

"Just over six months," I said, then filled my mouth with biscuit. The last time Drew and I dined here he'd claimed he needed to race back to his office right after dessert to finish up paperwork. He'd driven the girls and trusting old me home, then probably stolen over to Kristi's hideaway, which I envisioned as sporting scarlet satin wallpaper and mirrors over a circular bed. But why waste gray matter thinking about them? Someday I'd bring a new man to dinner with me, I mused, someone my parents would like even better than Drew. As I pictured the few single man I knew, my thoughts landed on Victor, whom I hadn't spoken to. "Dr. Huff is out of town," his receptionist had told me yesterday on the phone. Strange. He hadn't mentioned a trip while at the opera.

Mom handed the next plate to me. "In any case, we must do this more often," she said. "While we still have this nice big dining room to seat everyone."

"You moving?" Drew asked.

"We're considering it. In the meantime, Ed and I have decided to scale down and get rid of things we don't use." Pop came to life when she spoke his name. She arranged a small portion on a plate, then directed it to him. "If we have less to pack, our move into a smaller place will go much easier," she said.

"Move?" The folds around Pop's eyes rumpled.

"Yes, dear, we agreed this house is too big. We don't even use the upstairs anymore. And besides, we're going to find a situation that offers us special care."

"This seems sudden," Drew said. "Where would you go?"

"We haven't decided yet."

"I don't want to leave this house." Pop sounded for a moment like the man I used to know. "Not ever."

"No, of course, neither of us wants to," Mom said. "We've lived here for forty years. But it'll be for the best."

Pop's forehead creased as he stared at my mother with clouded eyes. "Why?"

"You know how I fell last week. I'm getting too old to manage such a big house."

"Maybe you're right." He jabbed into his meat, struggled to cut it.

"Would you help him?" she asked me. I reached over, took his fork and knife, and sliced the meat, then brought a piece to his mouth.

"I can do it myself," he said, snatching the fork out of my hand.

Drew and both girls stared. I'd warned them of Grandpa Ed's condition, but they hadn't seen him recently. It must have been a shock.

"Anyway." Mom's voice seemed too upbeat to sound convincing. "I'd like my granddaughters to each choose something from the house. You too, Ruth Ann and Drew." She glanced around the room until her gaze rested on the glass-fronted china cabinet.

I turned my head and peered into the case. Mom had collected china teacups for as long as I could remember. There must be over three dozen in there. She'd chosen each flowered vessel for a particular reason and knew its history and pedigree.

"Aren't you rushing things?" I asked. "You don't even have a place to live yet."

"Yes," Drew said. "Don't make any hasty decisions."

I appreciated his input. Selling this house and all its furnishings would be like dismantling the town I grew up in. I imagined my folks holding an estate sale, and strangers hauling away this cherry wood pedestal table with its six matching chairs, and the sideboard my great-grandparents gave Grandma Tessa as a wedding present. I grieved at the thought of losing the furniture, let alone the precious antiques Mom had accumulated over her lifetime. But I couldn't take any of it; my house was already bulging. When my marriage ended, I'd eventually move into a smaller place, maybe a condominium. When that happened, I'd have to give away or sell half of my own furniture. And I knew my brother and his wife preferred sleek modern pieces; they'd have no use for any of our parents' belongings.

Harriet pointed to a crystal vase housing an arrangement of dried flowers sitting on the sideboard. "I've always loved the way that vase sparkles. Can I have it?"

"Harriet!" I donned my sternest face. "What use would you have for that?"

"I don't know, maybe put a goldfish in it."

"Good, it's yours." Mom said, passing the butter to Drew. "And Nichole, I want you to choose something, too."

"This is crazy," I said. "You don't want us stripping the house bare, like a bunch of vultures." I cut into my meat, stuck a square in my mouth, and bit into a vein of gristle.

"No use holding on to things," Mom said. "Now, girls, I want to hear what you've been up to. Nichole, tell me about your college plans."

"Still up in the air," she said.

"I'm sure any college or university would want a lovely young woman like you."

"Thanks Grandma, but the competition's pretty stiff."

"Along with local colleges, Nichole's applied to Scripps, in southern California," Drew said, buttering a biscuit. "But it's small and doesn't take many students."

My mouth bulged with pot roast; I tried to chew quickly so I could enter the conversation.

"I'll pray you end up in the right school." Mom said, then smiled at Harriet. "And how about you, dear?"

She clinked her fingernails on her water glass in a most annoying way. "I'm not going to college."

"Yes, I know, not for several years."

"I mean ever. School and I don't mix."

Mom smiled. "You're a very talented young lady, who I'm sure will discover her calling when the time comes."

"Without a degree?" I asked, my mouth finally vacant. "How will she earn a living?"

Harriet's silver ball sneered at me through her parted teeth. "I'll marry someone rich, like you did, Mother."

"Kitten, I was almost penniless when your mother and I met," Drew said.

Pop cleared his throat. "That reminds me, Drew, did you bring your stock portfolio for me to review?"

Drew glanced to me for help, but I didn't know what to say. Then he turned back to my father and said, "No, sir, I don't have money invested in the market right now."

"Never mind." Pop scratched his head. "I've never heard of half the companies out there anymore. And I can't remember how to log onto my computer."

I wanted to say something to make him feel better, but there wasn't anything. Pop had never enjoyed the retirement pastimes most men look forward to, like golfing or fishing. His waking hours had centered around work.

Harriet shot to her feet and dropped her napkin on her dinner plate in spite of the many times I'd told her that was bad manners. "I've got to run."

"Now?" I asked. "You haven't had dessert. Where are you going?"

"To Alicia's for an overnight."

"Again? Maybe you should invite her to our house this time."

"Nah, our house is a drag."

"You need a ride?" Drew asked.

"No, I gave Alicia's mother this address. She's coming by at seven."

I checked my watch to see it was 7:05. "That seems like a terrible imposition. Please tell her we'll drive next time."

"She doesn't mind." Harriet placed her hands on Mom's shoulders and kissed her cheek, then blew a kiss to Pop, like a beauty queen.

He rustled in his seat. "I need to go, too."

"This is our home," Mom said, as if they'd had this discussion before.

"No, I mean—"

"Oh, dear." Mom started to rise, but Drew stopped her.

"I'll help him," he said, standing.

"I don't need help." Pop teetered to his feet but was unable to walk his chair back.

Drew slipped a hand under Pop's arm as he pulled the chair out of his way. "Come on, sir. This'll give us men a chance to talk privately."

As Drew and my father left the room, I glanced around to see Harriet had disappeared. I heard the front door open and close softly, then a moment later heard a car needing a new muffler pull away.

"Does this mean you've found a retirement facility?" I asked Mom.

"Not yet."

I gazed into her intelligent eyes. She was healthy and capable, her mind alert. If my father died first, which was probable, Mom might live in this house for another twenty years.

"Could you afford to hire a caregiver?" I asked as Nichole carried dirty dishes into the kitchen. "He or she could live upstairs."

Mom's features flattened, her cheeks sagging. "It costs too much."

"I'm going to start working less," I said, "so I can help you more."

"Thanks, but I don't want to be a burden."

"Mom, you and Pop raised me, and paid for my college education."

Drew took a step into the room to announce he was escorting Pop to the bedroom. "He turns in early." Mom got up to help Drew.

"Your Grandpa's getting old," was all I could say to Nichole as the two of us cleared the rest of the table, then filled the dishwasher and scrubbed the pots and pans.

Thirty minutes later, Drew drove us home. We sat in silence. I felt numb, my hands so weak they could barely open the car door when we reached the house. Once inside, the lump in my throat threatened to block off my windpipe if I spoke.

I hugged Nichole, then she mounted the stairs to her bedroom.

"I'm sorry about your father," Drew said. When I turned to him our eyes met. He had the bluest eyes, like a winter sky. There was no changing the fact he was good-looking, his features straight and manly. I hated that he still held any appeal to me.

Slowly, as if cloaking me with a shawl, he slid his hands around my shoulders. Don't trust him, I warned myself, stiffening. He pulled me closer, his arms encircling me. I wanted to ward off his embrace but couldn't move. My head, too heavy to keep erect, fell against his shoulder. Tears escaped past my closed lids and I wept, dampening his jacket lapel.

He stroked my back, my hair. "It's going to be all right," he said. "We'll find a way to help your folks, I promise."

Gulping, I nodded into his chest.

After several moments his muscles softened and his arms loosened their hold. I leaned back a few inches and gazed up to see his face only inches from mine. I inhaled his scent, the breath I'd known and loved for twenty years.

Then I watched his features blur as he moved closer. He was going to kiss me and I was going to kiss him back. In spite of everything, I would not, could not, resist.

His cell phone rang. I jerked back, a tumble of emotions ricocheting through me.

"You'd better answer." I blotted my nose with the back of my sleeve. "It might be Harriet."

After a moment's hesitation he extracted his phone from his pocket. Glancing at the screen, he let it continue to ring.

I yanked it out of his hand, then I stabbed at the answer button. My voice boomed into the receiver. "Who is this?"

Silence followed. Then the person on the other end hung up.

24

A SPLINTER OF LIGHT from under the guestroom door beamed into the hallway. On my way to the kitchen for a cup of milk—anything that might help induce sleep—my slippered feet padded closer to Drew's door.

I'd forced myself to lie in bed for over an hour, but my mind had wrestled with itself like a cat chasing its tail. I was stunned by how close Drew and I had come to kissing each other. It had felt natural, as if the last six months had been erased in a single wipe of a cloth. Then when I'd stormed away, Drew followed me. I'd locked myself in the bedroom. He'd stood in the hall imploring me to come out, but I'd turned up my bedside radio to drown out his words. "Go away," I'd yelled, and he finally did.

Now I was second-guessing myself. Had I reacted too swiftly when Kristi called? If it really was Kristi. I'd been the one to answer the phone. Drew had ignored the ringing. Maybe their affair was over and he would never speak to her again.

Staring at the guestroom door, I wondered what might have followed a kiss. Remembrances of our tender lovemaking heightened my senses. I recalled the luxurious feel of his body against mine.

Eyeing the doorknob, I reached out to turn it. No, I should knock first, I told myself. As my knuckles neared the door, I heard a quiet murmur drifting from the room. Was he talking in his sleep? He did sometimes. I held my breath and placed my ear to the door.

"Kristi, please—" I heard him say.

I felt like I'd just swallowed a vial of arsenic; my stomach clenched into a rock-hard knot. My hand, still balled into a fist, shook with outrage. I would rip Drew to shreds with my bare hands, was all I could think.

But what good would that do? We'd been round and round dozens of times and it never made a whit of difference. No good ever came from confronting Drew. I was the one who suffered when we argued. I gulped a mouthful of air as my ears strained to hear.

Drew spoke again, more clearly. "Yes, I love you," he said.

For a moment I stood, paralyzed, as though zapped by a blade of lightning, a field of red washing across my vision. I reeled around, shoved the door open.

His cell phone to his ear, Drew was sitting on the bed still fully dressed. His mouth gaped open as I rampaged across the room with my fingers clawing like a savage bear. I plowed him over onto his back and the phone flew out of his hand.

His face twisted. "What are you doing?" he yelped, blocking my punches.

I flailed out, every limb swinging. He rolled away from me and sprang to his feet. I came at him again, but he grabbed my upper arms and held them to my sides. My fists pounded his chest. Thud, thud—they sounded like a pile driver hammering into dirt.

Finally, he shook me. "What's wrong with you?" he said.

"I heard you!" A bead of my saliva spattered his cheek. "You told Kristi you loved her." I grabbed for his phone, which lay on the bed, but he reached it first and held it out of my grasp as he turned it off.

My eyes were as dry as the Sahara Desert. I might never cry again. "Get out!" I brandished my hands, and he leaned away from me.

"But I thought—"

"Get out of my house."

His mouth tightened into a half smile. "But my family's here."

"We're not your family anymore. You threw us away."

"No, I didn't. I'm here for you."

"You love another woman." I sounded like a cornered alley cat. "Go to her."

"But I love you, too."

I gripped the front of his shirt. "That's impossible."

He stared back, his face a blank.

I opened my mouth to speak again but was silenced by an inner voice warning me to keep quiet. Too often I'd let my emotions dominate my actions; I needed time to think this through. Was I being hasty by kicking him out? He'd dive into Kristi's open arms and the two would live happily ever after. Not only that, Nichole and Harriet, even Mom, would blame me for his departure. I'd be the bad guy. There was no way for me to win.

My mind grappled to formulate a strategy. One thing for sure, I'd find a way to get even with him if it was the last thing I did. Some day, he'd come begging and I'd laugh in his face.

My hands dropped to my sides. "Never mind about moving out." My voice returned to its usual timbre. "See you in the morning."

Minutes later, as I climbed into bed, my mind whirred like a flock of pigeons—touching down for moments then flapping off again on other tangents. I assumed I'd lie awake the rest of the night, but before I knew it eight hours swished by in dark serenity. Feeling refreshed, I swung my legs over the side of the bed and stepped onto the carpet to fetch my bathrobe. I glanced into my bureau mirror and saw a pretty face gazing back at me.

I jogged down the stairs with a bounce in my step. Where was all this energy coming from? Before heading to the kitchen to fix coffee, I reached out the front door to retrieve the Sunday paper.

I fed Bonnie before Drew could. I would not allow him to steal her devotion from me. As the coffee dripped, I sat at the kitchen table and sorted through the paper to find the travel section. "Maui, Island of Romance" read the headline. I eyed the photo of a barefoot couple, their arms woven around each other's waists as they strolled a beach at sunset. Drew and I had vacationed on Maui together, twice. Those weeks spent on the island paradise had been perfection in every respect. Remembering our candlelit dinners on the veranda of our condo should be making me sad, but it wasn't. I now saw our life together as a cheap novel I was ready to chuck into the recycle bin.

Drew cleared his throat as he stepped through the doorway. "Is it safe in here?"

I looked up to see a middle-aged man with pasty skin and beady eyes. Blinking, I turned back to the paper. "Sure, come on in. And help yourself to coffee." I scanned the photo again and wondered what it would be like traveling by myself. I'd probably meet interesting people and I could set my own schedule. And I could spend hours and hours in art museums and galleries, not to mention shopping, pastimes Drew found tedious.

He poured two cups, set one down next to my arm. "I'm glad you're not still mad." He landed on the chair across from me.

"No, I'm not angry." Not anything. I turned the page to check on the cheapest airfare prices and my gaze came to rest on a travel agency's ad promoting packages to Europe that might fit my budget if I started saving now.

He scratched his stubbly chin, producing a grating sound. "I've asked a certain person not to call me anymore. And I'll turn my cell phone off when I'm home."

"Whatever. I really don't care."

I glanced across the table to see confusion take hold of his face. "But last night—"

"Something must have snapped inside of me." I'd thrashed about like two-year-old Harriet embroiled in a temper tantrum. Never in my life had I come unglued like that; I rarely even raised my voice at the dog when she got into the garbage. "I promise that won't happen again." I shuddered as I recalled striking him. "From now on, I'm letting go—of you." I waited for a tweak of discomfort that didn't materialize. Sitting straighter, the corners of my mouth curved up. "I just figured out I don't love you anymore." Those words tasted better than a chocolate truffle, my favorite candy.

He rearranged himself in the chair, said nothing.

"You and I can remain housemates for a few months, until school gets out," I continued in an ultra-calm voice I barely recognized. "Harriet's done better in school with you at home. Nichole likes it, too." Plus, it meant more freedom for me.

He reached across the table, took hold of my hand. "Maybe I should stay, forever."

Feeling clammy skin, I withdrew my hand. "I don't think so."

25

A CLOUD OF STEAM escaped my mouth as I jogged down the front steps with Bonnie to head out for my first neighborhood walk since way before Christmas. That laziness would have to change, starting now. The thought of my legs in shorts this summer was enough to make me exercise every day of the week.

I'd left Drew sitting in the kitchen looking glum. What a pathetic excuse for a man. Why hadn't I noticed how scrawny he was until this morning? Sort of like that barren hawthorn tree up ahead in the neighbor's yard. Badly pruned, its stark branches scraggled out in all directions.

The nippy air prodded me into motion. "Come on, Bonnie, let's go." After traveling several blocks, my legs began to complain of fatigue, but I decided to keep going. Hadn't I heard about runners hitting the wall then being replenished with a second wind?

I crossed the street. A rumbling automobile approached, slowing as it neared me. I glanced over to see a man in his mid-forties behind the wheel of a Porsche. He tipped his head and smiled as he passed by. The unexpected compliment made me grin; it felt good to be appreciated. Just because Drew didn't find me attractive didn't mean I wasn't. I shouldn't allow his opinions to govern my self-esteem. When I thought about it, our tastes were completely opposite. I found his favorite TV shows about car and motorcycle restoration profoundly boring. And Drew sprinkled hot sauce on his eggs, which made my mouth pucker just looking at it. Why would I care what a man who liked eating that nasty combination thought of me?

In twenty minutes, Bonnie and I had covered over ten blocks. The aroma of sizzling bacon drifting from a nearby kitchen fan reminded me it was time to head home for breakfast. And Bonnie was lagging.

As I made my way back, I scanned the side street where I recalled Jackie said she lived and spotted her car parked in a driveway several doors down, in front of an aqua-colored Cape Cod shingled house. As I neared the home, I wondered if it was too early on a Sunday morning to go knocking on her door.

At that moment, the front door burst open and a tall youth lugging a vacuum cleaner stomped out. Approaching him, I smiled, but he didn't notice me. He opened the car doors, yanking the floor mats out and tossing them on the drive.

"Is Jackie home?" I asked, stepping closer.

His sleepy eyes zeroed in on me, and he pointed toward the house. "She's in there."

At that moment the maroon front door opened and Jackie strode out waving. "What a nice surprise." She beckoned me to enter. "Come in."

"But I have our dog."

"No matter, dogs are welcome."

"Are you sure?"

"Absolutely. What's her name?"

"Bonnie."

"What a pretty girl." Jacki reached down to stroke her under the chin.

"I hope you don't mind drop-ins." I crossed the threshold.

"They're my favorite kind of guests." Jackie set a bowl of water on the kitchen floor for Bonnie, who lapped with gusto. "I don't have to clean up before they arrive." She wore an olive-green skirt, a blouse a shade darker, and a necklace of chunky amber beads.

"You look great," I said.

"Thanks. I just got home from church, my one chance each week to get dolled up."

"You've been already?"

"I went to the early service. I've got work later."

We entered the living room where a collection of African masks hung in a diamond pattern on the far wall, a splashy modern painting hung over the fireplace, and silk sunflowers brightened the mantle. My jacket was suddenly too warm; I tugged the zipper down.

"Here, let me take that." she said, her hands out. "How about something to drink?"

"Thanks, but I'd better finish my walk before my legs realize they're too tired to make it home. Maybe we could do coffee again."

"Sounds fun. I've been all work and no play lately." She eyed her son out the window as he leaned into the car armed with the vacuum wand.

"What a wonderful son you have," I said. "To get Harriet to do that, I'd have to threaten corporal punishment."

Jackie chuckled. "He's not out there by choice. I present him with a must-do list every weekend from which he may pick three items. When he started griping a few minutes ago,

I told him he was welcome to clean the toilets instead, and I'd work on the car. But he insisted."

"You're a sly one. I wonder if that would work with Harriet. No, it's too late to retrain her. I'll just hold my breath until she grows up and moves out." I stepped toward the door. "I feel so good today I don't think Harriet could bug me. Of course, having her spend the night at a friend's helps."

Jackie chuckled again. "I'll wager you'll cry your eyes out when she leaves."

"I don't think you'd win that bet." I reached for the door-knob, then paused. "Do you know my father's neurologist, Dr. Huff?"

"Yes, I've worked alongside him at the hospital for twenty years. Your father's in good hands. Dr. Huff's an excellent physician and a fine human being." She came around me, opened the door.

"Have you met his wife?" I tried to sound offhand, when in fact I was digging for the inside scoop. "I hear she's beautiful."

"Yes, tall and stylish. Juliet helped put herself through law school as a fashion model."

"Did you know them when they got married?"

"I knew him, and I went to their wedding. Quite a fancy to-do, with a gown flown in from a New York designer. Caviar and champagne, a sit-down dinner for three hundred."

"Sounds fun, I love weddings."

Jackie shrugged. "Juliet and her family barely acknowledged me or any of the nursing staff."

I zipped up my jacket, descended a step, then turned back. "And they have a son in college?"

"Yes, but I've never met the young man." She raised a brow. "Why all the questions? You're not thinking of starting some-thing up with him, are you?"

"No, I'm just curious. Not that we won't both be single in the near future."

"You could be right. It's no secret Juliet's dating a city councilman. She doesn't seem to care who knows it." Leaving the front door ajar, she followed me down the stairs. "But I figured you'd get back with your husband, the way he was pining around the hospital. And didn't he move home?"

"In body only, for the sake of the girls. He sleeps in the guestroom. That's the way we both want it."

"At least you're in the same house. I believe that man loves you."

"I don't care anymore, it's too late."

Jackie shivered and rubbed her arms. "I've been there. When my husband cheated on me, I got to where I wouldn't have given a nickel for our marriage." The vacuum cleaner whirred, but she lowered her voice. "I went crazy and needed to prove I was still desirable, still a woman. So I found myself another man." Her head rotated back and forth. "There was this guy, a single parent, I kept running into at my eldest son's baseball games. All he had to do was smile and tell me I was pretty, and I was hooked. But I ended up getting a lot more than I bargained for."

Was she referring to a communicable disease? Emotional trauma? As my head did the math, I watched her son replace the floor mats. I brought my lips closer to her ear.

"Does your husband know?" I asked.

"Yes. Ray took off for a month, but then we got back together." She grasped my hand. "I'm only telling you to keep you from doing something you might regret later."

"But things turned out okay. You have a strong marriage now. And a beautiful son."

"True, but I live with a secret, one I guard every day of my life." She shivered again. "There's no way to avoid seeing that other man at school activities and sports events. I want to shrink up and disappear every time we meet."

"What you did wasn't so bad." I stood back to gaze into her eyes. "Your husband broke his wedding vows. He had someone else."

"That's true, but if I had it to do all over again—" She turned and crept up the stairs. A moment later the front door sighed shut.

I wished I could have found the right words to make her feel better. She was such a kind and generous woman. There was no reason for her to be ashamed. It was her husband who stood in the wrong.

As I turned to leave, a southwest wind lifted my bangs off my forehead and sent strands of hair over my shoulders. The sun lazing just above the rooftops warmed my cheeks. My lungs reached deep into my abdomen and I sucked in the breeze.

I could feel it: my life was about to take a turn for the better.

26

I DIPPED A SLICE of sushi into a puddle of soy sauce flavored with chartreuse wasabi, then tasted it. Savoring the smoky flavor, I said, "This is delicious. What is it?"

From across the table of our booth in a Japanese restaurant Victor said, "Unagi."

I swallowed the rest of the sushi. "Is it chicken?"

His eyes widened with amusement. "No, eel."

I gulped a mouthful of tea. "Maybe I should try something else this time." Although I'd liked it. Apparently, I was developing new tastes.

Victor chose a round of sushi—a paper-thin black band encircling rice around something pink and green—which he set on my plate. "This is California roll. Nothing scary in there."

I dipped it in soy sauce, brought it to my lips, then bit into rice, avocado, and crab. Much better, I thought, giving him a nod.

"I'm glad you were free on such short notice," he said. "It's been a hectic week. This is the first time I've come up for air. How are your folks?" Using chopsticks like a pro, he popped a slice of sushi into his mouth.

"That depends on your definition of fine. Neither one has broken a hip or gotten lost in the neighborhood, which I'm thankful for. But my mother's acting like a Pollyanna. It's hard to watch."

I knew Victor wasn't a family counselor, but I wanted his slant on things. I had few others to confide in.

"Mom wants to sell their house, but she doesn't have a clue where they're moving. With Pop so mixed up and frail, there doesn't seem to be a facility in town that will take them both, unless they reside in different units—which she refuses to do. Two days ago, she told me she had an appointment with a realtor and is going to list their house anyway. I asked her where they'd live if it sold right away and she said, 'God will take care of us.'" I rolled my eyes. "She thinks the big guy's going to fly in on his chariot and presto-change-o their problems will be resolved. Dad's dementia must be rubbing off on her."

"In my business, I've learned not to discount people's beliefs," he said. "I've witnessed some miraculous things."

"The only miracle that would help my parents is for them to shed thirty years and win the lottery."

Laugh lines deepened around his smile. "Those two might be hard for me to arrange, but I know a woman who helps elders find living arrangements. She might have some ideas. I'll give your mother her telephone number."

"That would be great."

His voice turned serious. "And, how are you?"

"Except for worrying about my folks, things are going well." I'd passed Drew in the house several times a day since that terrible fight and had barely noticed him. It felt like he was a distant cousin visiting from out of town. "I just realized I feel wonderful."

"You look wonderful."

"Thanks." Was he flirting with me? No, he couldn't be; that was the last thing either of us wanted. But I felt my cheeks warming.

He looked uncomfortable too. "By the way," he said, breaking eye contact, "I was out of town last weekend visiting my son at college. Juliet was there."

Not sure how best to react, I reached for another California roll, dragged it through the soy sauce, and nibbled into it.

"We told our son, Peter, about the divorce," he continued, his words strained. "He said he knew it was coming, but I could tell he was shaken."

"I'm sorry." I grieved for the young man. "Are you sure you want to go through with it? Maybe she'd give the marriage another crack if you asked her."

"She claims she's tried a thousand times, and she's done. I don't really blame her." He rubbed his neck below his ear. "I was unfaithful."

Oh, no, not him. I dropped my half-eaten sushi back on my plate, wiped my mouth.

"My other woman was work," he said, and I was relieved to hear the words. "I thought my patients needed me more than my family, that they couldn't make it without me," he said. "All the while, my marriage was decaying. In the beginning, Juliet begged me to spend more time with her, then she threatened to leave me if I didn't, which made me more obstinate than ever." He raked his fingers through his hair. "Then one day, she informed me she was in love with another man."

"How awful. Is she still seeing him?"

"No, that fling fizzled out. She's got someone else now and wants to marry the guy. There's no going back for us."

At that moment two women bustled past our table. I glanced up to recognize Mary Beth, the mother of one of Nichole's schoolmates. Mary Beth smiled at me and said hello. As her gaze fixed on Victor, her eyebrows raised. She paused for a moment, as if hoping to be introduced, but I looked away. Then she followed after her friend to a nearby table. Before sitting down, Mary Beth spoke to her friend and they both laughed.

My chest and arms began sweltering under my mock turtleneck. Their levity had nothing to do with me, I told myself. There was nothing to be embarrassed about. Victor and I weren't doing anything wrong. We were out in public, not hiding anything. Yet, the sooner I got my divorce finalized, the better.

The waitress presented our check on a small lacquered tray accompanied by two fortune cookies.

I reached into my purse. "It's my turn to pay." I handed the woman two twenty-dollar bills and she returned to the cash register for change.

Victor pushed the tray to my side of the table. "After you," he said.

I chose a fortune cookie, broke it in half, and read the narrow ribbon of paper. *An adventure awaits you.*

27

I'LL BE HOME *for dinner*, I'd written on a note now affixed to the refrigerator with a magnet. *If there's a problem, call my cell phone.*

On a Saturday morning, my two girls wouldn't be up for hours; they'd never miss me. And Drew was there if any problems surfaced.

Driving the highway north, I belted out a "Yuck," as I recalled how closely I'd come to kissing him the other night. Acting as Kristi's proxy—her temporary substitute—would have rated as a fiasco. I had to smile. If the past was the best predictor of the future, pretty soon Kristi and I would be paddling in the same canoe, with Drew cheating on her too.

Finally reaching the Island's exit, I steered the car, which Mom insisted was mine now, off the freeway and headed west through Stanwood. As I passed the sleepy town I wondered where Victor's mother lived. When he and I parted company yesterday, he'd mentioned he planned to dine at her house the next evening, and then asked if I could meet him at the island beforehand for a stroll on the beach. Without giving it much thought, I'd said I'd like to, although I hadn't planned to go up again so soon. But I reasoned I needed the exercise and had heard the weatherman forecasting decent weather. Anyway, the adventure my fortune cookie foretold would never come to fruition if I spent my weekends washing laundry and vacuuming.

Speaking of cleaning house, Gloria was rubbing me the wrong way. She'd phoned me the day before to see if I was free to attend Zumba exercise class today. I was thankful I had an excuse to say no. Then she casually mentioned Stephen Harrick had called to get my telephone number, which sent me into a tizzy. "The frog man? Why did you give it to him without my permission?" I'd demanded, but she managed to squiggle out of responsibility by saying he could easily find my number online. "And by the way," she said. "He's thirty-six, less than five years younger than you."

Descending our lane, I noticed smoke lacing up from Victor's chimney and saw his car sitting by the A-frame. I continued on and parked the Lincoln in my usual spot. Minutes later as I positioned the key in the front door, I heard a loud thunk followed by a splash, luring me around the porch to the beach side of the cabin. The wind rushing up the channel tossed my hair. I heard another thunk and splash, and noticed the high tide rolling driftwood logs against each other and sending spurts of foaming water flying. Mop-heads of seaweed intermingling with clam and crab shells, and a runaway buoy and several yards of line pressed against the shore. I should have checked the tide schedule before coming; there was no beach for walking. And in spite of the weatherman's optimistic prediction, clouds obscured the sun and even the foothills on the other side of the bay.

Once inside the cabin I shredded newspaper and tossed the curling strips into the fireplace. Atop the paper, I stacked kindling and several split logs, almost emptying the wood box. I'd

need to carry in more wood before leaving for my next visit—
if there was one. I selected a match and flicked it across the
hearth to produce a sulfuric flash but cool air descending the
chimney blew the flame out. Before tackling the chore again,
I decided I should let Victor know I was here.

I left the cabin and edged along the shore by balancing atop
one log then another. The low-growing bushes rimming the
shoreline reached out to hinder my progress. Water slapped
at my feet and the wind flung salty spray against my legs. As
I'd turned onto the path to his cabin, my footsteps shortened.
Checking my watch, I noticed I was an hour early. He might
get the wrong idea and think I was a woman on the rebound
throwing myself at him. As I stopped to glance up at the tree-
tops swaying like hula dancers and sounding like a rushing
stream I wondered if it was wrong for us to be alone together.
I told myself I should have considered that question before
accepting his invitation. And Jackie said Victor was a gentleman, someone you could count on. He'd been faithful to an
unfaithful woman for years. Not many men could boast of a
better track record.

A drop of rain splatted my cheek, then another landed on
my nose, causing me to hurry up the trail. As I neared the front
door, rain started plummeting down as if the sky had been
holding its breath until I reached safety. I rapped lightly on
his door; my timid knock brought him immediately.

I tried to tame my hair with my fingers. "I'm early."

"Me too. I couldn't wait to get out of the city."

"Did you notice the tide's up?" We'll have to postpone our
walk for a couple of hours."

"We could wait together."

Again I hesitated, not knowing if I should enter. He and I
had been alone here before, but that first day he'd thought I

was off my rocker and in need of a doctor's care. And then his mother was our chaperone.

"Okay," I said, not wanting to go anywhere until this cloud-burst let up. I tried to appear at ease as I removed my jacket. A balloon of toasty air lured me to the fireplace where burning wood hissed and crackled, spewing the fragrant aroma of damp cedar. I turned to find Victor standing nearby staring into the hearth.

"I've got an idea for something to do while we wait," he said. "I'll be right back." He disappeared into a bedroom and returned carrying a stack of flat boxes. "My buddy has three kids." He set them on the table. "What'll it be? Monopoly? Chess?"

"I'm not very good at games. You choose."

He shuffled through the boxes, opened one marked *Scrabble*, then unfolded the board on the table.

"It's been a while since I've played this game," I said, sure his vocabulary outdistanced mine. And my spelling wasn't that hot either.

"Don't worry, you'll do fine."

Sitting at the table, we each extracted a tile from the fabric bag containing letters. I flipped mine over to see a D and he showed me his T.

"You're first." He handed me the bag. I threw the letter back, then reached in to select seven more tiles. Placing them on the rack, my mind went blank. It was almost impossible to concentrate with a man with Victor's education sitting across the table. What was I doing? All of a sudden being here seemed like cheating on Drew. But that was crazy thinking. Drew was the cheater. I was only spending time with a friend who happened to be male.

I rearranged my letters several times, and finally placed *dream* in the center of the board.

"Good word." He wrote down my score. "I've been having some crazy dreams lately." He rifled through his letters and first placed an S at the end of my word, then added letters on either end to spell *sweet*.

"Sweet dreams?" I asked.

"No. My dreams have been anything but sweet."

"I'm sorry to hear that." I dug into the bag for more tiles. "Good grief." I reviewed my letters, which consisted of three O's, two U's, a V and an L. I fiddled with them, and finally realized the only word I could spell was *love*, using the E of *dream*. I dallied, fearful of sending the wrong message. Yet, would it be so terrible to fall in love with Victor? How many men of his caliber would come my way? If one of the girls, once they grew up, married a man half as wonderful I'd be thrilled.

Searching for another word, I juggled my letters around, but found none.

"Love." He watched me place the last tile down. An amused smile bloomed across his face. "That's a good word, too."

I couldn't bring myself to look at him. "I'm not very good at this."

"Quite the contrary."

Then why were my cheeks warming? As my hand fished for more letters, I glanced out the window to see a streak of blue peeking through the trees.

"Maybe we should take our walk now," I suggested, withdrawing my empty hand. "We could go up the road if there's no beach."

"Good idea, but first let me feed the fire."

I followed him to the hearth, where he bent down to shove in a log. The flames licked the new wood, then engulfed it.

He straightened himself and turned to me. His lips parting, he stared at me with such intensity that I wondered if he was about to say something life-changing. Yes, I decided, whatever came next would forever alter our relationship.

A sharp rap-rap-rap on the front door shattered the air. I watched his face blanch. Standing motionless, he looked more alarmed than anything, which made no sense.

"Aren't you going to answer?" I assumed Constance had come to check up on him. I had to smile; she was nosier than Mom.

Again, rap-rap-rap.

Finally, he walked to the door with measured steps and hauled it open.

"Your mother said I might find you here," a woman with a peppered voice said. Her mane swinging across thrown-back shoulders, she glided past Victor bringing with her a current of perfumed air. When she spied me, she came to a melodramatic halt. "What have we here?"

Victor followed her, then cleared his throat. "Ruthie, meet my wife, Juliet."

Juliet examined me like a doctor discovering the source of an infection. Then with nostrils flaring she cast her glare on Victor. "I was under the impression you came here to write." Her eyes scanned the room. "Where's your computer?"

I crept toward the door and reached for my jacket.

"Don't let me scare you away," Juliet said. I looked back to see her slipping an arm through Victors', then polishing her hip against his.

"If you have the hots for my husband," she said, "you and I have something in common."

28

I *DON'T BELONG HERE*, was all I could think.

As Victor and Juliet volleyed words at each other, their voices high and rough, I escaped out the door, stole around the side of the A-frame, and started down the path.

Juliet was even more attractive than her photograph. Stunning, really: finely honed features, eyes like a cat, long slender legs. And she still loved Victor.

I felt ridiculous as I imagined what she'd thought of me. *Short* and *mousy* were the most likely adjectives coming to her mind. Surely she couldn't have considered me her rival.

A low-hanging branch slapped my face, stinging my cheek. I slowed my pace. Listening to a tree limb squeaking overhead as the wind stretched it, and then a twig snap in the thicket, I longed to be back in my house in the city where all was familiar.

The earth pounded behind me. I turned to see Victor clipping down the path.

"Are you all right?" He panted like a runner after a marathon.

"Yes, don't worry about me, I'm fine." Not true. I felt like I'd been caught in a sniper's crossfire. "Did Juliet leave already?"

"No, in fact she found my friend's liquor cabinet, brought out a bottle of scotch, then went to get a glass."

"How did she know where to find you?"

"I'm guessing my mother suspected I was meeting you and gave her directions."

Constance must want them to reconcile. Any mother would.

"I'd better get back before she follows me," he said. "She's less than civil once she gets drinking."

Suddenly Drew's single glass of wine over a restaurant dinner didn't seem so bad. "Good luck." I wished I could articulate some sage advice. "It sounds like she still loves you."

Deep furrows dug across his brow. "Juliet's not capable of love." Then he disappeared up the path.

I trudged back to the cabin feeling too drained to get in my car and drive to town. I couldn't take the chance of falling asleep at the wheel, which I suspected was the cause of my accident, although that didn't explain why I was on the highway.

Inside, I noticed my unlit fire poised as I'd left it. Finding a match, I pressed it across the hearthstone, but the wooden stick snapped in half. The next match burst to life, but when I shoved it between the newspaper strips, it sputtered out. I felt annoyance quicken my pulse as I lit the third match, then was gratified to see the newspaper ripple into flames.

Relaxing on the couch, I reached for one of the several magazines sitting on the coffee table. When I opened the almost year-old *House & Garden* a rectangle of paper floated to the floor. I picked it up and recognized the Mother's Day card Drew had given me last spring while we were up here. A bouquet of flowers adorned the cover, with the words *To my dearest wife...* under them.

I frowned as I opened the card to read what Drew had written. *I'll love you forever, Drew,* in neat cursive script.

I'd eaten up those words and assumed I'd enjoy a lifetime union like my parents. "Your father and I made a commitment," Mom said one night when I asked her how she and Pop held their marriage together so long. "Without that promise we would have separated years ago," she admitted. "We weren't strong enough to make it on our own."

"A commitment isn't worth a can of beans when your husband's in love with another woman," I'd flung back.

I tossed the card into the hearth; it spun to the back and lodged upside-down in the ashes.

I leafed through the magazine, then another, and finally checked my watch. It had been over an hour since I'd left Victor's. I decided to head back to the city.

Had he sent Juliet packing or were they locked in a rapturous embrace, the kind you see at the end of movies where the hero and heroine kiss as if their love were holding the universe together? Which didn't seem fair. Why should Juliet enjoy the freedom to date other men and flaunt her escapades in Victor's face, and still be able to lay claim on him any time she felt like it? She'd treated him like dirty laundry—thrown him in the hamper until she was in the mood to wear him again. She and Drew were carbon copies, now that I thought about it. Neither one of them deserved a second chance.

I was tempted to sneak up there and find out, but if Mom were here, she'd remind me that meddling was wrong. Of course it was. The best outcome for any couple would be reconciliation, for the benefit of the children—for everyone's sake. I should go home and mind my own business.

I collected my purse and jacket, returned to the car, and started my ascent up the hill. As I neared Victor's driveway,

I heard an engine ignite, then a moment later I saw a sporty red automobile barreling straight at me. My first impulse was to slam on my brakes, which left me dead in the other car's tracks. Get out of the way! I told myself. Throw the transmission into reverse! But before I could act the red car lunged toward me. I recognized Juliet behind the wheel. At the last instant she swerved to avoid hitting me. Then her car, its low-profile tires spinning, tore up the road.

Victor stood outside looking in my direction. I imagined the verbal missiles and threats he and Juliet had launched like nuclear weapons. If they were anything like Drew and me, their argument had escalated into an ugly scene. As I drove to his house, then slid out, he continued to stare at the road. The whites of his eyes reddened, he seemed on the verge of tears.

"Would you rather be alone?" I asked.

He exhaled all of his breath, then caught another lungful of air. "Juliet said she's changed her mind. She doesn't want a divorce anymore."

"Good, that's wonderful," I said. Although he looked anything but pleased.

"She doesn't really want me. But she doesn't want anyone else to have me either."

Juliet wanted Victor waiting in the wings in case her latest affair disintegrated. As I considered his statement, I thought about Drew's reaction to my going to the opera. The next morning when he inquired about the evening, I'd heard possessiveness in his voice. And that night after dinner with my parents, perhaps in my weakened state he'd found me temporarily appealing. But always his pendulum shifted back to its position of indifference.

"I told her I'm through with her games," he said.

I thought about our Scrabble game, how one word could change the board's whole landscape. "Have you tried counseling? A diplomatic mediator might help."

"Yes, over the years we've gone, and after a couple sessions life would seem on track. But we'd sink into the mire again before we knew it, and Juliet would take off with I don't know who."

"Maybe give it one more try?"

"No, I'm done prolonging the charade. The marriage is over."

"I'm sorry," I said.

He was alone. Like me: a scrap of wood adrift in the channel. His pain made my bones ache. I wanted to console him, but didn't know him well enough to embrace him as I would my other friends.

I jammed my hands in my pockets. "If I can help in any way, please let me know."

What had I needed most when Drew left me? Solitude? No, but long conversations with Gloria and my mother hadn't fulfilled my needs, either.

"Ruth Ann, come in," Mom murmured as I entered my parents' home. She had asked me to stop by but seemed hesitant to let me enter. What had Pop done now?

"We have visitors," she said, and I relaxed, imagining several of their old friends gathered in the living room eating her Danish.

An exuberant voice filled the front hall. "Hello there, I'm Deanne Murray." A towering woman flounced over with her hand extended to shake mine. Wearing a bulky gunmetal gray raincoat and pointy-toed heels, she reminded me of a steamroller.

"I absolutely adore your parents," she said.

I bet she hardly knew my folks. "Thanks, so do I," I said, and withdrew my hand.

"This is the realtor who sold the house down the street," Mom said, her eyes brightening. "She has clients looking for a home just like this. A nice young couple, with two little girls."

I heard floorboards above us creaking. "They're here right now?"

"Yes, isn't it fabulous?" Deanne's teeth flashed behind bloodred lips.

"But the house isn't listed, and for a good reason." I turned to Mom and channeled my voice into a whisper. "Have you forgotten you and Pop need somewhere to live?"

"Don't worry about a thing," Deanne interjected as if we were close acquaintances. "We can choose a closing date months from now to give your parents plenty of time to find another place."

"It's not as easy as that. Mother, can we talk privately?"

At that moment a woman cradling a baby in her arms appeared at the top of the staircase. As she descended, a man and a little girl followed close behind. The girl wriggled past her parents to lead the way, but when she noticed Mom and me she stopped short. I'd been about her age when my folks moved into this house. Yet the thought of this lovely child sleeping in my bedroom made my insides groan. Why was this so distressing?

Deanne introduced the Largeant family, then guided them into the kitchen, avoiding the living room. "We'll have a look in the basement, then let ourselves out." She gave Mom a wink. "I'll be in touch."

I followed Mom into the living room to find Pop lounging on his easy chair. With his head rolled to the side and drool gathering at the corner of his mouth, only his open eyes revealed he was awake.

"Ed, honey, Ruth Ann's here." Mom jiggled his elbow, and he batted her hand away. She spoke to me while moving out of his range. "Aren't they a nice family? They remind me of you and Drew when the kids were little."

My shoulders jerked involuntarily. "I hope they have better luck than we did."

"Now, now, I haven't given up on you two."

"Mom, you didn't ask me over here to debate me about my marriage, did you?"

"No, of course not. I invited you over to ask if your father and I could move in with you."

Guffawing, I expected to see her smile, then hear her teasing snicker. But she stared back in earnest.

"Are you serious?" My voice must have revealed my shock.

"Yes, I've given it a great deal of thought," she said.

I'd always gotten along fine with my parents—better than fine—and I felt a great debt to them both. They raised me, fed and clothed me, and loved me. But my household was already topsy-turvy as it was. I imagined well-meaning Mom rearranging my kitchen cupboards and giving in to Harriet's ultimatums, while Pop dribbled soup on my couch or urinated on the rug. That amount of chaos just might propel me into a mental institution.

My brain scrambled for a kind but firm reply. "When Drew leaves and Nichole's in college, I won't be able to afford my house anymore," I said. "I'll have to move somewhere smaller."

"That's why my plan is so perfect." She gave me a hug. "With your father and me paying rent, you won't have to."

29

"THAT'LL BE $58.71," the checker at the QFC grocery store announced.

I reached into my purse to retrieve my billfold. When I extracted only two twenty-dollar-bills, my hand dove back into the leather wallet again, but I found it empty.

I visualized myself yesterday at the cash machine placing five, crisp twenty-dollar-bills into my wallet, then driving straight home. My brain strained to recollect where I might have spent the money. Nowhere.

Had someone stolen my sixty dollars? A sickening feeling sloshed through my stomach as I reviewed the possible suspects. I'd just spent the morning at work, but the day had passed quietly. My purse never left my sight.

The checker stared at me. "Ma'am?"

"Sorry." I found my debit card, swiped it through the machine, then punched in my PIN number: 0610, which represented June 10th, Drew's and my wedding anniversary date. Why hadn't I contacted the bank to choose a new number? I'd need to take care of that.

As the checker reeled the tape out of the register, my thoughts returned to my missing money. Was Harriet the culprit? Just because she was strong-willed and dressed strangely didn't mean she was a thief. But I'd have to risk her fury and inquire.

The checker set the two paper bags in my cart. "Would you like help out with this?"

"No, thanks." I grabbed hold of the cart's handle and started pushing it. Ahead of me a man in his early twenties carrying a six-pack of beer swaggered toward the door. He was what Mom would call rough around the edges: shaggy hair, in need of a shave, ragged jeans worn low on his hips. As he exited, he was met by a young woman wearing a pumpkin orange sweater. I could only see the back of the woman, her garish red hair cut at harsh angles and spiked out at irregular intervals much like Harriet's. The man languished an arm around the woman's shoulder and said something that initiated a burst of giggling.

I froze in horror. She sounded exactly like Harriet. But it couldn't be. Could it?

Shoving my cart, I charged after them, but a lady pushing a stroller with a fussy toddler blocked my path. I swerved to the left only to be stopped by an elderly gentleman coming from the other direction. As I sidestepped him, a bottle of dish soap flew out of my bag and rolled under a counter. I stooped down, grabbed the bottle, and threw it back into my cart.

When I looked up the man and woman were gone.

I plunged my cart outside; my eyes scanned the parking lot. I spotted the young woman standing with the man behind a car several rows over. The man pulled the woman close and planted an extensive kiss on her lips.

I stood on tiptoes, but still couldn't see the two clearly. Leaving my cart, I started running in their direction. "Harriet?"

The woman glanced my way, then both of them leapt into a black coupe. As I dashed closer, the car's engine revved and a rumble of heavy bass jarred the air. Before I could peer through the darkly tinted windows, it skidded backward, then peeled out of the parking lot.

My heart pounded like a conga drum; I stood in a daze for I don't know how long. It couldn't have been Harriet, I kept assuring myself. School wouldn't be out for another hour. She didn't own an orange sweater, and Alex wasn't even old enough to drive let alone purchase beer.

Finally a mini-van appeared behind me and the driver tapped on her horn. I moved out of the way, went to retrieve my cart, then found my car on the other side of the lot. My mind must be playing tricks on me, allowing my fears to materialize through complete strangers. I wondered if delusions were typical of head injuries or depression or anxiety. Maybe I needed to consider the medication Dr. Garcia recommended after all.

Ten minutes later, I coasted up to the front of the house. As I opened the trunk, Drew's BMW pulled up behind me and jerked to a halt.

I watched him get out. "What are you doing home so early?" I asked.

"I came to check on Harriet."

"What do you mean? Why would she be here?"

"I asked her counselor to call me if there were any more unexcused absences. Our younger daughter didn't go to any of her afternoon classes today. I assumed she went home ill, but when I called she didn't answer."

My mind replayed the scene in the grocery store. "I think Harriet stole money out of my wallet." I had no proof I'd seen her at QFC.

"Are you positive?"

"No, but pretty sure."

"I don't believe our girl would do something like that."

"Maybe not, but if she's on the straight and narrow, where is she right now?" I hefted up a grocery bag and handed it to him.

"Probably in the nurse's office or in the library researching a project."

Was he really this gullible? I snorted a laugh as I transferred the other bag to him.

"I saw your note, Mr. Templeton," a man said, and I noticed Harvey, our postal carrier, a wiry gent with thinning hair, approaching us. "You want your mail delivered here?"

Harvey pulled a white postcard from his satchel. Speaking to Drew, he said, "You'll need to fill out one of these or go online."

"I'll take that." I snatched the card and lobbed it in with the groceries. "Maybe you should leave one more for when he leaves again."

Harvey gave me another, then several letters from his bag. He sorted through the envelopes; his gaze paused on the last. I recognized my attorney's name and address printed boldly on the upper left-hand corner.

"I can take those." I grabbed them.

"Have a nice day." He started whistling as he headed to the next house.

I shoved the letters into my purse.

"Anything in there for me?" Drew asked, rearranging the bags in his arms. "If I'm paying the bills, I have a right to see them."

"Fine." I tugged the envelopes out of my purse and crammed them into one of the grocery bags. "One of those is a bill from my attorney. You're welcome to it."

"I'm not paying for your lawyer. I told you we can settle things ourselves. Why waste money on those lying snakes?"

I shut the trunk's lid. "And you're not a liar?"

"Quiet, the neighbors will hear."

I followed him onto the porch, then I reached around his bulk to unlock the front door. He pushed it open and tramped into the kitchen with Bonnie prancing at his feet. As I deposited my jacket in the hall closet, I heard Drew speaking to someone in the kitchen. I followed the voices to find Harriet sitting at the table with a torn-open bag of McDonald French fries spread out before her. I was relieved to see she was clad in black slacks and a black T-shirt, which solved the mystery of the woman at QFC. But where had Harriet been this afternoon?

Wondering how to start the cross-examination, I watched her dip a fry into a blob of ketchup, then chomp off the end.

"What?" Harriet said, eyeing me. She popped the remaining fry into her mouth. The mixture of her chewing without closing her mouth so I could view the potato particles caking her tongue stud and her impertinent attitude made my insides quake.

"That's my question," I said. "What are you doing home so early?"

She chose another fry and began stirring it in the ketchup like a witch blending a potion. "My last class got cancelled."

"There's our answer," Drew said. He reached into the grocery bag and pulled out a cauliflower.

I didn't buy her story. "The counselor called your father. You missed all your afternoon classes."

"That's a lie," Harriet said, indignant. "I was one minute late for fourth period and that old bat probably counted me absent. I couldn't help it. I was in the lavatory—an emergency."

"You should have told your teacher why you were late," Drew said.

"Like, I'm going to announce it was that time of the month in front of the whole class?"

"How about fifth period?" I cut in. "Late for that one too?"

Harriet gnawed on the fry, then swallowed it leisurely. "I don't remember, but I was there. Why are you on my case?"

My hands gripped my hips. "How did you pay for those?"

"A friend gave me a ride home and bought them for me." She grabbed another fry and waggled it at me. "You have a problem?"

"I'm missing sixty dollars."

"Oh, I get it." Like a coiled snake striking its victim, Harriet shot to her feet and hurled the fry at me, hitting my chest. Then she stepped forward, mashing it underfoot. "Anything that goes wrong is my fault."

I fought the impulse to slap her face, but, "You little brat," flew out of my mouth.

"Now Ruthie," Drew said, coming between us.

Harriet leaned around him to scream at me. "If you want to find the person who's screwed up, Mother, look in the mirror!"

30

I DASHED THROUGH SPRINKLING rain to find Gloria positioned behind the steering wheel of her beige Lexus SUV. Jogging around the vehicle, I climbed in on the passenger side.

"Where's Jonathon?" I asked. Her husband usually did the driving.

"He's running late." As my door closed, she pressed her foot to the gas pedal. "He'll meet us there."

"Where are we going, anyway?" Gloria had wanted to surprise me, and she asked that I wear something nice. I'd opted for a rust-colored pantsuit and a silk blouse. In Seattle the outfit would work anywhere.

"The Space Needle." She took us onto the main street.

I hated that place. Not the restaurant itself, but the fact it resided atop a 500-foot tower that looked like it might snap in half in high winds, not to mention an earthquake.

I fastened my seatbelt, cinched it tight. "If Jonathon's had a long day maybe we should eat somewhere closer to home," I said, not wanting to admit I was afraid of heights. The last time I visited the observation deck of the Space Needle I'd been clutched by the horrified feeling I might fall—no, jump—over the side, which was silly. I never would.

Yet I'd driven off the road. If I'd done that, in a blind spontaneous moment, I was capable of anything.

"Jonathon doesn't mind. He's coming from downtown." She aimed the SUV onto the freeway and took over the right lane. "They have valet parking."

My hand grasped the armrest. "We won't have any view tonight." The usual panorama of the Cascade and Olympic Mountains, Puget Sound and Lake Washington would be buried in cumulus clouds. "Let's wait for a clear day. Or never."

"Now, now, it's all arranged. This is our chance to treat you."

Fifteen minutes later she and I entered the glass-sided elevator along with a dozen other people, all laughing and chattering as if they actually looked forward to soaring fifty stories in forty seconds. I could feel my heart jitter when the door clamped shut. Then my stomach was mashed to the bottom of my abdomen as I vaulted upwards. I tried to comfort myself with the fact the restaurant revolved 360 degrees in the course of one hour, after which I could return to sea level and safety.

Exiting the elevator, all I could see through the restaurant's wraparound windows was an ominous black hole. Raindrops slid down the glass and the lights of the Seattle Center below barely found their way through the mist.

Gloria provided her last name to the host. "Be a sweetheart and seat us now," she said.

"Certainly, this way." He led us to a table set for four. I expected him to remove the extra place setting, but he ignored it and left four menus. Maybe that was the server's job I thought as I found a seat.

Gloria situated herself across the table from me; she rummaged through her purse to produce a pair of narrow reading glasses. "I hate these things." She balanced them low on her nose, then opened a menu. "They make me look like an old lady."

"No way, on you they're cute. I should start wearing them, myself." When peering into the mirror the other day I'd noticed a new squint line. And the print in the telephone book seemed to be shrinking.

I heard Gloria say, "Hi, sweetheart," and I looked up to see her husband Jonathon advancing in our direction. He was wearing his usual tweed sports jacket and tie loose at an opened collar. Behind him I could make out the top of a man's head and one shoulder. A moment later I was dumbfounded to see Stephen Harrick, his brown hair shagging over the tops of his ears.

Livid, I managed to get out, "What's he doing here?" before the two men reached the table.

"I hope you don't mind." Gloria acted as nonchalantly as if she were ordering an appetizer. "Jonathon and Stephen are working on a project together—"

"I do mind and you know it. I made it perfectly clear I didn't want to see him again." If I wasn't trapped in this floating prison I might have walked out. I sent her an icy stare, but she was busy smiling at the men.

"Hi, Ruthie, long time no see." Curly-haired Jonathon leaned over the table to give my cheek a kiss. Then he settled next to Gloria and worked his chair legs in.

"What a nice surprise," Stephen said, sitting next to me. Wearing casual khakis and a denim shirt, he didn't look like a man who'd known about our dinner before he left the house this morning.

"Yes, this is a surprise." I took in his short nose and boyish dimples; he looked even younger than I remembered.

"How have you been?" he said. Was he recalling our New Year's Eve kiss? It had been nothing more than a peck, really. Out of character for me, but he would have no way of knowing that. I hoped he'd forgotten it ever happened.

There was no way I'd bring up my car accident. "I've been fine, thank you," I said. As soon as we finished eating, I'd make my escape even if it meant paying for an Uber ride home.

"I haven't been up here for ten years." He scanned the window to observe the dismal abyss.

"Me neither," Jonathon said. "But we should have chosen better weather. I warned Gloria."

"Ease up," she said, elbowing her husband playfully. "This is fun."

My Caesar salad and beef tenderloin tasted delicious, and several times the conversation thrummed along in a relaxed manner, making me forget I'd been duped into coming. Toward the end of the meal, I watched Stephen as he and Jonathon compared notes on a new initiative to preserve wetlands in city and county parks. There wasn't a thing wrong with Stephen, I thought. Too bad I didn't know a younger woman hunting for an eligible bachelor.

When the server brought our check, Jonathon whisked it off the tray. "I'm getting this one," he said, keeping the slip of paper out of Stephen's reach.

"Then I owe you."

"Great, let's do this again soon," Gloria said, and I pressed my lips together into my mother's fiercest look of disapproval.

"Sure thing," Stephen said.

Finally, the four of us were standing in the elevator as it plummeted toward earth. My stomach clung to my esophagus all the way, but I kept telling myself freedom was only seconds away. We exited to find the rain had let up. I could see several stars twinkling above us and a jet cruising by. Frankly, I was so glad to be on solid land I wouldn't have cared if it were hailing.

We strolled to the valet stand, where Gloria had left her SUV. She handed the young man her ticket, then asked Stephen, "Would you mind driving Ruthie home?"

"Glor-i-a," I said.

"It would be my pleasure," Stephen said.

"But where's Jonathon's car?" I asked.

"Gloria drove me to work today," Jonathon said. "Stephen brought me here."

Here was final proof this was a set-up job. "I'll come with you two," I said.

"No, we're stopping by my mother's to pick up Shelby," Gloria said with determination. "And we're already late."

Before I knew it their vehicle arrived. The valet driver hopped out, and Gloria and Jonathon got in. I should have thanked them for dinner, but I was afraid what might flair out of my mouth if I opened it. As I watched their SUV roll away every annoying antic Gloria ever pulled nattered through my mind. Like the time she didn't show up for our lunch date at the exclusive Seattle Tennis Club, where she and Jonathon held memberships, and I was left feeling embarrassed and hungry. Later, she'd given me a long-winded explanation, but I don't remember her apologizing. And the time she gave me a chocolate cheesecake for my birthday when she knew full well I was on a diet and wanted to lose ten pounds before my high school reunion. And the time she told me I looked ghastly in green, my favorite color. I'd never worn it again without checking in the mirror to make sure I didn't look like a fern.

After each offense I'd forgiven her, although she'd never actually asked for forgiveness. But I'd told myself no one was perfect. Who didn't make a faux pas now and then, or stick their size-eight foot into their blabbermouth?

"My car's in the lot across the street," Stephen said, bringing me back to the situation at hand.

"Sorry if I'm taking you out of your way."

"No problem."

As we walked to his car, I considered who the woman behind Gloria's classy facade really was. As far as I could tell she was rarely home with Shelby. She trusted day care and her mother to raise her child even though Jonathon raked in plenty of income to support a stay-at-home mom. And I'd raised an eyebrow at her flirtations with waiters and salesmen more than once. I hated to admit it, but maybe Drew had her sized up right when he called her a pushy broad who lived by her own rules. Perhaps I needed to find a new best friend.

Minutes later Stephen drove his Saab along the perimeter of Lake Union. We spoke in self-conscious spurts. Finally, to fill the time, I asked him, "Do you have any family in the area?" and learned he'd moved here from Minnesota and had never been married.

"I was engaged once, but she broke it off while I was on a four-month trip to Central America. I don't blame her. What woman in her right mind would get involved with a wayfarer who collects amphibians?"

"Come on, you're being too hard on yourself."

He chuckled, sounding more at ease. "Does that mean you'd like to do this again, but without our matchmakers?"

"I don't think so." I tried to hear my words through his ears and hoped I hadn't been too blunt. "I can't."

Stopping at a red light he glanced my way. "I usually dress better than this," he said. "But Jonathon sprang dinner on me at the last minute."

"It's not your clothes. You look fine." More than fine, but that didn't matter. "I'm married."

Appearing confused, he was probably wondering why I wasn't wearing a ring. "Sorry, I thought your divorce went through ages ago."

"Is that what Gloria told you?" My anger toward her ratcheted up another notch. "Look, it's a long story. Not only am I married but my husband is living with us."

"Gee, I'm sorry. I mean, that's great you two are back together."

Did I have the stamina to shepherd him through the whole saga? No.

"Isn't it?" he asked when I didn't respond.

"Let's talk about something else. Okay?"

When he brought his car to a halt in front of the house, I said, "Thanks for the ride, and I apologize for the mix-up."

"Good food, good company. I enjoyed myself."

I reached down to retrieve my purse, which gave him time to sprint around the car to open my door. As I stepped out, I scanned the house and was glad not to see Drew's eyes in the window.

"Well, goodbye," I said.

At that moment Nichole's friend Emma's car pulled in behind us, and Nichole got out.

"Mom?"

I was hoping Stephen would withdraw into his car unnoticed, but he stayed put.

"Hi, sweetheart." I glanced at Stephen, who seemed to have grown younger. What was Gloria thinking? "This is Stephen Harrick."

Almost as tall as Stephen, Nichole put out her hand to give his a shake. I could see her eyes appraising his face.

"And this is my daughter, Nichole." I felt a wave of pride followed by an unexpected pang. Was this jealousy? No, ridiculous, I would never compete with my daughter over a man I wasn't even interested in.

"Nice to meet you," she said, her eyes hesitating on his.

"Same here."

Emma's car pulled away from the curb, but Nichole didn't bother waving goodbye to her friend. "Where have you two been?" she asked, as if she were the parent quizzing her children.

"Out to dinner with Gloria and Jonathon," I said.

"At the Space Needle," Stephen added.

"I wish I could have gone," she said, and I wondered if she meant in my place.

"Maybe you and I can go there for dinner sometime." I hated the distance between us; this could be the icebreaker.

"I don't know, I'm pretty busy."

"Come on, you must have one free hour."

"I'll say good night," Stephen grinned my way. "Maybe I'll see you next New Year's Eve?"

"No, I'll be out of town," I kidded. "I'm planning a trip to China where they don't celebrate it on December 31st."

"Excellent idea, I hate that night." He chortled. "But seriously, I hope to see you sometime."

"Nice to meet you," Nichole said and shook his hand again. She lingered as he got into his car and drove away.

She made no move to go inside. "Who's the guy?"

She'd called him a guy, not a man. Did that mean she saw him as her peer rather than mine?

"He teaches biology at Shoreline," I said. "I suppose that makes him Professor Harrick."

"And he was your date on New Year's Eve?"

"No, I barely know him. He was at Gloria's and Jonathon's party. Not a big deal."

"Are you planning to go out with him again?"

I could hear Bonnie yapping inside the house. "I wasn't out with him. He only gave me a ride."

"But you're seeing someone, aren't you?"

Her grilling was beginning to ruffle my feathers. "If you mean dating, the answer's no, I'm not."

"But you went to the opera with a man. You wouldn't get fixed up like that for a woman: high heels, gobs of lipstick and mascara."

I remembered passing Nichole in the hall that evening, but I hadn't mentioned whom I was meeting. "Since when do you know what I would or would not do?" Exasperation was coming to life but I tried to hide it.

"And you've disappeared several times, off for the weekend with who knows who." She'd never spoken to me with such disrespect. I could feel my annoyance increasing. I shouldn't have to defend myself.

"I have every right to spend time with whomever I want."

"So, there is someone?"

"Did your father put you up to this?" I glanced at the house and saw the curtain in the front window move. Was Drew spying on me?

"I have a right to know," Nichole said.

"Sweetheart, you're young, you don't know what it's like to love your husband for twenty years, then have him flush you down the drain like sour milk."

I made a move toward the house, but she stepped in my path.

"You're wrong about Dad," she said. "He told me he still loves you."

31

THE HOSPITAL'S GLASS doors skimmed apart like ghosts. As I entered the lobby, my mind repeated fragments of Mom's phone call from thirty minutes earlier.

"Your father, unconscious, in the hospital, room 506."

In the lobby at 7:00 AM only a handful of people lingered near the front desk. I found the bank of elevators and rode up to the fifth floor.

Mom hadn't given me many details, only that Pop had fallen, but would be fine. But if he was fine, what was he doing here?

The elevator swayed to a halt, but the doors remained closed. Great, I'm stuck in here, I thought, feeling the walls attempting to suck away my breath. But maybe being trapped in an eight-by-eight cubicle would be easier than seeing my father.

The doors finally slid open and I bolted out. I glanced down the corridor and was gratified to spy Victor striding toward me reading something on an iPad. In spite of the circumstance, I couldn't help feeling happy to see him. I'd grown to depend on his friendship. We'd spoken on the phone twice over the last week. I'd called him with a question about Pop, and Victor and I ended up discussing the visiting Impressionist exhibit at the Seattle Art Museum. We both declared our love for Monet and Renoir, and decided to see the show together, if it worked out. Then he'd called back the next day to fill me in on a vitamin E therapy that helped some memory-loss patients. I could tell he wanted to chat longer because pretty soon we were comparing notes on why single people never dine at restaurants alone.

As he moved my way, my anxiety began to subside. If anyone could help Pop, Victor could.

He continued to peruse the iPad until we were ten feet from each other.

"Doctor Huff," I said, not wanting to diminish his stature by using his first name.

When he heard my voice, he stopped for a moment and looked up, but his expression remained distant, preoccupied. Then he continued toward me with deliberate steps that told me something was very wrong.

"Have you seen my father?" I asked.

"I just came from his room." His gaze finally landed on my face. "I believe he suffered a ministroke."

"Mini? Is there such a thing?" The only person I'd ever known who'd suffered a stroke was a neighbor, an eighty-plus woman who lost the use of her left arm and leg, then died of a massive stroke three years later.

"A transient ischemic attack, also known as a TIA." He grasped the iPad as he folded his arms across his chest. "If all goes well, he could recover completely."

"Then he'll be okay?" I needed more words of assurance.

"Most likely. I'm sorry, I'm on my way to see another patient and need to run." He sidestepped me to hurry into the open elevator. Inside, he went back to studying the iPad.

He must be worried about the other person's health more than Pop's. That was a good sign, wasn't it?

As I continued down the hall, I began checking room numbers. My stay in this hospital seemed like ancient history. In fact, I hardly remembered being here, only that I'd met Jackie and Victor. I guessed something good came from everything.

Glancing through a doorway, I saw an aged woman—her face the color and texture of cottage cheese—lying in a bed and staring at the ceiling. The rancid odor of urine and antiseptic wafting from her room caused a wave of nausea to clench my throat. I hated hospitals. How could Jackie stand working here? Turning away, I continued down the hall until I found room 506.

Inside, Mom sat on a chair by a hospital bed. Her head was bent and her hands held under her chin as if she were meditating. Much like the old woman in the other room, Pop lay flat on his back, his bottom half disappearing into the mattress. A drip bag was emptying its contents into the back of his hand; a heart monitor blipped its lament in monotone. As I moved closer, I surveyed the square bandage covering his forehead and the quarter-sized scab on one cheek. I'd always been able to stand the sight of blood, but my legs weakened. Pop looked like a corpse. Maybe Victor had erred in his prognosis, or perhaps he was trying to delay my agony. Only the monitor's steady rhythm confirmed Pop's heart was still pumping. But was he brain-dead?

I understood he and Mom would die someday. Like sandcastles, they'd erode, then collapse into nothingness. But I thought when the time came, I'd be able to deal with my loss the way I handled everything. Now I realized my parents were the roots of my tree, stretching back from my ancestors to the present and holding me erect.

"Mom," I said, coming to her side.

"Ruth Ann, I'm glad you're here."

"What happened?"

"He complained of a headache so I went to fetch an aspirin and a glass of water. He was more confused than normal and insisted on following me into the bathroom. Then all of a sudden, he fell against the sink. I tried to stop the fall but couldn't."

I remembered from helping Pop how heavy he was. "It's not your fault," I said. "He weighs twice as much as you."

She got to her feet and I wrapped an arm around her trembling shoulder.

"At least nothing's broken," she said.

"That's good." A broken bone might multiply his problems tenfold. "When did all this happen?"

"Last night around midnight."

"Why didn't you call me?" I'd told her it was never too late in the day to ask for my assistance.

"I didn't want to wake you. I dialed 911, and two medics arrived five minutes later. Such nice young men, and so polite."

I could imagine the deadly silence as they checked Pop's vitals, then lifted him to a gurney, and strapped him on. "And you spent the night here?"

"Yes." She nodded toward an armchair sitting against the wall. "I managed to get a little rest."

I reached out to stroke my father's bare forearm. It felt smooth and cool, not like living flesh.

"Pop, it's me, Ruth Ann." He didn't respond.

"He's been like that ever since we got here." Then she sank back into the chair.

"Mom, why don't you go home and rest for a while. I'll stay." Although I felt like running away, hiding.

"No, I need to be here if he wakes up. But you could do me a favor. Find the cafeteria and get me some coffee with cream and sugar."

"Sure." I was glad for an excuse to leave for a few minutes; I couldn't think clearly in here. "I'll be right back."

Out in the hall, I asked a nurse's aide for directions, then took the elevator to the basement. When I stepped out, the heavy cafeteria smell engulfed me, setting off another round of nausea. With no appetite, I purchased a cup of coffee and a muffin for my mother.

As I walked to the elevator, I recognized the back of Victor's head as he leaned against the wall using his phone. I was surprised he'd come to this area of the hospital, but maybe he wanted to talk where none of his coworkers would overhear him.

Not wishing to interrupt him, I waited at a distance. Then he raised his voice and I heard him say, "Juliet, why now?"

I should back away, I thought, to give him privacy. But just as I'd lingered outside Drew's bedroom door, I didn't move a muscle and strained to hear his words.

Victor held the phone against his ear. "Yes, I love you and probably always will," he said, his voice trailing off as if he'd been interrupted. A long pause followed, then, "All right, I'll meet you there."

His words assaulted my eardrums. My thoughts sped ahead of me like a team of horses pulling a runaway wagon. I reeled back and spun around, staggering in front of a woman pushing a man in a wheelchair. The man's foot clipped my shin, but I barely felt the impact. Ahead lay the bank of elevators with all its doors clamped shut. To the side, I spotted an exit sign above a door. I wrestled the door open and dashed into a stairwell.

As I clambered up the first flight of stairs my shoes felt full of lead. Had I misunderstood Victor? No, he was speaking to a woman named Juliet. It was his wife and he'd told her he loved her. And why should that bother me? Wouldn't their reconciliation be for the best? Yes, and I had no right to think differently, no right to interfere. Yet somehow his choosing to love her made me feel as though I'd been jilted all over again.

Had I fallen for Victor? No matter; he would never love me. I could not compete with Juliet. I could see her symmetrical face, her hair as smooth as a river, her critical eyes studying me like I was a second-class citizen below her majesty's status. I hated her and I hoped she choked on her smugness. I hoped she fell off a cliff or left town and never came back.

I rebuked myself for my malicious thoughts. What kind of an evil person was I? My throat tightened around a lump the size of a golf ball.

Several flights up, a door opened. Voices mingled as a man and woman entered the stairwell and descended the steps. I continued up the stairs past them. I kept my head down so they wouldn't see my face. I must look as ugly as I felt.

By the time I'd reached the fifth floor, all my senses had turned numb.

Entering my father's room, I glanced down at the paper bag, which hung limply in my moist fingers. I attempted to smooth it out without much success.

Mom stood inside talking to Jackie.

I thrust the bag out between us. "Here's coffee and a muffin, Mom."

"You're white as a ghost." She took the bag. "I think you'd better sit down."

"No, I'm fine. Just worried about Pop."

At that moment, my father rustled, as if straining to move.

Mom hastened to his side and took his hand. "Ed, it's Mildred. Can you hear me?"

His lids popped open like a doll's, but his glassy eyes stared past her. Then fear washed across his face, and a moan from deep in his chest gurgled out of his mouth.

Jackie came around to the other side of the bed. "It's all right, Mr. Jacobi," she said, her voice soothing, but firm. "Mildred and Ruthie are right here. You're in the hospital and we're going to take good care of you."

"Why can't he move his fingers?" Mom asked. "Dr. Huff said he'd come around."

Then Pop's eyelids slid shut again and he withdrew into his sleeping state.

"Jackie, do something," I said.

"It may take him awhile to wake up. We'll let the doctor tell us what's going on when the test results come in."

"When's Victor coming back?" I asked.

"I believe Dr. Fletcher, one of Dr. Huff's associates, will be looking after your father," Jackie said. "Dr. Huff will be out for the rest of the day."

And I knew why.

32

I PITCHED MY JACKET over a hanger in the front hall closet, but it slid off like melting butter and landed in a heap on the floor. Lacking the energy to pick it up, I shut the closet door. If only I could dispose of all my other problems as easily.

An hour earlier, my father had awoken again and watched my mother with what seemed to be recognition. But except for the tips of his right fingers, he didn't move and couldn't speak. Along with dementia, I thought, he could be a vegetable for the rest of his life. He couldn't stay in the hospital forever. What would happen when they discharged him? There was no way Mom could care for him by herself. Maybe their moving here was the only option, but how would we all fit in this house? And how would I maintain control over Harriet with so many distractions?

Something thumped above me on the second floor. As I climbed the stairs to investigate, I expected to see one of the girls, but instead found Drew extracting his suitcase out of the hall closet.

When he noticed me his hand relaxed and the suitcase scudded to the floor. "I spoke to your mother on the phone," he said. "I'm very sorry about your father."

I was too exhausted to pretend I was all right. "It's been one of the worst days of my life."

"I can imagine. Your mother sounded so upset I asked her to sleep here tonight. I hope you don't mind."

I was touched by his sensitivity. "Of course not. I should have thought of that myself. She can have my bed and I'll sleep on the couch."

"No need. The guest room will be available in twenty minutes."

I eyed the suitcase. "You're moving out?"

"Yeah, I'm going back to my apartment. I couldn't find anyone to sublet it, so it's still vacant."

"But I thought you said—"

"My being here hasn't helped anyone. I don't think Harriet's doing any better in school and I drive you crazy. Anyway, I can't stand sleeping alone in that guestroom another night. I've never been so lonely."

Finally, he was getting a dose of what I'd endured for six months. That fact should have filled me with elation, but I experienced a wave of compassion.

I stepped closer. "Drew."

His hand jutted up. "You don't need to say a thing. I brought this misery upon myself and I'll never be able to make things right again." His hand finally landed on his chest. "But if you're honest with yourself you'll agree this split's been coming on for years. We've had a loveless marriage. We've lived like two single people under one roof."

I felt my face droop. The truth in his words stung. There had been times—lots of them—when I'd treated him the way Harriet treated me.

"I gave up Duchess for you," he said, referring to his Harley Davidson, which he'd sold shortly after Nichole's birth as a favor to me because I feared he'd slip under a truck some rainy night. He adored that bike, and I couldn't remember properly thanking him for his sacrifice.

"And I all but stopped traveling out of town."

True, he rarely attended the conventions he claimed were vital to his growing business, because I'd convinced him his absence damaged the girls. Which was true. However, they were older now. And when he'd invited me to join him at conferences, I always declined.

"I tried to make you proud of me," he said.

"That's no excuse."

"Yeah, I know." He glanced through my open bedroom doorway. His gaze came to rest on the bed, which I hadn't bothered to make. "You and I did have good times, too."

"Yes, we did." A vision of us entwined in each other's arms swirled through my mind, yet I hardened my features. "But apparently not good enough."

A tear welled up in the corner of his eye. He looked so pitiful; his shoulders bent like a man twice his age. I felt like comforting him. But that would only complicate matters.

"Coexisting like this hasn't worked for either one of us," he said.

"You're right." Yet I didn't want him to leave. I'd grown to rely on his presence again—of all crazy things.

"Dad?" Nichole said, her voice urgent. She must have been in her room or just come up the stairs.

"How long have you been standing there?" I asked.

"Long enough to hear that Dad's leaving." She angled her body away from me to face Drew. "I want to live with you, Dad."

Stunned, I grasped for words. "Nichole, sweetheart. Please."

"Dad has an extra bedroom," she said without looking my way.

"You're upset about Grandpa Ed." I'd spoken to her before she left the house this morning, then called her after school.

"This has nothing to do with him. I want to be with my father." At that moment she looked a carbon copy of Drew, as if she hadn't inherited any of my genes. "At my age I have the right to live with whichever parent I choose."

"I realize you're maturing into a woman." I steadied my voice to hide frustration and panic. "But you need to do your growing up here in this house."

"No, I don't." Nichole's voice sounded mechanical, as if she'd rehearsed the words before. "I can legally decide where to live." Had she been contemplating this move since he left?

"But I'd miss you."

"I doubt it, with all the men you're chasing after."

I moved closer, tried to capture her gaze. "That's not true. There's no one. And I love you more than anything." I did love her more than Drew and Harriet, which I realized was wrong. How could I have been so foolish?

She finally looked me full on and said, "How can you love me? You don't even know who I am."

"Honey." Drew's arm reached around her shoulder. "I've never been more flattered in my life, but it isn't fair to dump this on your mother when Grandpa's in the hospital."

She leaned into him as if they were one being with four legs. "But maybe you can spend next weekend with me," he said.

THE NEXT MORNING, I found my mother sitting on the living room couch reading the newspaper she must have brought in.

"Did you get any sleep?" I came to roost next to her.

"Not much." She folded the paper. "I called the hospital several times to check on your father. He's resting fine."

I wondered what that meant. Was he exactly the same? I decided no improvement was better than the alternative. At least he was alive.

"We'll go see him in a bit," I said. "Let me wake up first." I'd barely slept.

"I hope Drew didn't take off on my account." Leave it to Mom to be thinking about the welfare of others at a time like this.

"No," I said. "It was time. His choice."

"I didn't hear Harriet come in last night."

"She's at a girlfriend's. She went there straight after school."

"Does she know about her grandpa?"

"Just what I told her before school yesterday." Harriet had seemed upset as she gnawed into her thumbnail, but distracted, as if her thoughts resided elsewhere. "We should pick her up on the way to the hospital and take her with us."

"That would be nice. If anyone can pep Ed up it's that girl."

I found Alicia's phone number, and moments later her mother, Karen, answered on the fourth ring.

"Hi, it's Harriet's mother," I said. "Sorry to bother you so early."

She gave a brief yawn. "That's all right, I should get up."

"I hate to wake the girls, but I need to speak to my daughter."

"Harriet? She's not here."

I scoured my memory to retrieve the conversation I'd shared with Harriet yesterday morning. "Alicia has a TV in her bedroom and her mother buys us pizza," Harriet had said when she told me of her plans.

"Is it possible she's in Alicia's room?" I asked, thinking Karen might have forgotten. The poor woman was obviously in a half-sleep state.

"No, I haven't seen Harriet for months."

I felt topsy-turvy. Had I dialed the wrong number? Was I speaking to a different Karen? No, I recognized the Midwestern twang in her voice.

"But she's spent the night at your house almost every weekend," I said.

Karen sounded perturbed, almost hostile. "I think I'd know who's staying in my own house."

"Of course, sorry. Good—"

Karen rang off before I could finish saying goodbye.

I remembered seeing Harriet's shut door this morning. She must still be in her own bed. Mom had been sleeping more soundly than she thought. But that didn't explain all the other nights my daughter said she was at Alicia's.

I felt relief mixed with trepidation as I mounted the stairs. I cracked Harriet's door a few inches and saw a slice of her room. What a pigsty. My gaze landed on dirty clothes strewn across an empty bed.

My heart went wild. I shoved the door further and barged in. No Harriet. I scanned the rest of the room and noticed a swatch of orange fabric peeking out of a half-opened bureau drawer. Yanking the drawer open, I pulled out a sweater like the one I'd seen in the grocery store.

Nothing made sense. Tossing the sweater on the bed, I grabbed my phone and called Drew. After several long rings his recorded message picked up.

"Harriet's gone." I couldn't contain the tremor in my voice. "Please tell me she's with you."

A moment later my hand shook as I punched in 911. "My fifteen-year-old daughter's missing," I said as soon as the operator answered.

"When was the last time you saw her?" a woman asked.

"Yesterday morning before school. She was supposed to go to a friend's house, but she's not there."

"Can you think of anyplace she might be?"

"Not a clue."

"Has she done this kind of thing before?" Her voice remained steady, like she'd heard every possible horror story and then some.

"No." I thought of the many times Harriet had stormed out of the house, slamming the door. But she'd always returned in a few hours. "She's been ornery, but nothing like this."

"Do you think she was taken against her will?"

"No, I don't think so." I wouldn't let myself believe she'd been abducted.

"Then she left on her own volition?"

"Yes."

"We'd classify her a juvenile runaway."

I hadn't thought of that. With all the turmoil in our household would she choose to live on the streets? Unlikely, the way she enjoyed her twenty-minute showers and our full refrigerator. "I can't imagine her running away."

The operator took Harriet's name and description. "I'll let our patrol cars know," she said. "They'll keep their eyes open for her."

"Good, thank you." I wondered where they'd think to look. Under the freeway with the homeless? Out on Aurora with the prostitutes? In the morgue?

"Ma'am, I'll warn you we have hundreds of kids out on the streets and living in tents. Even if we locate her, your daughter's not breaking the law. We can't bring her home unless she agrees to come with us.

"Seriously?"

"I'm sorry." Then she hung up.

33

A HISSING SOUND LIKE white noise flooded my ears, but I admonished myself to keep a clear head. If the police wouldn't help me, I'd do my own detective work. Harriet wasn't with her friend, then where? With the ratty-looking man from QFC? Recalling them leaving the store together made me want to break something.

As I hung up the phone, I forced my face to take on a composed façade. I didn't want to scare Mom, who was watching me from the couch.

"I'm going to look for her," I said in as calm a voice as I could muster. If the man was shopping at my local grocery store, I figured he lived close by. I'd drive up and down every street, and maybe spot his car. But it could be hidden in a garage or over the border into Canada by now. I moved to the closet and snatched my jacket off the floor.

Mom set the paper aside. "Do you want me to come with you?"

"No." I shoved my arms in the sleeves. "But could you stick around in case Harriet shows up?" I felt terrible asking her to man the phone while her husband's fate dangled between here and Neverland, but there was nothing I could do about it until Drew showed up. If he did.

"Yes, glad to."

"Thanks, Mom. I'll take my cell phone."

Once in my car, the disgusting possibility of what Harriet and that man were doing together tormented me. I decided I'd have him charged with statutory rape. Send him to jail. But that wouldn't change what was happening to my daughter right now. In my mind, I envisioned her mangled body sprawled in a ditch, the police wanting me to identify her corpse.

As I cruised the neighborhood, I used my cell phone to call Harriet's friends, even Alex, whose mother roused him from bed to answer. But the kids all gave me the same story, that they had no idea where she was. I passed house after house. Newspapers dressed in blue or orange plastic adorned front porches; a woman walked a black Cairn terrier; a dad and his pint-sized son played catch in their front yard. The world appeared normal.

I check the QFC parking lot to find a sprinkling of cars. Most were white or beige; the one black automobile was a Mercedes with a massive chrome grill I wouldn't forget. I scavenge through my memory trying to recall what the man's automobile looked like. Did it have mag wheels or some kind of sticker in the window or on the bumper? It tore out of the parking lot so quickly I'd only noted it was a coupe slinking low to the ground, and the engine rumbled like angry protestors. I was tempted to go into the store to ask the checkers if they've seen Harriet, but her photo in my wallet was taken over three years ago, back when I could still cajole the girl into smiling for the camera. With shoulder-length hair and a trace of makeup, she'd looked a whole different person.

I guided my car back onto the main street and headed for the University District, where I'd heard homeless kids sometimes hung out and drug deals were consummated. As I drove, thoughts of Harriet's birth swam through my head. I remember missing my period sixteen years ago, then my excitement when revealing my pregnant condition to Drew. "I think it's a boy," I said toward the end of the nine months, and he was thrilled. I carried the baby low and all in front, I craved salty foods, and the little fellow was as active as a kickboxer—everything the women in my Lamaze class said predicted a son.

"Don't believe old wives' tales," Mom had warned me, but I paid no heed. A boy would make our family complete; he would carry on the Templeton name. I went so far as to choose his first name: Peter. Peter the Great, I'd think when feeling the unborn baby stretching its limbs against my ribs. As I converted Drew's home office into the baby's room, I grew to love little Peter and spoke to him often. I painted his bedroom walls powder blue for a boy.

I knew it was wrong not to rejoice over the birth of my healthy daughter, but when Harriet blew onto the scene I declined into a period of grieving. Maybe it was normal postpartum depression, but my disappointment squelched all gratitude. I felt like something wonderful had been stolen from me.

Things got off to a bad start. It took weeks for Drew and me to settle on a name. "Petrina or Petra?" I suggested, but Drew grimaced, then proposed calling the baby Maxine, after his mother. With much debate we finally agreed to name our daughter after Mom's sister, Natalie, who, now that I thought of it, had much the same temperament as Harriet.

Harriet rejected my milk—she preferred the bottle. She rejected my arms—she preferred to be held by her father. She rejected me. As she grew, I tried to give her all the affection and attention I showed Nichole, but Harriet never loved me in return. She only needed me for a meal ticket, allowance, or a ride to a friend's house.

As I turned onto University Way—what Harriet called "The Ave."—I considered if I truly loved her. Or was I simply resigned to a lifetime of dodging her verbal punches?

The wailing of an approaching siren bombarded my eardrums. The car in front of me swung over to the curb and stopped. I also pulled off to the side just as a fire engine, its lights flashing, screamed past me. I'd heard seventy percent of fire department calls were summoned to administer first aid rather than extinguish fires. I wondered if the massive truck was on its way to help Harriet, and I was tempted to follow it, but knew the trip would be futile.

I imagined attending her funeral. I wondered if I'd be wracked with pain or if my senses were so dulled I couldn't feel emotions anymore. I knew these thoughts meant I was an awful person, the worst mother on Earth. I tried to reframe the event with me dressed in black, tears slashing my cheeks, my eyes swollen. I'd wear a veil to conceal my devastation, or my lack of it.

I must be going nuts.

I started driving again, toured the length of the five- or six-block strip, then hung a U-turn and retraced my route. But all I saw were folks sequestering parking places, college students jostling each other as they strolled from Fraternity Row to eat at a restaurant, a bag lady with a shopping cart, and two bums on a bench chugging something from a brown paper bag.

I glanced in my rearview mirror to see I was being tailed by a squad car. I was relieved the patrolman hadn't noticed my illegal U-turn, but had that meant he'd overlooked Harriet too?

An hour later, the hole in the pit of my stomach gaped larger than a crater on the moon. I started contemplating if Harriet's disappearance was my fault. Why hadn't I seen a crisis growing earlier? My vision had been pointed inward, at myself.

Mom finally called to report Drew was on his way there, and she was leaving for the hospital. As I started home, I got it in my head I needed to speak to Jackie. Minutes later I entered the intersection by her house to see her sedan backing out of her driveway. I took a quick jog onto her street. She coasted to a stop when she saw me; we both got out. She hugged me, then stepped back to listen. I didn't know where to start. As I recounted the last twenty-four hours, my words came out like marbles rolling across a hardwood floor.

Her hands found mine. "Would sitting and waiting with you help?"

"I don't know." I stared at the pavement: colorless, cracked, stained. Like me.

"You have a lot on your plate," she said.

I nodded my head. "I feel like running away but I'd better get home in case she returns."

34

WHEN I GOT home, I noticed Drew's car parked out front where Mom's had been. Half of me breathed a sigh of relief he was here, but the other half couldn't wait to unleash my wrath at him. If he'd stuck around maybe this wouldn't have happened.

I found Drew in Harriet's room sitting at the IKEA desk he and I had assembled. He'd been unfolding a scrap of paper, then rotating it to read Harriet's clumsy handwriting. At his feet milled Bonnie, happy to see me but intent on sniffing each paper scrap.

"Hi," I said, and he swiveled the wheeled chair part way around. His expression didn't reveal fear or even worry. Maybe Mom hadn't filled him in sufficiently. "Did my mother tell you what happened?"

"Yes, Harriet's not where she's supposed to be and you were out looking for her. Any luck?"

"No." I moved closer to examine the hodgepodge scattered across Harriet's desk and spotted half-finished homework assignments, an empty Diet Pepsi can, a book of matches, and some chewing gum.

"Anyone call?" I'd just spoken to the 911 operator again, so I knew the police hadn't picked her up.

"Nope." He tossed the paper aside. "Are you sure this isn't some kind of silly mix-up?" His hand found another square of creased and folded paper. "Maybe Harriet knows two girls named Alicia."

"Not according to her friends. And Alicia's mother said she hasn't seen our daughter for months.""Still—"

"Drew, Harriet's been claiming to spend the night with this girl every weekend."

"But she's been so compliant lately. She's followed all our rules."

"No, she hasn't." I walked to the bed, scooped up the orange sweater, and brandished it as evidence, but he stared back without comprehension. "I have strong reasons to believe she stole the money for this sweater," I said. "Or maybe she stole the sweater."

"Now, look, you're jumping to conclusions. She could have borrowed it from a friend."

He had me there, but that didn't change what I'd seen. "Drew, a Harriet look-alike wearing an orange sweater exactly like this one was in the QFC parking lot during school hours." I regretted not telling him of the incident earlier.

"That doesn't prove anything." He unfolded a paper, which looked like notes taken in science class. "One of her friend's mothers could have taken Harriet and her daughter there to buy lunch."

"She was with a man."

He spun around, let go of the paper. It sailed under the desk. "A man or a tall high school-aged kid? At sixteen young men start filling out in the shoulders and grow chin stubble."

"A man, as in, in his twenties."

"What would she be doing with someone like that?" His brows lowered. "Are you positive?"

"No, and I might be all wigged out, as Harriet's called me more than once. But if she's not with Alicia, where is she?"

He turned back to the desk and rifled through the papers. "I was hoping to find a clue—a name and a telephone number."

He's worried, too, I thought, noticing the severe angle of his shoulders, his jerky movements. He was shielding his fears from me. This realization caused a fresh round of dread to clutch my chest. Should I contact the TV stations? Give them Harriet's photo so they could ask viewers to be on the watch for her? No, the police said it was too early for those measures. But did we have to wait until she was dead to get their attention?

I couldn't laze around doing nothing. "I'll look, too. Maybe she has a diary tucked away somewhere."

Harriet was supposed to dust and vacuum her room. I tried to give her privacy, so I hardly ever rooted around in here. With Bonnie at my feet, I scanned one side of the room, which seethed with messy activity. My gaze landed on her Snoopy collection. Ceramic and stuffed canines controlled the top shelf of her shoulder-high bookcase, backdropped by a Snoopy poster with the words *Joe Cool*. She stopped collecting the black-and-white pups several years ago, but she must still like them. In many ways Harriet was a little girl inside. My daughter, a girl who liked Snoopy, was missing. It seemed absurd.

I noticed on the bottom shelf several spiral notebooks that didn't look familiar. I leaned down to pluck one out. I opened the pad to discover the portrait of a girl, her long tendrils of hair weaving out gracefully like branches of a tree. With a minimum of what seemed to be spontaneous pen strokes, the artist captured the girl's pert nose, her sassy eyes, her flirtatious personality. I check the lower right corner and read

H. T. Harriet's initials? I hadn't seen Harriet sketch anything beyond doodling since grade school.

I looked the drawing over again and marveled at the artist's skill. I was creative in high school, but my ability paled compared to this. I flipped through the notebook to find page after page of drawings, some executed in ink, some in colored pencils. Most were portraits of women or female figures clothed in medieval attire, although I came across several drawings of flowers. I reached for another notebook also teeming with sketches, all with the initials H. T. inscribed at the bottom.

I held up the opened notebook. "Look at this."

Drew glanced at it. "Her drawings?"

"You knew about these?"

"She's shown me some, but not for a while. Hey, she's gotten really good."

"But why would she keep this from me?" She must have gone to great lengths to hide her artistry. "Does she hate me that much?"

"Now, don't take it personally. Teenagers are secretive. Weren't you?"

"Not like this. If I'd had half her talent, I would have been thrilled to show my folks."

"Well, that's our Harriet. Full of surprises."

He stood and walked to the foot of the bed. In one swift movement he yanked up the corner of the mattress to check under it. Then he whisked around to the other end and did the same.

"What are you looking for?"

"Drugs, money. I don't know."

"I didn't realize you were such a good detective." It occurred to me if I had been nosier, I would have discovered Drew's infidelity on my own. I couldn't help myself from asking, "Where were you this morning?" I was sure he'd say, "With Kristi."

"I went to the club to work out, then I visited your father."

"Oh." I was taken aback. "How was he?"

"Not bad. He called me *son*." Drew seemed to be choking on the words. He forced a cough into his palm. "Then he said he was hungry."

THE REST OF the day crawled by in stop-and-go motions. I could feel the air shift as Drew and I passed each other every now and then. I noticed his bare feet and his jeaned legs in my downcast vision, but our eyes never met. I heard him ask Nichole if she had any ideas about Harriet's whereabouts, but Nichole said, "No, she doesn't confide in me anymore." I was used to her counseling us to ignore Harriet's antics, but she offered us no advice and was obviously alarmed as well. Then she sealed herself in her bedroom to study for a physics test and write a paper. Even Bonnie, her ears folded back and her low-slung torso sagging, moped in the front hall anticipating Harriet's return.

When my phone—sitting on a kitchen counter—rang, Drew and I raced to answer it. I bolted across the room, but he beat me by a giant step, then allowed me to hoist the phone to my ear. It was my mother asking after Harriet.

I wanted to allay her fears. "You know Harriet, always trying to keep us guessing," I said. But I didn't believe Harriet would intentionally pull a stunt like this. Although she enjoyed tweaking my strings, she wouldn't cause her father this discomfort. Would she?

Mom said, "I have good news. Your father ate lunch and complained bitterly about the food. He's almost back to his old self." Which old self? I wondered, but didn't ask. I was just glad he was alive.

An hour later she rang again. "Your father's watching the news and he remembered the president's name. He hasn't been able to do that for months." His memory gaps seemed inconsequential at the moment.

"That's wonderful. Keep me posted." Of course, I was pleased, and I sure didn't want to burden her with the beehive of anxieties infesting my mind.

In the old days I would have turned to Gloria for support, but not anymore. Two days ago, she phoned me at work, and had the gall to ask about Stephen. Had he called, and if not, why didn't I make the first move? According to her, today's women took the initiative; they make things happen. "That's how Jonathon and I met," she said. "He was in line behind me at Starbucks. I bought two mocha lattes, offered him one, then found us a table." I'd already heard the story several times. As I recall Jonathon was dating another woman at the time, but that didn't stop Gloria. No way would she come in second place.

I should have said I was offended by her questions, but I waited out the call—all the time drilling my fingernails into the desktop—then hung up, vowing not to speak to her again. But if I let our friendship lapse, I'd be out of allies. I ran an inventory of the women I called friends and came up short. Which left me Jackie, who I don't want to bother again. Anyway, I must keep my phone line clear in case the police called.

The dog barked and I heard a rattling sound at the front door. I dashed into the hall only to see a piece of mail ease through the slot. As the lime-green flyer skated to the floor, I read Emerald Garden Services across the top.

"Someone's canvassing the neighborhood looking for jobs," Drew said. He fetched the flyer, crumpled it into a ball, then lobbed it into the wastepaper basket.

"Would you like something to eat?" he asked. "I'll make tuna sandwiches—if that's all right with you."

I looked into his face for the first time in hours. His eyes looked weary, his skin weathered.

"Sure," I said. Save for several cups of coffee, I hadn't eaten all day. I followed him into the kitchen and watched him assemble the sandwiches. Brown bread heavy on the mayo, sliced tomato and cheddar, a little lettuce. He knew my routine. He set one on a plate and positioned it on the counter in front of me.

"Thanks." The first bite hit my stomach like a rock in a swimming pool. My hand moved to my abdomen. I tried without success to rub the spasm away.

As Drew sat at the kitchen table my phone chimed again. I nabbed it and brought it to my ear to hear Alex asking for Harriet.

He hadn't given his name, but I said, "Hi, Alex, still no sign of her?"

"Uh, okay."

He started to say goodbye, but I interjected, "Are you sure you don't have any idea where she is?"

"Like, I haven't seen much of her recently." He paused. I sensed he was gathering his thoughts, evaluating his words.

"Alex, please, anything you can think of."

"I guess she has a new boyfriend."

"Does he go to your school?" When he didn't answer, I said, "I promise you won't get her in trouble." A blatant lie because of course she was in trouble. The stress had aged me ten years.

After an extended pause, he said, "He's older. I don't think he goes to school."

"Do you know his name? Please, I beg you, if you know his name tell me."

"I'm sorry Mrs. Templeton, I never met the guy."

As I rang off and set my phone aside, I noticed Drew had gotten to his feet and was pacing several feet away from me.

"That was her friend, Alex," I said. "He confirmed Harriet has a new boyfriend. Someone older."

I saw anger and anxiety distort Drew's features. He was finally in the same state as I. His brain was flipping around like a beached herring battling to find the safety of water. I was glad to share my anguish with him. But a moment later I realized his distress hadn't eased my fears one bit, only heightened them.

"Now what?" He looked to me for an answer, but all I can do is shake my head.

35

I T IS 5:00 when the front bell rings. Just a chirping sound,
as if the person outside is barely pressing his fingertip to
the button. It can't be Harriet; she has her own key. I figure it's

Mom, who must be exhausted. I need to be strong for her,
I tell myself.

Between barks, Bonnie sniffs under the door with long hard
drags. I nudge her aside with my foot.

"Quiet, girl, it's just my mother."

I open the door and see Harriet. She's in the same knit top
and slacks she had on when she left for school yesterday. Her
cheeks are blotchy under foundation a shade too light; her
mascara has melted down into the hollows beneath her eyes.
She stares at me without blinking.

The dog is deliriously happy and prances in circles at Harriet's feet, but she pays no attention.

"Thank God you're home." I am overflowing with gratitude
and love. Yes, I realize, I love Harriet, my daughter, my precious child.

"Are you all right?" I step aside to let her enter and she starts
to walk past me. I reach out with both arms, wrap them around
her, and hug her. This crisis has drawn us close to each other.

I take a breath and detect a smoky, pungent odor on her hair. It's not from cigarettes or firewood, rather something sweeter. I want it to be incense, but I've smelled enough incense to know it's not. My best guess is she's been smoking marijuana. A wave of revulsion curdles in my gut, but I refuse to let it take hold. I only want to revel in her return. My happiness is pushing all else aside.

I tighten my hold around her shoulders and feel the girl's ear is like an ice cube against mine.

"You're freezing," I say.

"I walked home."

"From where?"

"Kitten," Drew says.

I see he and Nichole are standing behind Harriet.

She shrugs off my embrace, then glances at Nichole, who gives her head a slight nod. It's a secret language between siblings. I remember my brother and me signaling each other across the dining room table when one of us was in trouble.

I decide to keep quiet and let Drew conduct the interrogation. He can be the bad guy.

"Where have you been?" he asks. "And no more lies. We know you weren't at Alicia's."

Harriet moves into his shadow and looks up at him. "I'm sorry, Daddy," she says.

"You didn't answer his question." I'm unable to silence myself. "Where were you and with whom?"

"Someone you don't know," she says, then chews at her fingernail.

"What's his name?" Drew asks.

"Slam."

The enemy has a name. I consider how much I despise him. "Slam must be his street name," I say. "No one would call their child such a ridiculous thing."

"What would you know?" Harriet says.

"I know you walked home from somewhere. Slam steals your virginity, but he can't bother to give you a lift?"

"Ruthie." Drew sends me a disapproving frown. "For all we know she was raped."

He's right, but judging from her demeanor, I doubt it. Her hair is slightly mussed, just the way she likes it. Her clothes seem in order. Which is good news. The last thing I want is for her to have been brutally violated.

"Were you?" I say, and finally she gives me her attention. "Did he rape you?"

"No," she answers, loudly.

My volume increases to match hers. "Then you were a willing participant?"

She doesn't reply, but I presume she's had sex with this man.

"Let me put the question another way, young lady." I feel my pent-up emotions loosening my tongue. "How long have you been sneaking out to meet Slam?"

She ignores me, moves toward the staircase. And that move tells me everything.

"Did you bother to use birth control?" I am terrified she might be pregnant, let alone have picked up a disease. "Please tell me you did."

"Ruthie," Drew says. "This can wait."

"You want us to pretend nothing happened? Act as if we haven't been frantic all day, scared out of our minds? That we didn't call the police?"

Harriet whirls back to me. "Police?" she asks.

"Yes, we were very worried," Drew says. "Your mother drove all over town searching for you."

Harriet tosses me a sneer I've seen more times than I can remember. "If you'd give me my own cell phone," she informs me.

"Don't you dare try to make your appalling behavior my fault. You brought this on yourself." I feel like a loaded revolver ready to fire. "What's Slam's real name?"

"Why do you want to know? Will you tell the police?"

"Yes. And have him charged with statutory rape."

"But he didn't rape me."

"That doesn't matter. He's an adult and you're a child." I know she despises being called what she is, but it's too late to take the words back. Anyway, she is a child.

"I hate you!" she yells in my face.

The dog scurries to the kitchen; Nichole retreats up the stairs.

"Get it?" Harriet says, her finger targeting me. "I hate you."

She's lied to me often, but I believe her this time. She loathes me. Her words are like a butcher's blade cutting through my bones. I almost collapse from the pain. I feel tears pressing at the back of my eyes.

"I'm sure you don't mean that," Drew says. His voice is ultra-calm and I understand he's restraining himself. "And your mother is correct. If Slam is as old as we think he is, we can press charges."

"You wouldn't do that to me, would you, Daddy?"

"Your mother and I will decide later."

"But you can't. All the kids would find out. I'd never be able to show my face in public again." She clutches his forearm. "Don't listen to Mom, she's trying to turn you against me."

"That's not true, she wants to help."

"No, she's never on my side."

"Kitten, no one's taking sides. We both love you."

As I watch him enfold her in his arms and kiss the top of her head, I wonder for the first time if I am the person who's wrenched this family apart.

36

I DROP MY MOTHER off in front of the hospital and let the engine idle. I watch her follow a man carrying a vase overflowing with long-stemmed roses through the front door. Maybe his wife had a baby. At least one person entering this building is on a pleasant mission.

Mom and I got up early this morning, not that I'd slept much. I first checked my bedside clock at 2:00 AM to see its illuminated dial watching me like a jackal lining up its prey. I slammed my lids shut, but sleep continued to elude me. I wonder if I will ever feel rested again or if I'll continue in this state of exhaustion.

When I arose at 5:30 I found Drew hibernating on the couch, just like in the old days when we had fights. Now I realize those were mere spats, nothing worth talking about. I had a tendency to inflate our disagreements out of proportion, which drove him away. And I was always comparing Drew to Pop. My allegiance should have transferred to my husband when we married, but it remained locked to my childhood idol, my father. And Drew knew it. I never treated him with the respect he deserved. And some of my snide comments were plain mean-spirited. I am an angry person, destroying others to elevate myself.

I think about Harriet and wish I could relive yesterday. When she came home it took me all of three minutes to plunge down to her maturity level. I wonder about my judgment, my self-control. How could I have been so stupid to rip into her, especially in front of her father and sister? That tactic never works. To Harriet, I am a tape recorder set on repeat, teeth grating into ice—she shuts down when she hears my voice. And I don't blame her. I imagine what I look like through her eyes: The Wicked Witch of the West soaring in on her broom, Medusa consuming her children. I wonder what facial expression I wear when she gets home from school. Probably one of reproach. Anything but welcoming. How did I get like this? Mom was always generous with her love; her grace flowed from a bottomless font.

Harriet is still sleeping and might not wake up for hours. Before she tromped upstairs, she informed Drew and me that Slam is twenty years old. But that still makes him five years her senior. I am just as horrified. Any man is too old for her, as far as I'm concerned. When I was Harriet's age, I loved horses; my favorite movie was *National Velvet*. But those days of innocence are long gone. Today's girls are taught to flaunt their sexuality like fishermen trolling with live bait. I remember the first time Harriet wanted thong underwear. I should have said no, but I was weak. I let her buy those seductive clothes; it seemed easier than sparring with her. Mom never caved to my demands, but I took the easy road, then found myself convincing Drew that Harriet's attire was appropriate.

Last night she stalked off to bed without dinner, although later Drew brought a tray with peanut butter sandwiches and a glass of milk to her room and set it on her desk in case she woke up hungry. He is kinder than I, who hadn't understood her humiliation. I wouldn't blame her if she demanded to live with Drew along with Nichole. They'd be better off with him. Far away from me.

Thinking about this makes me feel small, a dwarf against an endless horizon. I am barely visible, a speck of dust. As I steer the car into the hospital's parking garage, I feel tears threatening. I want to cry, to let myself submerge below the sadness. I yearn for that deep space, where I belong, but I mustn't smudge my makeup. I need to stroll into Pop's room with poise and dignity. He's the sick person, not me.

Taking the car up the ramp, I stop to allow a minivan to back out of a spot, then I pull into it. As I open my door and step out, I hear an eagle shrieking, and my mind is transported to the island. Out of habit I suck in through my nose trying to catch the crisp briny aroma of the beach, but instead I smell exhaust and oil on damp cement. I'm startled. I look around in confusion to see I am standing in a cavern filled with automobiles. Again, I hear a screech. I realize it's a car's tires powering around a turn on the floor below. As I walk past the end of my car, I see an SUV's headlights descending upon me. I imagine myself stepping out in front of the vehicle, its whipping me off my feet—the impact killing me.

Would that be so terrible? I could have died not long ago and it would have been a blessing, when I think about it. It's unlikely Harriet would have thrown herself at Slam. She would have been more concerned with Drew, who would have moved home where he belongs. Things are becoming clearer to me now. I had everything backward. I'm the one who should leave, not Drew.

After the SUV lumbers past me, I head toward the door under the exit sign just as a male figure moves through the doorway. I recognize Victor, whom I expected to see inside the hospital. Last night when Mom mentioned he'd be checking on Pop when making his early rounds I realized how much I've missed Victor. I'd learned to rely on his friendship, not to mention his insights on understanding my father. And Victor empathized with my abrupt singleness in a way no one else had. None of my friends or family could understand the depth of my sorrow or my feelings of powerlessness. I remember Victor and my evening at the opera. The expansive sweeps of music, the sumptuous stage and costumes, and my attentive escort had elevated me out of my humdrum existence to a higher place. I'd been happy. I'd felt attractive.

I watch him dip his hand into his pants pocket for keys. I wonder why he left Pop's bedside without waiting to speak to me. Maybe Mom forgot to tell him I was parking the car. Or was he avoiding me? I recall overhearing his telephone conversation with Juliet. He'd said he loved her. But I could have misinterpreted his words. For all I know, he meant he cared for her in a platonic way. And even if the two were reconciled, I reasoned, he and I could remain friends. Although Juliet didn't seem the type who'd allow such a thing.

No, of course not. Our friendship would end like the flame of a snuffed-out candle.

He is nearing the first car, inserting a key in the lock.

"Victor," I say, but he must not hear me because he opens the car door without looking up. I pick up my speed. "Victor?"

His back is to me, his left hand on the door. I spy something shiny on his finger. Then my breathing thuds to a halt as I make out a gold band.

He turns to me. His features are pulled in as though he just swallowed something sour. Finally, he says, "I was going to call you," without animation.

I wait.

"There's something I need to tell you," he says.

I glance down at his hand again. There is no doubt he's wearing his wedding band.

"Juliet and I," he starts to say, and I look up. "We're back together."

I feel as though I'm standing in waist-deep water being pummeled by waves, each smacking me harder and harder. I don't know where the anguish is coming from. Am I jealous of Victor and Juliet's reconciliation—of their happiness together? Could I be that selfish and petty? Have I secretly harbored dreams of Victor's falling in love with me, of our eventually getting married?

Get real, I tell myself. No man will ever love you. You're not worthy of love.

I am doubled up inside. If I don't leave immediately this agony will shred me to ribbons. I reel around, hurry to my car, and dive in. Victor says my name, but I am a hollow reed; his words pass right through me. I shut my door, ram the key in the ignition, and listen to the engine flare. I don't want to hear his explanations. I don't want to know about Juliet's and his joyous reunion. I toss the transmission into reverse, throw my foot on the gas pedal. The tires blurt out a squeal as the car springs out of the stall. I glance over my shoulder to see Victor is standing behind my car. My foot strikes the brakes and the car jolts to a halt, just inches from him.

"I'm sorry," I whisper. How could I be so careless? If I hurt him I would never forgive myself. I am inundated with shame.

He is striding to my door. I hear him speaking through the window, but his words sound like gibberish.

"Leave me alone," I want to say. "Let me escape gracefully." But I don't have the strength to push the window down.

Anyway, we've said enough. I am certain I will never see him again.

I continue to back the car out then proceed toward the exit. In my rearview mirror I see him watching me. I hurry to get out of his sight. The further away from here the better. I pick up speed as I descend the ramp, then leave the garage. Once on the street, I don't know where to go.

Not home. I have no home.

My temples are pounding, crushing my brain. I would do anything to abandon this body, to escape. I notice the freeway entrance up ahead and I hang a quick left, surge up the ramp. My speedometer is gliding up to sixty, then seventy, as I race into the far-left lane.

I see the car in front of me resembles Drew's BMW, but this one is several years older. In an instant, time spins back on itself like a scroll rewinding. Memories of the day of my accident gel into opaque images. I was having a good day, I recall, a very good day—the first I'd enjoyed in months. Drew was coming to dinner. That morning I admitted to Mom I still loved him and wanted him back, and she encouraged me not to give up. Feeling optimistic, I took the afternoon off to get my hair trimmed and styled, and my eyebrows sculpted. As I glanced at myself in the beauty salon's mirror, I decided I looked pretty; with a little makeup Drew would find me irresistible. I went to Nordstrom and asked the Christian Dior representative for help. No doubt about it, after her camouflaging and artful brushstrokes I appeared ten years younger. And beautiful. Later, I felt giddy as I piloted my cart up and down the grocery store aisles. Tonight, I would light candles, use cloth napkins, the works. I was sure Drew would move home after sitting down to his favorite meal with his daughters and me looking so snazzy.

With grocery bags stowed in the trunk, my car rolled out of the parking lot and onto the main street just as Drew's BMW streaked by. Seeing him brought a flush of joy. My hand flapped up to wave hello, but his gaze remained fastened to a woman sitting in his passenger seat. As I swerved onto the road and trailed behind them, I saw the woman was a strawberry blonde. It wasn't his secretary, who's a brunette, or anyone I knew. Which meant it was Kristi. In the past, I'd found her hairs on his jackets.

Like a scrap of metal being dragged by a magnet I followed them onto the freeway heading north. He still hadn't noticed me; he was immersed in their conversation. He'd forgotten about our dinner. Or maybe he had no intention of coming. He couldn't care less. As they talked and laughed—were they laughing about me?—she tossed her head. Then her hand moved to his shoulder, and her fingertip traced his earlobe.

He drove faster and faster. I could barely keep up. He must be in a great hurry to whisk his darling away to somewhere special. Where were they going? To the island, our Shangri-La? He wouldn't dare, would he? It was ridiculous to follow them, but I had to find out. However, thirty minutes later he flew right by the island's exit without even tapping his brakes. I figured they were journeying all the way to Canada, too far for me to follow. They would probably stay at the Sylvia Hotel in Vancouver, where Drew and I spent our honeymoon. I was outraged for a moment, then resignation steered me off the next exit.

"You win," I said to Drew's vanishing car. I got myself turned around and headed back to town.

As I drove along the lifeless highway, I considered how disappointed the girls would be their father wasn't coming for dinner, and how crushed I was—crushed to a pulp like a strawberry in a blender; a shapeless mass. I adjusted the rearview mirror enough to catch a glimpse of myself. The woman in Nordstrom had applied too much makeup. I looked like a streetwalker. Or worse, a clown. I was relieved Drew hadn't seen me like this. How could I have been such a fool?

The weight of despair fell upon me, invading my body. I looked in the mirror again and my gaze locked onto my eye. I was mesmerized by the flattened orb. My pupil was a pinprick being consumed by a murky pool.

I felt the ground shift, then heard hailstones pelting the car. An earthquake? I glanced out the window to see the scrub brush growing by the side of the road leaping up at me. The earth snaked around the car, spinning and whirling in slow motion. My purse and papers, everything launched through space. Weightless, I floated in the eye of a hurricane.

Then blackness, and all was still.

37

I WISH I HADN'T remembered that day. It only makes me feel worse.

I begin to cry. Wrenching sobs take over my body and I bend forward against the steering wheel. Over and over again I am seized by long blubbering sobs. I cannot stop them. They launch through me like blasts of wind shaking my body until I am empty of air. Then I gasp and weep again. I make hideous sounds, deafening moans.

I look out the windshield to see the road is a serpent unhinging its jaw, ready to swallow me again. I will enter its warm belly and find rest.

The car is skimming like a water bug across the next lane toward the center median, a grassy area that dips into a ravine. My tires begin to bounce and wobble as I leave the paved surface. The ocean's roar turns to thunder. Gravel is battering against the bottom of the car.

I hear myself scream. In that second the desire to live grabs onto me. But it's too late. My hands are frozen to the wheel. I might as well be hurtling over a cliff.

My palms burn against the plastic as I wrench the wheel enough to alter the car's trajectory, then aim it back onto the shoulder. My foot slides off the gas pedal and onto the brakes. The car limps to a stop.

As I gasp for breath, I see blue lights flashing in my rearview mirror. A moment later, a state patrolman who looks young enough to be my son taps on the window and signals me to put it down.

When I do, he says, "Are you all right?" He sniffs the air. "I'll need your driver's license and registration."

"Yes, sir." My voice quivers.

My purse, once on the seat next to me, sprawls on the floor. I reach for it and find my wallet. My fingers feel like rubber as they struggle to remove my license. I pass it to the trooper.

"Your vehicle registration?" he says, all business. I locate the folded paper in the glove box, hand it to him, and he returns to his patrol car.

My heart beats against my ribcage, and my chest swells and collapses. I feel tired but invigorated. I remember begging to wear Grandma Tessa's massive fur coat as a five-year-old. When I took it off, I felt twenty pounds lighter and an inch taller. That's exactly how I feel right now. Free. And grateful to be alive.

The patrolman returns. His eyes narrow as they appraise my face. "You sure you feel good enough to drive?"

"Yes, I'm fine, really." I am trembling all over.

He passes me the registration and license. My hand shakes as I take them.

"Thank you, sir." I wait for him to enter his patrol car to expel a breath. In a blink he is driving out of sight. When the traffic lets up, I pull back onto the highway, then negotiate my car to the far right-hand lane. Usually a confident driver, I am overly cautious, even more than my mother, who hates the freeway.

Which reminds me, Mom must wonder where I am. I had planned to stroll into Pop's room and hug him. But I'm too shaken up to visit or offer comfort.

I chide myself for wishing Drew was here sitting behind the wheel to do the driving. He's not and never will again. When will my thoughts stop returning to Drew?

38

FOR THE FIRST time since last summer, Drew and I are walking the beach. We are traveling in the same direction. Like two strangers strolling down an avenue, perhaps, but Drew and I are at least moving side by side. Our footsteps beat out a harmonious rhythm as the soles of our shoes sink into the rocks.

Our plan was to have one last look around the cabin, decide which belongings to keep and what to let go. I've already determined not to bring much back to town. If I have any brains, I'll toss my agates, the driftwood—all our collected treasures—back on the beach. Let Puget Sound reclaim what she's lent us.

Hal Vandervate has prospective buyers even though we have yet to list the cabin. The market analysis he sent me still lies dormant in an unopened envelope somewhere on my desk. "I was showing some people, a real nice couple from Bellevue, around the island, but they didn't find anything they liked," he told me on the phone yesterday. "As you know there's not much low-bank waterfront for sale. There never is. I mentioned your cabin might be on the market soon and they insisted on stopping by. They fell in love with the place. I know they'll pay top dollar."

I suppose that's good news, but I will miss coming here. It never fails. Each time I arrive I am awestruck by the beauty of the island.

I turn toward the center of the bay and see scuffs of wind chopping the water's surface. Shallow waves slap atop one another as the breeze pushes them against the shore. I fill my lungs to the fullest and try to fix the almost intoxicating aroma of drying seaweed into my memory store. But I know I will forget it just as I always do when I return to the city.

Drew has barely spoken since we got here. He and I happened to wander to the water's edge at the same time, then he started moving along the shoreline and I fell in next to him. The afternoon sun is sitting low, casting our shadows out to sea. I sneak a sideways glance at him and take in the even plane of his nose, his strong jaw, his lips pressed together as though his mind is a scale weighing a heavy burden. He doesn't know what took place on the highway, so I suppose he's ruminating about Harriet, who's back at the cabin with Bonnie. Although Harriet fumed about accompanying us here, she soon discovered an unopened puzzle left over from last year. A moment later she dumped the thousand almost identical shapes onto the table and started jiggling the outside pieces together.

She's grounded and Drew took her phone away until she's proven herself trustworthy. We're talking six months of good behavior. She isn't allowed out of our sight unless she's in school. If that means my being home afternoons and evenings until she moves out on her own, I'll be there. Janet Caddish, her school counselor, has instructions to call if Harriet's late to class and her teachers agreed to sign daily tally sheets stating Harriet has her homework turned in.

Nichole is spending the weekend with my parents—a gift to them and to me. This summer, when school's out, she's agreed to work for Mom twenty hours a week as a housekeeper and nurse's assistant. Drew and I are chipping in to pay her, too. "Money for when you're in college," I told Nichole. "Wherever you land I'll be happy for you." Her hug gave me goose bumps. Our relationship is on the mend.

The tide is receding. I notice a giant blue heron posing in a foot or so of water. As we approach, the bird grunts, then spreads its wings and flaps them clumsily. Once in the air, however, it transforms into a graceful sprite floating on an invisible stream—giving me a glimpse of hope. To fly he must believe in what he cannot see. Which is hard for me to do.

In the past it bothered me to hear Mom putting herself down. My pride insisted she was perfect, and I was a good person who didn't need forgiveness, either. Now I see how my ambivalence toward Harriet revealed a mean-spirited and callous nature. I've treated Nichole badly, as well. And to think a week ago I was willing to skip out on both of them. No matter how bad things get I have no right to abandon my children. Drew at his worst didn't do that.

We rarely see other people on this stretch of beach, but I catch sight of a rower gliding out to a buoyed powerboat that wasn't there the last time I came.

A sign of spring. And the air is decidedly heavier and warmer today.

I recall my first encounter with Victor just down the way after I'd whooped and cried out like a banshee. No wonder he thought I needed therapy. Bringing the car down the hill thirty minutes ago we passed his cabin, not that the A-frame is really his. An SUV with all its doors flung open dominated the driveway, and a family with several kids was unloading groceries and boxes. They must be the owner and his family. I'm glad we won't be running into Victor today.

My eyes canvass the beach and I spy a peach-colored agate couched among the thousands of pebbles. Without hesitation I bend down to scoop it up. As I caress the stone's cool surface, I am struck by the notion that old habits die hard. I don't want new habits. I drop it in my pocket.

"We need to talk," Drew says and slows his pace.

I brace myself for what is coming next. He's getting married and wants our divorce yesterday. I wait for disappointment to hit me, but I must be stronger now because I feel fine. I can make it on my own. This is the inevitable course neither of us can alter.

He says, "I can't go on living in limbo." He is rubbing his mouth, which tells me this conversation is difficult for him. I appreciate his trying to spare my feelings. He is basically a caring man. I hope someday we will be friends.

"It's okay, I understand." I want to help him navigate this discussion to its completion. "Let's get the divorce finalized," I say. "We both want it."

"If you could ever forgive me—"

"I have," I say, and mean it. "I'm over thinking, I'm always right and wanting to punish you." I recall his visiting my hospital room to apologize. All I'd sought was retaliation. I wanted him to writhe in agony like a man dangling from a hangman's noose.

"You're free to do as you please," I say. "I won't stand in your way."

"I don't want to be free. Not the way you mean."

I see the swallows are back from Central America, where they spent the winter. I watch a half dozen swing through the air like acrobats. Another sign of spring.

"I've treated you horrendously," he says. "I'm sorry."

"I told you I forgive you. Don't worry." I'm amazed how easily I grant this gift.

"It's over between Kristi and me, I swear. Forever."

"You don't owe me an explanation." I listen to the power-boat's engine jump to life, the blades churning the water. In a burst the boat takes off for the marina on the other side of the bay.

"Please, Ruthie," Drew says.

I remind myself I've never been a good listener. Let the poor man say his piece, I tell myself.

"I'd like another chance," he says.

I look at him to see he's gazing straight ahead.

"What did you have in mind?" I notice the swallows, their iridescent backs glistening, have landed on the beach not far ahead of us.

"I want to move home to my own room," he says. "Our room, that is."

Is this a proposition? No, he doesn't come across as a man who wishes to share his bed with me, which means he wants me to move out. I've considered this scenario—his return-ing home and my renting a studio apartment—but now that it's presented itself, I hate the idea. I listen to our footsteps, which are all out of whack. His stride is long and even, while my feet drag into the rocks.

"I don't understand," I say.

He glances in my direction, and when our eyes meet, the corner of his mouth raises a smidge.

Then it dawns on me: he wants me back. This is the moment I've waited for. But what do I want?

I see the swallows have paired up. Within weeks, twosomes will be gathering mud and bits of straw to fashion nests under the eaves of our cabin. They mate for life, unlike us capricious humans. As I ponder this fact, I commit a daring feat. My pinky finger reaches out and hooks onto his little finger.

For several minutes we walk like this: little fingers locked. Nothing more.

"I was thinking." He finally slows his pace.

As I wait for him to continue, he disentangles his finger from mine. My hand slaps against my pant leg. I must have misinterpreted his message. My disappointment is crushing, my self-esteem flattened. But I continue to stroll along as if nothing unusual happened.

Then I feel his hand surrounding mine like a glove. He slows to a halt, faces me, and says, "I was thinking you and I should try again." He lifts my fingertips to his lips and nibbles them. Then his mouth finds mine and our lips meld together into a luxurious embrace. The kiss I've longed for.

But can I truly forgive him? I feel as though I've survived a war and I'm embracing my enemy.

"Ruthie, I swear, no more cheating. No more lies. I've started seeing a counselor and joined a support group that meets weekly to hold me accountable."

"You have?"

Knock me over with a feather, Pop would say.

"I'll do anything to regain your trust." He dips his hands into his pocket, fishes out a box I recognize is Tiffany's signature robin's egg blue, and opens it to show me a ring—a gold band supporting a row of diamonds. "Will you marry me again, Ruthie?"

"You mean have a second wedding ceremony?"

"Yes," he says to my astonishment. "Maybe right here on the island."

"Exchange new vows and invite witnesses?" I scan his face trying to read his sincerity.

"If that's what it takes, Ruthie. Whatever you want."

I recall the little white church I admire each time I drive onto the island. Or do I like the beach better?

"There's your father to consider." Drew surprises me again. "Maybe we should have the ceremony in his hospital room so he can attend."

I imagine a short service—with Isolda officiating after conferring with Jackie. The two of them will coordinate the ceremony. Nothing grandiose, but special because Drew and I will promise to love each other for ever.

I decide to not invite Gloria.

"Sounds wonderful, Drew." Better than any dream I could have imagined. "But are you absolutely sure?"

"Yes. More sure than I've ever been about anything." His arms encircle my shoulders, and he pulls me close. "I love you, Ruthie. With all of my heart."

We kiss again—a long and leisurely embrace. Electricity zings between us and I allow him to support the full weight of me.

I feel as though I've awakened from a nightmare. I hesitate, then I say the words that have never left me. "I love you too." I'm already writing my new wedding vows in my head.

He steps back and displays the opened Tiffany's box. "Is it too early to wear your new ring?"

"Never." I put out my left hand. As he slips it on my ring finger I say, "A perfect fit." I can't contain my happiness. I know I can make it on my own, but I don't want to.

BLUEBERRY FRENCH TOAST

INGREDIENTS:

1 (12-14 ounce) loaf French bread, sourdough bread, or challah, cut into 1" cubes (about 12 cups). Stale bread works best

1 cup fresh or frozen blueberries*

8 large eggs

2 and 1/4 cups whole milk

1/2 teaspoon ground cinnamon

3/4 cup packed light brown sugar

1 tablespoon pure vanilla extract

Streusel Topping

1/3 cup packed light brown sugar

1/3 cup all-purpose flour

1/2 teaspoon ground cinnamon

6 tablespoons unsalted butter, cold and cubed

optional: extra blueberries, fresh fruit, maple syrup, and/or confectioners' sugar for topping

Instructions

1. Grease a 9×13-inch pan with butter or spray with nonstick spray. Spread bread cubes into the prepared baking pan and top evenly with blueberries. Set aside.
2. Whisk the eggs, milk, cinnamon, brown sugar, and vanilla together until no brown sugar lumps remain. Pour over the bread. Cover the pan tightly with plastic wrap and stick in the refrigerator for 3 hours – overnight. Overnight is best.
3. Preheat oven to 350°F Remove pan from the refrigerator.

Prepare the topping: Whisk the brown sugar, flour, and cinnamon together in a medium bowl. Cut in the cubed butter with a pastry blender or two forks. Sprinkle the topping over the soaked bread. Bake for 45-55 minutes or until golden brown on top. Serve immediately. Cover leftovers tightly and store in the refrigerator for 2-3 days.

For variation, use strawberries, blackberries, or thinly sliced apples or pears instead of the blueberries.

A Letter from Kate

THANK YOU SO much for reading *Reinventing Ruthie*, book that is very close to my heart. I hope you liked my storyline and characters—maybe a couple not so much. Even though I know the final outcome when I write, I love to stir the pot and wait to see what happens.

If you enjoyed Reinventing Ruthie, I'd love it if you would leave a short online review. I learn so much from my readers! Your feedback is invaluable.

If you'd like to learn more about my future books and monthly Giveaways subscribe to my newsletters at

WWW.KATELLOYD.COM

You may unsubscribe at any time. Or email me at info@katelloyd.com. I will not share your e-mail address with anyone.

All my best,
Kate

ACKNOWLEDGEMENTS

M Y READERS MEAN everything to me. Thank you for reading my books! I can never thank Mary Jackson enough for her continued encouragement and support. A big shout out to my fabulous Kate's Review Crew! Hugs to author Peg Kehle for answering my many questions and helping me improve my writing. Thanks to fellow authors Rachel Hauk, Nick Harrison, Judy Bodmer, Kathleen Kohler, and Marty Nystrom. Thank you Phil Bransford, who has helped me with pertinent facts in several of my books. Much gratitude to birder and author Constance Sidles. Applause to crime prevention specialist Mary Amberg, who has helped me on numerous occasions. Thanks for proofreading, Lori Wilen. Many thanks to Keri Barnum of New Shelves Books. Thank you to my fabulous webmaster, Lisa-Ann Oliver of Web Designs by LAO. With every novel I forget to thank someone who helped or encouraged me. Please forgive me if I neglected to mention you by name. It really does take a village to write a book.

ABOUT THE AUTHOR

BESTSELLING AUTHOR KATE Lloyd is a passionate observer of human relationships. A native of Baltimore, she lives in the Pacific Northwest with her husband and Piper, her Cairn terrier. She still misses her dear Welsh corgi. She has two grown sons and two marvelous grandkids. Kate has worked a variety of jobs, including restaurateur and car salesman. Always, she is writing in her head. Her favorite pastimes other than writing are daily journaling, walking her dog, reading, and strolling the beach.

KATE LOVES HEARING FROM READERS.
CONNECT WITH HER ON HER

Website: www.katelloyd.com
Instagram: @katelloydauthor
Facebook: www.facebook.com/katelloydbooks
Pinterest: @KateLloydAuthor
Email: info@katelloyd.com